TRULY DARKLY DEEPLY

TRULY DARKLY DEEPLY

VICTORIA SELMAN

QUERCUS

First published in Great Britain in 2022 by

QUERCUS

Quercus Editions Ltd
Carmelite House
50 Victoria Embankment
London EC4Y 0DZ

An Hachette UK company

A CIP catalogue record for this book is available
from the British Library

HB ISBN 978 1 52942 064 7
TPB ISBN 978 1 52942 065 4

10 9 8 7 6 5 4 3 2

Typeset by CC Book Production
Printed and bound in Great Britain by Clays Ltd, Elcograf S.p.A.

Papers used by Quercus are from well-managed forests and other responsible sources.

In memory of Maggie (2006–2020)
Deeply loved. Desperately missed.

This book was inspired by a number of different real-life serial killer cases. True crime fans will no doubt spot psychological or behavioural traits familiar to them from the Shadow and monsters like BTK, the Zodiac, the Green River Killer, Albert DeSalvo, Richard Ramirez and many others. However, the characters in the novel, their actions and motivations, are all entirely the product of the author's imagination and are wholly fictitious.

Sophie—

There's so much to tell you, I don't know where to start. The kite, maybe. It's not the beginning exactly, but I suppose it's as good a place as any.

You watched it transfixed, your nose pressed up to the glass as it circled, a black shadow creeping across the lawn. Flying on the spot, you said. The way you liked to dance.

There are kites in Massachusetts, but you'd never seen one before. Or maybe you just didn't remember, you were so small when you moved to London. Certainly you never expected to see one here. They get pigeons in the capital; sparrows, the occasional robin. Birds of prey, not so much.

'What's it doing?' your mother mused. 'Lost maybe. Poor thing.'

'It's hunting,' you said.

And you were right.

The sparrow was hopping about in the fallen leaves

on the trampoline, didn't see it coming. Didn't stand a chance. The kite didn't swoop so much as drop out of the sky, snaring its victim, pulling it apart right where you practised your tuck jumps.

Your awe turned to horror, gripping you the way the kite gripped its prey.

Sated, the killer returned to the clouds, leaving behind only the sparrow's legs spat out and discarded on the muddy, leaf strewn canvas. An avian crime scene.

I think of it often. An omen for the darkness readying to descend into our lives. For the wreckage that would follow. For the incomprehensibility of it all.

You cried; nose running, choking on your tears.

'It'll be okay. There's nothing to be afraid of,' your mother told you.

She lied, Sophie. You had every reason to be afraid. And it was not all going to be okay.

ONE

You think you know this story. I think I do. But how much do any of us really know?

I'd like to think I always had a feeling. That a part of me always suspected something was amiss. Though the truth is I didn't suspect anything. Of course, there are things I look back on now which make me think, Was that a clue, a sign? But if so, it's only because of what I learned later. Back then, it wasn't a clue. It wasn't an anything.

That's the problem with hindsight. It distorts memory, superimposes warning flags where before there were none. Makes you question yourself. Turns the past into a series of whys and recriminations.

Why didn't I see what was happening? Why didn't I realise sooner?

I know the answer. It doesn't help though. If anything, it makes it worse—

No one saw. No one realised. I wasn't the only one who was fooled.

*

The letter lands on the doormat with a soft *plmp* as I'm tying my Merrells; steeling myself to take the dog out and brave the biting rain. Wishing I'd drunk a little less last night. Fighting a hangover. Same old, same old.

I pause, hunched over my shoes, laces looped around my fingers, eyes snared by the flat Manila rectangle. By the name I know it contains.

The air has gone still. I'm conscious of my breathing; of a dull ringing in my ears, the drumbeat of my heart.

BATTLEMOUTH PRISON

The words are stamped in bold red lettering across the top of the envelope the way a farmer might brand a lamb.

My stomach knots. I bite down on my tongue, taste the backwash of acid mixed with my morning coffee. Smell the alcohol-stained sweat breaking out over my skin.

He broke out too, escaped his cell just six months after his incarceration. Another of his smoke-and-mirrors tricks.

I run my thumbnail under the flap, pull out the letter. Under-lined at the top:

Re: Matthew Melgren

'Matthew', even though everyone always calls him 'Matty'. Us, the press, the true crime shows. All the channels have run them.

Matty fascinates people; his apparent normalness, his charming smile. Handsome and educated. A killer who doesn't fit the stereotype. He wasn't a loner, wasn't socially awkward, held down a good job.

4

He had a girlfriend too, so no markers in that direction either. There was one of those straight-to-DVD movies made recently about his relationship with my mother. The producers got some stick for using such a handsome actor. It was all over Twitter; how they were playing up Matty's golden good looks. How it was an affront to his victims.

They missed the point though, those up-in-armers. Never mind that he still has more than his fair share of female fans sending him panties and porn, playing down his attractive-ness would have been the real insult to the women he killed. Revisionist history. After all, if Matty had been some socially awkward troll, he'd hardly have been able to lure his prey, to get them to trust him. I should know.

Re: Matthew Melgren

My eyes move down the page, the air thickening in my gullet. I speak to my mother as I reach the end; head pounding, mouth dry. At first, I deflect.

'I broke up with Tom,' I tell her, steeling myself for what I need to say, gathering my thoughts.

'Oh, Soph, I'm sorry. What happened? He seemed nice.'

I scoff.

'Everyone's nice at the beginning.'

The words hang between us, conjuring the same face in both our heads.

'Did he hurt you?'

I laugh – it's hollow.

'He told me I should wear skirts more.'

'Oh Soph,' she says again.

It'd sound stupid to anyone else, but I knew she'd get it, just like I'd know she'd been knocking back the pills long before the slur hit her words.

'There's something else, isn't there?'

She could always see through me too. No point covering it up, not now.

'I got a letter. From Battlemouth.'

'Matty . . .'

I hear it in her whisper. It's still there after all these years, after everything that's happened. The yearning, the questioning, the love that won't leave. Straight away I think of the pearl-handled penknife I keep in my dresser drawer, the relief that comes from exorcising the guilt. God, I really am Pavlov's bitch.

Buster, my dodgy hipped German Shepherd rescue, has Pavlovian reactions too. Whenever he hears a man shouting, an unexpected bang or thump.

He senses my mood, stumbles over nosing at my thigh. I rub his ears. *Good dog.*

'Matty's dying,' I tell my mother. Not gleeful, but not sorry either. 'Pancreatic cancer.'

'How long?'

I shrug.

'Couple of weeks? Possibly less.' I take a breath, let it out slowly. 'They say he wants to talk. To meet.'

'A confession?'

I hear the hope in her tone, the desperate need for closure. My skin prickles. I need that too. And yet . . .

'Maybe a confession,' I say. 'Though who knows with him? Last I heard, he was still saying they got the wrong man.'

'Will you go?'

'I'm not sure.'

A yearning for answers. The fear of getting them.

I glance down. My hand is trembling.

In it, the letter trembles too.

TWO

'I got a letter too,' my mother says.

'From Matty?'

'No.' There's disappointment in her voice, she covers it quickly. 'From the prison chaplain. A guy called Bill.'

'Old, is he?'

'What?'

'Nothing. Sorry. Ignore me.'

Old Bill is British slang. Something as an American, she never quite picked up. Just as I never picked up the ability to sit with my discomfort.

I resort to lame jokes when I'm nervous. A defensive mechanism, according to my therapist, Janice. Another deflective tactic. I've acquired a few over the years.

Let your guard down, one of my mother's Post-it notes reads. *Let people see the real you.*

Yeah, right.

'So, what did this chaplain say? Bill.'

'That forgiveness is healing. That I'd feel happier if I could let go of my resentment. That I'm the one it's hurting.'

'Christ's sake.'

'Don't talk like that.'

Bet you and Chaplain Bill got on like a house on fire, I think.

'I hope you told him where he could shove his forgiveness speech.'

'I didn't write back. I kept the letter though.' I know she did. It's in the box with the photos. 'You can read it if you want.'

'I'll pass, thanks.'

'I wish the way I feel would pass.'

Her sadness evokes a responding wave of emotion in me. I wish I could hug her, tell her everything's going to be okay. But it's too late for that.

'When I think of my life with Matty, I don't know what was real. And what I just wanted to be real,' she says.

'Does it matter?'

'It does to me.'

The pause is pregnant. There's so much I want to say to that, so much I shouldn't say. I settle for the thought so often in my head.

'That last girl he killed was eight. Same age I was when we first met. Her sister, twelve, just like I was when he was arrested.'

'We don't know for sure he killed her.'

'Jury was pretty sure.'

I hear her sigh, take a sip of whatever she's drinking. Gin, I imagine. It became her morning tipple during the trial. By the afternoon she didn't care what was in her glass so long as it kept her drunk.

'Don't you ever wonder if they got it wrong?' she asks.

'No.'

I'm lying though, of course I wonder. How could I not?

What he did, what they said he did, has haunted me for so long I can't remember what it's like not to feel as though I'm suffocating, not to have to remind myself to breathe.

Even now, a part of me thinks one day I'll wake up and find it's all been a bad dream. That my hero's name has been cleared. That he didn't hurt those women, slaughter a girl who still slept with a teddy.

I followed the trial every day in the papers, have read and watched everything about the case since. I've seen the photos, read the crime scene reports. But as long as he protests his innocence, I'll always wonder: Did they convict the wrong man? Did I make a terrible mistake? Was my childhood a lie? Or is the lie the story I've told myself?

'He wrote me, you know. After his conviction. A love letter. Poured out his soul. Begged me to believe in him, in what we had. Told me he was embracing his spiritual side. He'd taken up meditation, he said. Was getting involved with the prison charities. Even counselling some of the inmates struggling with depression.'

You'd have lapped that up, wouldn't you? I think. Matty turning over a new leaf, you prompting it. Proclaiming his undying love for you.

'Bill said he asked him to read it over. That he wanted to get the words just right.'

Why dupe one person when you can dupe two?

Her tone changes, a balloon deflating.

'I never wrote back. He must have been so upset.'

'Good.'

My voice has hardened, varnish on rotten wood. A façade. The slightest poke and I turn to sawdust.

'Will you go?' she asks. 'To visit him?'

For a long time, I don't answer. She waits, pulls at her drink. I dig my nails into the scab on my wrist, hard enough to draw blood.

'I'm scared,' I tell her finally.

'I know,' she whispers.

But she can't. Not without understanding what I did.

From the blog *True Crime Files*

Why do serial killers so often feel the need to issue press statements after their convictions? Showboating? Getting the last word? Their insatiable egos?

Matty Melgren's post-sentencing statement is eerily reminiscent of Ken Benito's (the San Francisco Strangler) who was arrested ten years after Melgren was sent down.

This has led some to speculate whether Benito's crime spree was inspired by Melgren, who famously asphyxiated his victims with their own underwear, leaving the ligature tied in a bow around their necks.

If so, he's not the only person to hero-worship Melgren, who receives fan mail, money, and even saucy snaps from female admirers who appear to be turned on rather than off by his gruesome attacks.

Matty's statement (read out by his lawyer):

A terrible miscarriage of justice has taken place here today. I am innocent of these murders which have rocked the world and caused women everywhere to fear going out alone.

If anybody is guilty of a crime it is the police who have fabricated a case against me based on deception and phoney evidence. Nothing has been proved, least of all my guilt.

The sentence I've received belongs to someone else. I hope with all my heart he is found soon and brought to account, not just for my sake, but for the victims' families too. They deserve to know what really happened to their loved ones.

As do I.

Whatever the motivation behind Melgren's statement, plenty of people are still wondering if he was telling the truth. And whether the real killer is still out there . . .

THREE

I was six when my mother and I moved to London from Newton, a sleepy suburb on the outskirts of Boston, Massachusetts. She'd met my father in college, married him in her first year, dropped out in her second, given birth to me in what would have been her third.

By the time I was two, he was gone. My grandparents, fish on Friday Catholics, weren't happy.

What did you do, Amelia-Rose? He just disappeared?

Divorce wasn't something they or their neighbours approved of. In our town, there was a church on practically every street corner. Someone who knew you on every street corner too.

'Why would he just leave?' Nanna G asked for the umpteenth time, the pair of them forming a makeshift factory line at the kitchen sink. Nanna soaping the dishes, my mother drying them. 'A man doesn't just walk out on his wife and daughter.'

'Well, this one did.'

My grandfather folded the *Globe*, set it on the coffee table, WOMAN'S BODY RECOVERED FROM THE CHARLES cut in half by the crease.

'Your ma's just trying to understand, sweetheart.'

He'd come over to the States when he was a boy. Over time he'd lost his hair but managed to keep his soft Dublin lilt. Nanna said she'd fallen in love with the accent then the man. *In that order*. His kindness is what would have drawn me, but his accent was beautiful, especially the jig of it when he sang.

My mother said my father had an accent too.

I don't remember that.

Well, no, you wouldn't.

It had been a lifetime since I'd heard his voice.

She put down the dishcloth, tucked her hair behind her ears.

'Scooch over, Soph. Look at the funnies, shall we?'

I snuggled up to her, leaning my head against her shoulder as she read aloud. She could never get Jon Arbuckle sounding quite male enough but she did a great Garfield.

Nanna G tutted.

'I'm trying to have a conversation with you, Amelia-Rose.'

That's my abiding memory of her. Tuts and eye rolls and the face powder she applied so thickly it looked as if her skin were made of dust.

We lived with them after my father left, my mother and I sharing a bedroom in their clapboard house on Goddard Street, with the raccoons that woke me every night rifling through the garbage cans.

Fed up of the racket, I threw a cup of water out of the window one time, thinking to scare them off. The cup smashed into about fifty pieces leaving china splinters all over the driveway that 'anyone could step on.'

'You need to learn to think before you act,' Nanna G scolded, sending me out with a dustpan and brush the following morning. 'You're too rash, missy. It's going to land you in serious trouble one of these days.'

This was about Tommy Sinclair, not just my attack on the raccoons. My grandmother didn't seem to care that the snotnose deserved the bashing I gave him. Or that he fought like a girl.

'The behaviour has got to stop, do you hear? I can't have you ending up like—'

Grandad shot her a warning look, gave his head a little shake.

'Georgia . . .'

Sensing an ally, I stood my ground.

'He said he didn't blame my daddy for leaving us. I gave him a chance to take it back. What else was I supposed to do?'

Nanna waggled a finger in my face.

'You need to be less of a hothead, Sophie Brennan. Next time try using your words instead of your fists. Or better still, just walk away.'

'You can't teach someone a lesson with words.'

My grandfather smiled.

'You'd be surprised, muffin.'

Nanna had some experience in that department it seemed. I heard her and my mother talking one night when I was supposed to be asleep, disjointed words floating up through the floorboards.

'I know what I saw . . . People are talking . . . Better if you . . .'

Not long after that we left the clapboard house with three suitcases, a Ziploc bag of cheese sandwiches and two plane tickets.

'London, baby,' my mother said.

'I don't want to go,' I said, trying not to cry.

'You win more arguments with smiles than tears,' Nanna G used to say. 'And smiles don't make your eyes puffy.'

One of her 'precious pearls of wisdom'.

'It's never too late to turn your life around,' was the particular gem she gave my mother as we said goodbye that day, her and my grandfather standing side by side on the stoop, arms folded. Looking anywhere other than in our direction.

Was this why we were leaving, to find my mother a new husband? If so, what was wrong with the States? There were plenty of men here. Mr Benson, who ran the Candy Kingdom in Newton Center, was my not-so-secret ambition. A man for her, a lifetime supply of Red Vines and strawberry laces for me. Win-win, my grandfather might have said, though for some reason my mother didn't see it that way.

'Do you know what a confirmed bachelor is, Sophie?'

I considered the question.

'An unmarried man who's an adult in the eyes of the church?'

'Not quite.'

I glanced at her, sitting up in the cab; chin raised, shoulders pushed back.

Let's put on our happy faces.

Her happy face was a mask, a poor disguise for her vulnerability.

I wasn't sure what made me think she was fragile. Her slightness perhaps? Her little bird wrists, that long slender neck.

People always said she looked like a curly-haired Hepburn. Not *Breakfast at Tiffany's* Audrey with her choker of pearls and long cigarette holder, my mother was nothing like a film star. But Audrey, make-up-less in a turtleneck and ponytail, I could see the similarity there. They shared an innocent sort of beauty, fresh-faced and timeless.

Those long slender necks, heart-shaped faces and huge Bambi eyes. Though my mother's are more amber than brown, the colour of whisky when the light shines through it.

I didn't know the word 'vulnerable' then, just sensed it about her. That she wasn't made of stone like Nanna G. That she was more cardboardy. That if she got wet, she'd crumple.

'Why do we have to leave America?' I asked, a squirmy feeling in my belly. The same feeling I got when I woke in the night convinced there were monsters under my bed.

'We don't have to leave, Sophie. We choose to.'

'We choose to?'

Did that mean we could just as easily choose not to?

'We're choosing freedom. No one breathing down our necks. A fresh start.'

'I don't want to go.'

She sighed to show her patience was wearing thin. It wasn't the first time I'd voiced my objections.

'Didn't you know, the streets of London are paved with gold?'

'Really?'

'We'll see, won't we?'

She got a job as a secretary.

'Hired me on the spot. It's about all I'm qualified for, but it'll pay the bills.'

'If there are so many bills to pay, why don't we just go home?'

'We are home, Sophie.'

After a week camping out at the Holiday Inn, we rented an apartment; the second floor of a two-storey walk-up near Parliament Hill. An oasis of green in the heart of North London, with ponds people actually swam in, a big adventure playground and a running track. A café too, that sold ice cream and pain au chocolat. Our go-to spot on a Saturday morning.

'It's where they did the Twilight Bark in *101 Dalmatians*, remember?'

She was wrong, that was Primrose Hill. An easy enough mistake though. To our American ears, the names were deceptively similar. You only see nuance when you look for it.

We watched *101 Dalmatians* that first night in our hotel room, curled up in the same bed eating the Twinkies we'd picked up at Logan, both of us too jet-lagged to sleep.

It became a habit, eating in front of the TV, something Nanna G would certainly not have approved of. *Uncivilised*, she'd have called it. I could practically hear her saying it, see the appalled look on her face at the murky depths we'd sunk to.

Being civilised was very important to Nanna. I had an idea it meant holding a knife and fork properly and not eating with your mouth open. *Manners maketh the lady, Sophie*. Not much of a carrot. I was six, being a lady wasn't high on my list of priorities.

I suspected my mother was the same when she was my age, though it was hard to imagine given how big she was on manners these days. From the scraps I pieced together, I figured she'd been a Tom Sawyer type; catching frogs, whittling wood, collecting little animal bones.

I don't know what happened to the frogs, but she kept the bones in a cigar case at the back of her nightstand; *Amelia's Treasure Box – Hands Off*, scratched across the top.

I thought the collection was a bit morbid and told her so.

'There's beauty in everything, Sophie,' she said. 'You just have to look.'

And we did look. One of our favourite things to do became scavenging about on Parliament Hill, searching for feathers and flint and bits of worn-down glass which I was convinced were emeralds. At night we'd cuddle up on the couch eating spaghetti and watching *Columbo* re-runs or video rentals from the Blockbusters down the street. *Return From Witch Mountain. Grease. Sgt. Pepper's Lonely Hearts Club Band.*

Sgt. Pepper's was my mother's favourite. She was mad about The Beatles, had all their albums on vinyl. We used to play them on the turntable in our new living room, dance along. Her swaying from her hips like she was melting, me mostly jumping on the spot.

In Boston my bedtime had been seven o'clock, here it was creeping closer to nine.

'Well, you're older now,' she said, though looking back I suspect it had more to do with her not wanting to sit up by herself in an empty living room. I wasn't complaining though, not about that at any rate. Des Banister, the odd-jobs guy who lived in the apartment downstairs, was my real *bête noire*.

'He's creepy,' I told my mother. 'He smells like cheese and his teeth are horrid.'

'Looks mean nothing, Sophie. It's what's in a person's heart that counts.'

'I don't think he has a very nice heart either.'

She ding-donged my pigtail.

'You don't even know him.'

'I know how he treats his dog. Its ribs are sticking out. He's obviously starving it.'

'For all you know, it's just a picky eater. You remember old Gabe Robinson from down the street back home? How kind he was?'

'Yes?'

'His wolfhound's ribs stuck out too. But no way Treacle was being starved, not the way Gabe loved him.'

'This is different.'

She sighed heavily, tilted her head to the side the way she always did when thinking how to put something.

'I know this move has been hard on you, that leaving what you know behind feels unfair. But one day I hope you'll understand it was for the best, that I was thinking as much about your needs as my own. In the meantime, you've just got to try and make a go of things. Okay?'

'I can make a go of things and still know what Des Banister is.'

I ground my toe into the dirt, bit my lip to keep the tears in. My mother crouched down, took my hands in hers.

'We don't know Des. We don't know what he's been through in his life, what drives him.'

'So?'

'So, you can't judge a person till you've walked in their shoes.'

I thought about the clompy army boots Des wore with his ugly camouflage trousers. The way I'd seen him kick over a homeless girl's money cup outside the station.

'I don't need to wear that guy's shoes to know what sort of person he is.'

'Okay, so you don't like him. But that doesn't mean London's all bad. I can think of plenty of things that are better here.'

'No Grandad bribing me to be quiet in church?'

She laughed.

'Since when have you minded Junior Mints, missy? No, I was thinking of the weather. Do you have any idea how cold it is in Massachusetts right now?'

'Pretty cold, I guess.'

'Pretty cold? Snap your fingers off freezing, more like.'

She grabbed my hands, pretended to bite them. *Nang*.

'And it's nice being able to walk places, don't you think?'

I shrugged, unwilling to concede the point, though she did have one. Back home, you couldn't get anywhere without driving. 'The local high street' was a completely new concept for me.

But that was precisely the problem. This wasn't home. Everyone talked like Prince Charles. When I asked for jelly on my toast, they looked at me as if I was nuts. And literally nowhere stocked Lucky Charms.

'I hate Weetabix,' I told my mother. 'It tastes like straw.'

'How would you know?' she teased, looking up from the Post-it note she was writing on.

There were quotations tacked up all over the apartment. Inspirational messages, she called them. Wise words. Maybe deep down she missed Nanna G.

'What's that one say?' I asked.

'The only person who can define you, is you.'

'How about the dictionary?' I asked, proud of myself.

She shook her head.

'No book. Just you.'

Nanna G would have likely brought up the Bible at this point, but I wasn't about to risk reminding my mother she still hadn't enrolled me in Sunday School. Instead, I played the pragmatist.

'The only person who can define you, is you. That's actually pretty good.'

And it was. Though 'Beware wolves dressed as sheep' would have served us rather better.

FOUR

I find one of my mother's old Post-it notes down the back of the couch, the paper soft and curled with age. Her writing – blue felt tip, perfect cursive – is faded. A ghost. A whisper down the years.

What would I say if whispers worked the other way? If I could leave a note now, for the me then? A warning from the future. A tip-off.

It's a fantasy I often indulge in, although it inevitably leads to guilt and recriminations. Of me, of my mother. And there are so many of those already.

I still do it though, can't stop myself. A scab you're not supposed to pick but which itches like hell if you don't.

I turn the old note over in my hand, play the game. What would I say?

Beware wolves dressed as sheep?

Trust no one?

Run?

But what if it was all a terrible mistake? What if it's true he's innocent? Would I really want to have missed out on what was truthfully the happiest time in my life?

Yes, I think. No.

God! No wonder I'm such a mess.

I trace my mother's handwriting with the tip of my forefinger. There's a tightness in my throat I recognise as a sign my black dog is on the prowl. The spectre that's always lurking, waiting for its chance to pounce and pin me down. Stealing weeks. Locking me inside myself. Sapping my energy so all I can do is sit and stare.

The tight throat is there but the other symptoms are missing; the feeling you get behind your eyes just before you start to cry. The lead in my muscles. The inertia.

This isn't the onset of another depression then. It's not about shutting myself away. It's the thought of doing something that frightens the life out of me.

My mother's note: *No time like the present.*

A portent maybe, although I don't make the call immediately. Deciding on a course of action is one thing, following it through is another. Forgiveness works the same way.

I wait till Buster and I have had our lunch, he eats most of mine as well as his. My appetite is shot. A silver lining, perhaps. Ever since I hit thirty, weight has been harder to shift.

I reach for the phone, the letter with the prison phone number printed at the top. I hesitate, replace the handset, cover my eyes.

I can't do it. The tightness in my throat chokes me.

Tomorrow, I think, standing up, wondering if it's too early for a glass of wine. Just a small one to take the edge off.

And then in my peripheral vision—

No time like the present.

I grit my teeth, inhale deeply, dial.

I sound out of breath when the receptionist picks up, as if I've been running up and down the stairs, rather than sitting at the kitchen table racked with indecision for the last two hours.

I hate myself for letting Matty get to me. I'm an adult now, so many years under the bridge. And yet still the slightest thing recalls him to me.

Bows. Footprints. A discarded earring. The past isn't a foreign country. It's a prison sentence with no hope of parole.

I hear the women whispering to me at night, though mostly it's the girl. Angry, accusing.

'Why didn't you do it sooner?' she asks. 'I'd be alive if you had. I had a mother too. How do you think she feels?'

Other times she's crueller.

'Why me? What's so special about you?'

I ask myself the same thing. All the time.

The receptionist wakes up as soon as I mention his name. The magnet pull of notoriety.

'Matty Melgren?'

'When's convenient?' I ask, as if making a dentist appointment.

Down the line; a keyboard tapping, the cluck of a tongue.

I think of the girl from Hogarth Road, what they say he did to her tongue. There isn't a bridge big enough to traverse the years.

'You'll need to arrive half an hour before your check-in time. Bring identification. A passport or driver's licence,' the receptionist says. 'And a pound coin for the lockers. Tuesday. Four thirty.'

It's not a question, she's not asking if that works for me.

As usual Matty is calling the shots.

FIVE

I woke to the sound of shots. At least, that's what I thought they were until I realised it was actually just a car backfiring. This was London not Boston. A city without guns. Safe, we thought.

It was a Sunday morning in early fall. Autumn, I corrected myself.

'We're in England now,' my mother kept reminding me, as if I could forget. 'You'll never feel at home here if you keep talking like an American.'

'It's not home,' I told her. 'And my tummy hurts. I think I'm sick.'

'Oh, it's your stomach today, is it?'

I'd been feigning maladies ever since starting Hampstead Hall School. (Hampstead Hell, I called it.) I'd even tried biting my nails in an attempt to get a tapeworm but, contrary to my grandmother's dark prophesies, my endeavours were as unsuccessful as my efforts to get out of class.

Being the new girl sucked. *One of these things is not like the others . . .*

The kids made fun of my accent. Nicknamed me Yankee Doodle. Asked if my mother was married to Ronald McDonald.

'For your information she's not married to anyone.'

Yankee Doodle became 'Seppo bastard'.

Cockney rhyming slang. Septic tank, Yank. 'Bastard' was rather more obvious.

'Take it back,' I snarled, hands curling into fists.

'Why? You just admitted you don't have a daddy.'

In those days, in that part of the world, being from a single parent household wasn't as common as it is now. Plus, like all children, the blazer wearers had a nose for weakness. The tiniest spot of blood would get them circling.

'Did you see the way she was watching me and my dad at drop-off this morning?'

'She had to give her Father's Day card to her grandpa.'

'What a loser.'

'You're the losers. You and your bunch of idiot dads.'

I used my fists to ram home the message, but there were more of them and, unlike me, they'd learned words were more powerful than punches. Plus they left fewer bruises, a.k.a. 'proof'. Nanna G would have been impressed.

I was sent to the Head's office and given a letter to take home to my mother. Two days later, I was sent home with another.

My teacher – all angles and elbows with the ill-fitting name of Miss Bacon – had called us up to her desk in turn to collect our homework assignments.

'Very good, Allegra.'

'Lovely descriptive language, Eugenie.'

I was at the back of the line. She handed me a sheet graffitied in red pen corrections. No smile.

'Colour has a "u" in it. So does "neighbour". There's no "z" in "apologise", and two "l"s in "travelled".'

She shook her head, made the sort of sniffing noise I associated with my grandmother.

'You're in Upper Trans, Sophie. You shouldn't be making mistakes like this.'

I explained politely that I'd got a medal in the spelling bee at my old school and had been reading since I was three.

'They're not mistakes,' I concluded.

The barcode lines around Miss Bacon's mouth deepened. Her brows drew together.

'Are you arguing with me?'

I felt the other kids watching from their desks. Several snickered behind their hands. I raised my head a little higher, tried again—

'I'm just saying, I know how to spell colour.'

It didn't occur to either of us that there might be two ways of spelling it.

Miss Bacon stiffened, narrowed her itty-bitty eyes. Asked, didn't they teach manners where I came from?

'Not at school,' I said.

Her lips disappeared into a thin line.

'I'll be sending a letter home to your mother. I must say, I'm very disappointed in you, Sophie.'

I'm disappointed in you too, I thought. You're a teacher, and you can't even spell.

'What did you say?'

'Nothing.'

It wasn't an auspicious start. But auspicious beginnings aren't everything. Just because something bodes well, doesn't mean it'll turn out that way.

The sunlight filtered through the slats in my blinds, painting the walls butter yellow. I stretched under the covers, thought about getting up and watching *Wacky Races*. Weighed that up against the pull of my warm bed.

My mother had been out the previous night with a friend from work – Linda, the only friend she'd made since we'd moved to London. If Linda hadn't been so insistent about it, I don't suppose she'd have even made friends with her.

She was never very social. *I like my own company, that's all*, she used to say. The other mums at school had invited her to join their coffee mornings to begin with, but she'd always found an excuse not to go and in the end they gave up asking. I expect she was pleased.

'Remember what Dr Norman told you?' Nanna said. 'It's not good for you to be by yourself all the time.'

I could empathise with that. I could also see Linda was good for her. *Gets me out of my shell*, she used to say.

I don't know about shells, but the woman certainly talked enough for both of them.

I'd tried to stay awake, listening for the reassuring sounds that she'd returned. My mother didn't go out much in the evenings. When she did, I'd torture myself worrying what would happen to me if something happened to her. Would anyone even think to tell me?

As far as I knew, Linda was the only one in London who had our phone number and she was the only person my mother ever went out with. The math wasn't in my favour.

'Let's go let our hair down!' she'd said as they went out last night.

'Amen to that,' my mother replied.

Her tone sounded fake. I wasn't surprised. Letting your hair down seemed a pretty boring way to spend an evening.

I rubbed my eyes now, glanced at the clock on my bedside table. A fat green sphere with frog eyes on the top and glow-in-the-dark numbers. A present for learning to tell the time.

A minute tick-tocked by, two, three and, just as my eyes were starting to close again, a creaking sound from the living room made me freeze. Footsteps, too heavy to be my mother's.

I tiptoed to the door; chest tight, breath held. Then eased down the handle; carefully, carefully so its squeal wouldn't give me away. Opened the door a crack. Just wide enough to peek out.

I saw a man – burnished blonde, cashmere sweater, brown Oxfords – standing by the couch, picking up the framed photographs my mother displayed on the end table. Examining them, putting them neatly back. There was something methodical about his actions, unhurried. At ease.

I figured a burglar wouldn't move like that, wouldn't be interested in family snaps.

My heart rate steadied, my respiration returned to normal. I pushed the door wide.

'Who are you?'

He turned and smiled as if he'd been waiting for me.

'Hey Sophie.'

I was both confused and comforted by his relaxed manner.

'How do you know my name?'

'I'm an old friend of your mam's.'

He had an open face and an accent like my grandfather's that straight away made me think of home.

As I stood there equivocating, he sauntered over, extending his hand. It made me feel grown up, as if I mattered. Adults tended to ignore me or else call me 'cutie', like I was a puppy dog wanting to be petted.

I shook his hand, felt its warmth envelope mine.

'What's your name?'

'Matty.'

There was something familiar about him. Something about the eyes.

He did a little dance, put on a silly voice. That put me in mind of Grandad too.

'How do you do? Do you like the zoo?'

I laughed, the final pressure valve releasing.

'I was going to make your mam pancakes. Want to help?'

Pancakes were my favourite. Among the photos on the end table was a picture of me eating a cream covered stack of them at the IHOP.

'Is Mummy coming?'

Not 'Mommy' any more.

'She's still sleeping.' He gave me a conspiratorial look. 'Thought we'd surprise her. What d'you say?'

'Sure.' Then, 'She likes them with chocolate chips.'

She didn't, that was me.

He grinned, like I wasn't pulling the wool over his eyes, but he let me have my win.

'All right then, partner. Chocolate chips it is. We're going to need a spatula, ladle and pan. Any idea where they are?'

'Not in the living room.'

SIX

Matty started coming over all the time after that, pitching up in his black Mini Cooper, waving at the picture window where I'd be watching out for him. He'd stick out his tongue, flap his hands on either side of his face, or else put on a silly dance right out there on the sidewalk for the whole world to see.

My mother called him a show-off. To me he was magical.

'Your car looks like a big ant from up here,' I said, letting him in one time.

'And you look like a princess.'

He picked me up, swung me upside down. Made me squeal – inaudible over his fake roars and 'Hey Jude' playing on the turntable.

As McCartney started telling Jude not to be afraid, Matty made to drop me.

'Oh, you want me to put you down?'

'Nooo!'

Next thing, I was on the floor, a victim in what we called the Prisoner Game – Matty pinning me down, me struggling to get away. We had a 'safe word', *smelly feet*, but it was a point of pride not to use it, a point Matty was only too conscious of.

You're admitting defeat? You're sure? Well, okay, but you realise that makes me the overlord?

My mother appeared in the doorway, wiping her hands on a tea towel. Her hair was loose the way Matty liked it, her Bambi eyes bright.

'You guys are making me feel left out.'

Matty released me, went to kiss her ('Hey, you') started dancing her around the room. I grabbed at his legs wanting him to capture me again, ready to run away screaming if he did. *Can't get me . . .*

I was making a gnat of myself, deliberately so. I'm here, I was saying. Pick me.

He was my mother's boyfriend, but I loved him too. More than anyone apart from her. And some days more.

'So, what have my two favourite ladies been up to today?'

Matty was putting ADT stickers on our windows. We didn't have a security alarm but he said the labels would make anyone think twice before breaking in. He was big on personal safety, always telling my mother she needed to be more careful. *A woman on your own, you're easy prey.*

'We played hide and go seek on Parliament Hill,' I told him.

'You didn't close your eyes, did you Ams?'

'Kind of spoil the game if I looked, don't you think?' my mother replied.

'It's not safe. You never know who might be lurking in the bushes.'

She raised her eyes to the ceiling, shook her head.

'Overreact much? It was fine. There were plenty of people about.'

'Crimes don't just happen in secluded alleys.'

'Good to know.' She nodded at the carrier bag he'd left on the kitchen counter, changed the subject. 'So what's in there?'

'Steak. Thought you might need a bit of cheering up, like.'

John Lennon had been killed a few days ago. My mother was grieving, along with thousands of other women who'd never met him.

Shot in the back. What kind of coward shoots a man in the back?

'I got us a Rioja too,' Matty said. 'A reserve. Should be good.'

She kissed him.

'My prince.'

Matty gave a bow, stirred up the air with his right hand as he bent over.

'My lady.'

'Princes don't bow,' I said. 'People are supposed to bow to them.'

He grinned.

'Aye, reckon I could get used to that.'

'Shall I open the bottle?' my mother asked, brandishing the Rioja by its neck.

'How about changing into a skirt first? Figure like yours, you should show it off.'

I mimed sticking a finger down my throat.

'Don't you want to look like a lady, pumpkin?'

I told him, no, not especially.

My mother was keener to please. *I was going to change anyway.*

Matty caught me between his legs, gripped me in a vice.

'Gotcha!'

'Let me go!'

He put on a *mwahahaha* voice—

'You're my prisoner now . . .'

I kicked and struggled. He tightened his hold.

'She wasn't going to change anyway,' I told him, still panting from the exertion.

He'd released me, decided I'd struggled enough.

'If it wasn't for you, she'd live in her jeans. Same as me.'

Matty just smiled to himself, started unpacking the groceries. I went over to inspect the purchases.

'Rocky Road, excellent!' I said pulling out a big tub of ice cream with a triumphant flourish.

'Your favourite, right?'

They didn't sell that at Safeway up the road. He'd have had to make a special trip to Baskin-Robbins all the way over in Golders Green.

'Thanks, Matty. You're the best!'

He did a Mickey skit, started capering.

'Aw shucks, you're making me blush.'

My mother returned, in a blue and white boho dress similar to one Lady Diana had been wearing on the front of that week's *Woman's Own*. She leaned against the door jamb, watching the show. Her eyes big and wide and filled with love.

'Quite the actor, Mr Melgren.' Then with a wink at me, 'Or should I say, Mr Mouse?'

I looked from one to the other, a warm buttery feeling spreading inside me. Wondered if this is how it would feel to have a dad, to be a proper family.

My mother kept a snapshot of my real father in her dresser drawer along with framed photo of a child cut from a newspaper. A girl who'd lived down the street, she said. Died when she was just three.

'Why do you have it?' I asked.

She shrugged, head tilted to the left.

'To remember her by.'

'And the photo of Daddy?'

'To remember him too, I suppose.'

I thought about that, wondered what it meant. If she wanted to be reminded of him, did she also want to get back together?

'Did it used to be on the wall?'

'No. Why?'

I pointed out the pin marks.

She just smiled to herself, told me I'd understand when I was older. I wondered if I'd understand why he left us when I was older too.

He never called or tried to visit. Every year on my birthday I'd make the same wish. Every year it failed to come true.

I figured he'd forgotten about me, got a new life. A family he loved more. Much later, I learned it wasn't that at all, though I never did find out the full story.

Meanwhile, the photo disappeared from my mother's dresser. It must have been around the time Matty became a part of our lives. I didn't ask about it, reckoned my mother must have thrown it away. Turned out she'd assumed the same thing about me, that I was the one who'd chucked it. Neither of us thought to suspect Matty.

*

'Bedtime, young lady.'

Matty was over again, my mother trying to get me out of the way so she could have him to herself.

She was working to keep her cool, trying to impress Matty with her mothering skills. I wanted to impress him too.

'I'm not nearly tired.'

'It's late. You need to go to sleep, Sophie.'

'Not yet.'

It was Matty who broke the deadlock.

'How about I tell you a story first?'

I grinned widely, head nodding up and down like one of those plastic dogs people put on their rear parcel shelves.

He made up the best stories. Crazy adventures about dragons and monsters and curly-haired princesses trapped in towers until the brave knight, Sir Mattalot, charged in on a flying steed to save the day.

'Stop pandering to her, Matty. She needs to learn to do what she's told, when she's told.'

'Have you heard the one about Princess Sophie and the Mountain of Doom?' he asked me, paying no heed to my mother's protests.

'No, tell me!' I giggled, delighted he was taking my side. I could always rely on him for that.

'Ah, well this is a good one.'

He scooped me up in a fireman's lift, carried me off to my room while she followed all tuts and tight lips. A first-rate impression of Nanna G.

'Once upon a time, there was a beautiful princess.'

'Called Sophie?'

'You know her?'

He flipped me upside down, hanging me by my ankles.

'Matty, stop. You'll make her sick.'

She might as well have been talking to herself.

'Princess Sophie's the most beautiful princess in the world,' I said, making sure he got that part in.

'With the smelliest feet.'

I laughed so hard I thought I'd wet myself.

Matty Melgren. My hero.

A man who organised trips to Regent's Park and Hampstead Heath Fair. Who played Ludo with me on Sunday mornings and made waffles while my mother slept. Who bought me presents and dragged all the way to Golders Green for my favourite ice cream.

A man I loved. And a man who killed.

So they say.

From *Debate-it.com*

Could Matty Melgren be innocent?

Barry Altman, self-employed, proud grandfather

If Melgren is innocent then the world is flat and Scientology is the one true religion. This is just a ploy to stir up interest before *A Mask For All Seasons* hits our screens – not mine, I may add. No way I'm watching a film that glamorises a vile predator like that.

Matty Melgren was a manipulative psychopath who got off on other people's pain and conned everyone he knew into believing he was just a regular guy. Watch *Sessions with a Psycho*, the look in his eyes when the interviewer asks about his victims. It tells you all you need to know. The man is pure evil.

Charlene Fulton, sceptic, true-crime enthusiast

I honestly think he might be innocent. When you look at the court transcripts, you can see that the evidence against Matty was basically all circumstantial. Plus, the witness statements are very conflicting in terms of the offender's appearance and the shoes he was wearing.

I can't help wondering if maybe it's a case of mistaken identity??

On top of all that, he EXPRESSED SYMPATHY FOR THE FAMILIES:

"The victims weren't the only people who suffered, their families have suffered horribly too. In some way their pain is actually worse, given the length of time it has gone on for. But locking up the wrong person is hardly going to give them the closure they need."

Does that really sound like something an evil person would say? I don't think so.

SEVEN

'That doesn't sound like . . .'

My mother was on the phone to Nanna G. I was listening down the line, eavesdropping on their conversation about the nightmares I'd been plagued with ever since we'd moved to London. In the beginning, she'd let me crawl into bed with her, but once Matty had started staying over, everything changed.

'The bed's too small for three.'

Matty shifted across, made space for me to get in.

'It's fine, Ams. I can lie on my side . . .'

My mother was firm.

'Sophie's a big girl, she needs to sleep in her own room.'

'I'll be so quiet. Please.'

'I said, no. Now back to bed.'

'But I'm scared by myself.'

'How about I sit with you till you fall asleep?' Matty said, swinging his legs out of bed.

'Will you sing "On Raglan Road"?'

An Irish folk song about enchanted roads and carrying on in

the face of danger. My grandfather used to sing it to me back in Newton.

'Sure I will. Trust me, I'll have you snoring in no time.'

'I don't snore.'

'Your mam says the same thing. But she's like a train coming through.'

'Nightmares are the brain's way of processing fear,' Nanna G was saying now. 'Has Sophie come across anything to make her afraid?'

Something in her tone jarred, but I couldn't quite put my finger on what.

My mother started to answer, 'No, of course not. I—' She broke off. 'Sophie Brennan, are you listening in on my phone calls again?'

'No.'

'Put it down. Now.'

That night it was more of the same. A dungeon. A dragon. No one to hear me scream.

I woke up, heart thrashing, pyjamas damp with sweat. The dark room changed the shape of everything, brought the dream to life. The branch tapping against my windowpane was a witch's gnarly finger. The clothes on my chair, a crouching monster.

'Just a tree. Just a chair,' I whispered, my night-time mantra.

But could I be sure it was just a tree, just a chair?

I began to pant, to shake.

'Just a tree. Just a chair. Just a—'

I stopped, ears pricked. Graveyard still.

What was that?

A shuffling sound coming from the other side of the door. Someone taking care not to be heard.

My heart beat louder, so too the noises in the corridor. I wanted my mother, the sanctuary of her arms. But how to get to her without being eaten?

Oh God . . .

I took a deep breath, willed myself to the door, inched it open. Every fibre taut, adrenaline surging through my veins.

'It's you.'

My shoulders dropped, my body becoming suddenly heavy. In my nose was a fizzing as if I were about to cry.

Matty was crouched by the window, shirt rolled up to the elbow, examining his forearm. On his skin, a deep red scratch illuminated by the street lights.

'You hurt yourself?'

A whiff of cologne drifted over. The only time I'd ever known him to wear it.

He put a finger to his lips.

'Don't tell your mam. She'll only worry.'

I rolled my eyes. *Tell me about it.*

'She worries about everything.'

It felt good to know something my mother didn't. Our club of two.

'You want a Band-Aid?'

'What I want is for you to go back to bed. You won't grow if you don't sleep, pumpkin.'

I didn't think about that night again until four years later when the police showed us the photos. And by then it was too late to share Matty's secret with anyone.

EIGHT

My mother is on the floor kneeling by the coffee table. In front of her, a shoebox full of old photos. She's poring over them, pausing only to sip her gin. I can smell it from the doorway. Juniper berries. Lemon. Pine. The smell of my childhood. My childhood after him, although of course the pills were her real poison. My little helpers, she called them.

She tried to hide her dependency from me, but she wasn't very good at it. And then when she lost her job, she just gave up. Accepted she had a problem, didn't accept she needed to deal with it.

'I'm too much of a coward for suicide,' she told me once. 'These babies are the next best thing. If only it didn't take so long to reach oblivion.'

I was fourteen. Matty had been in prison for over a year. My mother, a whole lot longer.

'Don't judge her too harshly, Soph,' Linda said, helping clear up the place one afternoon while my mother slept off whatever she'd recently taken. 'She's one of the bravest people I know.'

I thought of the woman currently comatose in the bedroom.

'Brave? What makes you say that?'

Linda put down the rubbish bag she was holding, wiped the back of her hand across her brow.

'Leaving everything she knew to make a fresh start for the two of you. An ocean between her and her family. No man, no support system, nothing to fall back on. That takes guts.'

I glanced at the debris, the mess of our lives.

'Not exactly the best trade-off.'

Linda pressed her lips tightly together, gave me a sympathetic look.

'It's just a blip. I promise.'

I hoped she was right but couldn't muster her optimism.

'You have no idea what it's like,' my mother told me later that same day. 'The guilt I lug around. This bag of rocks stuck to my back.'

'You couldn't have known what he was doing. It's not your fault.'

'That's not what the rest of the world thinks. I can't walk down the street without people staring and pointing. Yesterday, an old guy stopped me in Safeway, told me I should be ashamed of myself.'

'What did you say?'

'That I *am* ashamed.'

She doesn't look up as I watch her now, but she knows I'm there; this woman with bird-like wrists and big wide eyes who the wind could carry off with a single puff.

'What are you looking at?' I ask, not that I need to. That shoebox comes out a lot.

'Do you think he ever loved us?'

How many times are we going to have this conversation?

'I don't think men like Matty are capable of love.'

She shakes her head like she knows best.

'The way he used to smile at me, the warmth in his eyes. You can't fake that.'

'Can't you?'

A sigh, right down to her soul.

'I don't know. Maybe you can. It seemed real though. The things he said, the way he was with me. With us.'

'What's real is he was a liar.'

She shakes her head again, this time as though it weighs the world.

'What he could have been. It's a tragedy. You remember what the judge said?'

Remember? How could I forget? It's brought up on every documentary ever made about Matty, in every film, on every podcast.

You had so much going for you. The pity of it, Mr Melgren.

Never mind the victims. The violence. The families who'll never recover. Olivia Paul's mother still leaves the porch light on, just in case this is the night her daughter will finally come home. Lydia Deval's family still haven't been able to give her a funeral.

The judge's remarks captured the problem though, Matty's ace in the hole. How conventional he looked. Someone you might work with. Meet for a drink. Take home to your parents.

A mask of normalcy. No graphic photos or witness testimony has ever quite ripped it off.

I'm still not convinced he did it.

He just doesn't look like a killer.

He seems too nice.

And through it all, Matty has given interviews, protested his innocence, filed appeals. It's both sickened me and given me hope. A demon and an angel whispering in each ear.

I nursed the doubt, couldn't bear for him to be guilty. Despite what I'd done, despite what it would mean if he wasn't.

I didn't want my childhood to be a lie, didn't want to hate the only man I'd ever loved. The father I'd never had.

I give my mother a hard time, but we're not so different really. Even now, decades on, I'm still rehashing the past, trying to make sense of it. Unable to let it go.

Which is why I have to see him, I think. To get answers before it's too late.

Despite the price I know I'll have to pay.

NINE

Love can't be purchased. Affection has no price.

A candy-pink Post-it note written in gold marker pen.

For the first year, my mother's relationship with Matty was picture perfect, a fairy tale. He'd dance her around the living room, the two of them singing along to 'Love You Inside Out'. Surprise her with flowers. Bring her breakfast in bed – *Because you looked too pretty to wake.*

But then things started to change; gradually, the way the tide comes in. Inching closer so you don't notice it until your shorts are wet and your sandcastle's a shrinking mound.

The building tension advanced in increments up the shoreline. Silence where there used to be conversation. Frowns where there had been smiles.

Matty and I still played the Prisoner Game, but whereas before my mother had watched us with sparkly-eyed approval, now she was twitchy. Matty's sense of fun seeming to destroy hers, to bring out the worst in her.

'You're a bit old for that,' she'd snap. Or, 'That's enough now.' And when that didn't work, 'Time to set the table, Sophie. I'm not going to ask you again.'

'Not going to ask again? Sounds like a result to me, eh pumpkin.'

'You're not helping, Matty. Sophie, come and do what you're told.'

Why did she have to nag so much, to be such cold water? What had changed? Since when had she become so stern, so like Nanna G?

You'll drive him away, I thought. Can't you see?

Is that why my father had left? Did she drive him away too?

Matty stopped coming over as much as he used to. He'd make plans to see us and not show up. Then when we were together, it was as though a light inside him had gone out. If he smiled, it looked like he was working at it. If he laughed, it sounded hollow.

I blamed Nanna G as much as my mother. I'd listened in on enough phone calls to tell the damage she was doing with her dust-bowl discontent.

'It's been over a year. What are you waiting for, Amelia-Rose? Don't you want a normal life?'

'You're not suggesting I propose to him?'

'Of course not. But you could nudge things along. Does he even know you'd like to get married?'

'I think so.'

'"I think so", isn't good enough. You need to be clear about what you need.'

'I don't want to pressurise him.'

'So what, you'd rather sit around playing house without a ring on your finger?' She clucked her tongue on the roof of her mouth, a knock of disapproval. 'You're sleeping with him, I suppose.'

'Mom!'

'What I'm saying is, where's his incentive to tie the knot? You're already giving away everything for free.'

'I—'

'And what about Sophie? Do you really think it's a good idea for you to be parenting on your own?'

It wasn't just about what was good for me though. Or Nanna's notions of respectability. Truth is, she had wedding fever. Same as pretty much everyone on Planet Earth right then.

My grandmother didn't own a passport and had never ventured further from home than New York City. But that didn't stop her being a massive fan of the royals. And with Charles and Diana about to get hitched, she was fizzing over like the baking soda volcano I'd made for the school science fair.

'Your father and I are getting up to watch it live on TV,' she told my mother, voice crackling over the speaker phone.

'Five in the morning,' Grandad grumbled in the background. 'It'll still be dark.'

Nanna ignored him.

'Did you hear, the dress cost £9,000? Nine thousand,' she repeated in a way that I knew meant she was shaking her head. 'There's even a back-up one in case something goes wrong.'

I knew all about Diana's dress. I'd been keeping a wedding scrapbook of magazine cut-outs, every detail about the big day stuck in, from how many bridesmaids the soon-to-be princess was having, to the number of beads on her ivory satin shoes.

I don't remember why Matty didn't watch the ceremony with

us. He can't have been working, it was a public holiday. He did come over in the evening though to join us for the highlights.

'Isn't she beautiful?' I purred.

For someone with zero interest in fashion or femininity, I was surprisingly sucked in by the theatre of the Royal Wedding.

Matty helped himself to a handful of M&Ms from the bowl on the coffee table, tipped the lot into his mouth in one go. When I attempted to copy him, I got a telling off from my mother.

'Beauty's only skin deep. It's what a person's like underneath that matters,' he told me.

'That's what Mum always says.'

He gave her knee a little squeeze.

'Wise woman, your ma.'

The schmoozing was annoying, though she seemed pleased, rewarding him with a little kiss and a private smile.

'Diana's lovely,' I persisted. *One, two, three. Look at me.* 'You can tell by her eyes.'

'Can you though? Your eyes are much prettier.'

I gave him a dig in the ribs.

'What's that for?' he said, rubbing his side, pretending to be hurt. 'I was paying you a compliment.'

'Complimenting yourself, more like. My eyes are exactly the same as yours. Even the shape.'

He grinned.

'Pair of beauties, so we are.'

That earned him another rib dig and me another satisfying 'ouch'.

This last coach which we can see comes to a stop at the bottom of the steps of St Paul's. The door opens and for the first time we see in all its glory, that dress. What a dream she looks . . .

I dug a handful of popcorn out of the mostly depleted bowl.

'They won't be calling her Lady Di any more.'

'Don't talk with your mouth full, Sophie.'

That was my mother, of course.

Matty gave me a wink. An ally in the ongoing war on manners.

'Lady Di. Ominous nickname, when you think about it,' he mused.

'What's ominous mean?'

My mother tutted, shook her head.

'It means, I don't know what's got into Matty.'

'But I bet I know what's got into you two. Chocolate and popcorn and very little else. Am I right, pumpkin?'

The royal wedding coverage eventually gave way to the local news.

The naked body of a young woman has been found on a towpath by Regent's Canal near Hampstead Road Lock . . .

'Hampstead Road Lock?' I whispered.

It was less than a mile from our front door. The three of us had taken an ice-cream stroll down there only the other day.

The body was found by a jogger at 6.30 this morning, partly concealed in undergrowth which may have been dislodged during the recent winds. The woman, aged between eighteen and twenty, appears to have been dead for at least three weeks and has not yet been formally identified.

A cordon has been set up at the scene and police have appealed for witnesses to come forward.

'There'll be more,' Matty said. 'You see.'

His tone sounded almost boastful, although that might just be my mind playing tricks. Knowledge of what was coming, colouring my recollection of what actually happened.

A false memory, Janice calls it. One that can't be trusted.

My mother flashed him an odd look.

'What makes you say that?'

There was a sharp note in her tone, disapproval.

Matty angled forward, looked from one to the other of us, his voice lowered even though it was only us there.

'Don't repeat it, but one of the victim support officers I work with says the woman had been strangled with her own underwear. A stocking tied in a big old bow around her neck like a Christmas present.'

My mother shot him a 'not in front of the children' look. Lips tight, dark scowl.

'Why does that mean there'll be more?' I asked, never one to be left out of anything.

As a bereavement counsellor Matty knew all about human psychology. *An expert in dark matter*, he used to joke.

'The fetishism and level of rage in the attack indicate a special sort of killer,' he answered, addressing my mother rather than me. It was something adults did all the time, though I expected better from him.

I tried again.

'Special how?'

'Someone who's killed before and who'll likely kill again. A person who enjoys taking lives and thinks of very little else.'

He didn't say 'serial killer'. That term hadn't been coined yet. But it wouldn't be long before it was.

TEN

I didn't see how Matty could be so sure the killer would strike again, but he was right. The murder at Hampstead Road Lock was just the beginning.

The victim was identified as Sheryl North, an eighteen-year-old homeless woman who'd come down to London from Liverpool six months before in search of a better life.

'Like Dick Whittington,' my mother remarked.

'Dick Whittington didn't get his head caved in,' Matty said.

I was curled up on the sofa watching *The Smurfs*. Matty had my feet in his lap, playing 'This Little Piggy' with my toes.

'Turn it up,' he said as the cartoon wound up and the news came on.

Before I'd had a chance to react, he'd taken the remote from me and done it himself, Little Piggy abandoned.

'Sheryl came to London looking for work, same as me,' a woman was saying; sleeping bag up to her armpits, arms wrapped tightly around her knees. 'You think it'll be different down here, more opportunities.' She scoffed. 'It ain't what it looks like on TV though.'

The camera switched to a reporter holding a furry micro-phone. Behind him, the backdrop of Euston station where Sheryl had disembarked on her arrival into the capital. That night she'd slept in a hostel. Two weeks later her money had run out and she was sleeping on the streets.

'A growing number of young people come to London every day in search of new opportunities. But with two and a half million unemployed and more joining the dole queue each week, work isn't easy to find. Which makes these newcomers easy targets for exploitation, and the city an increasingly dan-gerous place in which to live.'

'Switch it over, Matty. It's time for *Jim'll Fix It*.'

He usually made fun of the presenter. Worzel Gummidge with a medallion, he called him. *There's something off about that guy and it's not just his haircut.*

Today though he just held up a finger. *One minute.*

I harrumphed, kicked at the coffee table, but he didn't take any notice.

Meanwhile Olivia Paul, a student from North London, also in her late teens and bearing a strong physical resemblance to Miss North, has been missing since March.

A picture of a smiling girl with long curly hair filled the screen.

'Do you think she's been killed too?' I asked Matty.

His left eyebrow angled upwards.

'Maybe.'

I don't know why his frankness took me aback, it's not as if Matty was in the habit of sugar coating. But something in his tone or manner stung.

He gave me a sideways look, raised his arm for a cuddle.

'Come here to me, pumpkin.'

The burning behind my eyes receded. I breathed in the chocolate and cedarwood smell of him, felt my body relax.

We sat like that a while; him listening to the news, me listening to the soft tick of his watch, the internal sounds of his breathing and swallowing.

Miss Paul's mother, Carol, today issued an emotional appeal to her daughter to make contact:

'I love you, Livy. If you're watching this, please call me and let me know you're okay. We both said things we didn't mean that night, but I'm not angry, I promise. I just want you to come home.'

My mother and I had exchanged angry words earlier too.

'You said you needed extra sandwiches in your lunch box because you were hungry. You didn't tell me you were selling them to your classmates.'

'You're the one who's always saying I need to learn the value of money. I make 50p on your egg salad rolls.'

'Which you'll be giving to the collection plate this Sunday.'

I burned with resentment until dinner time. After that, fresh concerns took over.

'Do *you* think Olivia Paul's been killed?' I asked her.

Her hands hovered in mid-air over the salad bowl, frozen in the act of tossing the lettuce.

'Who said that?'

'Matty.'

Her lips tightened.

'Well, he shouldn't have.'

A pressure lifted.

'So, you think she's alive?'

'I think you should stop worrying. Supper's nearly ready. Have you washed your hands?'

I walked away scowling. From now on, I knew where to take my questions.

Later she and Matty had a row that had clearly been brewing all through supper. I listened in, ear to my bedroom door.

'What possessed you to tell her that girl's been murdered?'

'It was on the TV.'

'What were you thinking?'

'She asked me a question. Was I supposed to lie?'

'About that? Yes.'

'Seems to me you're best answering a kid honestly, Ams. Else how will they ever trust you?'

A warm feeling settled inside me. Finally, someone I could count on. It didn't occur to me till a long time afterwards that might have been exactly what he wanted me to think. And as a chronic eavesdropper, it was a safe bet I'd be listening.

Turned out Matty's pronouncement about the killer had been a safe bet too.

He and my mother were whispering on the sofa, discussing a surprise for my birthday. I was secretly hoping it would be the new BMX I'd been dropping not-so-subtle hints about. I strained to hear but it was all sibilance and sea sounds.

Matty seemed to be the one pushing for whatever it was. My mother had her arms folded, clearly more reticent.

He gave her a wry look.

'Don't tell me you wouldn't get a kick out of it,' he said, back to normal volume.

He glanced over to where I was sitting at the kitchen table surrounded by paint pots and brushes.

'What you doing there, pumpkin?'

'Maths homework,' I told him.

He wasn't the only one who could do wry.

'Cover the table please, smarty-pants,' my mother said. 'I've finished with the newspaper. Use that.'

I fetched it, pulled the pages apart. As I did, a headline caught my eye—

ANOTHER BODY FOUND IN NORTH LONDON

Olivia Paul?

My spine prickled. A hundred insects crawling along the bone.

I stole a look in my mother's direction to make sure she wasn't watching, then quickly scanned the article before she cottoned on to what I was reading and whipped it away. Recently she'd become rather over-protective about the current events I was exposed to. 'Unsuitable' her new favourite word.

Police today confirmed that a body discovered in an area of woodland in Highgate, North London is that of schoolteacher Katie Epstein who went missing last Friday after a night out with friends.

Not Olivia. Someone completely new.

Miss Epstein was found naked, a ligature tied so tightly around her neck her larynx was fractured. Although police say there are notable similarities between this crime and the murder of Sheryl North whose body was found on a canal towpath at Hampstead Road Lock, they are yet to confirm whether they believe the murders were committed by the same perpetrator.

Below the article was a photo of the victim. My muscles froze. My stomach writhed with worms.

Two women from very different walks of life; stripped naked, butchered and dumped like trash. Each slim and petite, with dark curly hair worn to their shoulders, just like Olivia Paul, who was still missing.

Even more disconcerting though, they were all the spitting image of my mother.

So much so they could have been sisters.

ELEVEN

Looking back through hindsight-tinted lenses, it's easy to think the murders consumed me. That I did nothing but watch the news and obsess over what was happening on our side of the river.

In reality, they were little more than a backdrop to our daily lives – to begin with, at any rate.

But, as more women started going missing, fears in the community heightened. Strangers discussed the murders in line at the supermarket. Mothers whispered about them at the school gates. Even our teachers drummed into us the importance of personal safety, *Stranger Danger* no longer just for pre-schoolers.

The killer liked petite, slim, white women with curly brown hair, but he was an opportunist. He wasn't interested in his victims' backgrounds or jobs, only whether they were easy targets. Lone targets out at night, his speciality.

Women started carrying whistles. Phoned their families and roommates to say they were on their way home, held their keys between their fingers as they approached their front doors. And yet still he struck.

If he'd operated in a particular area or gone after a particular group, I imagine the police would have had an easier time catching him. But he was clever, never hit the same place twice. Went after homeless people as often as professionals.

It meant anyone in the wrong place at the wrong time was a potential victim. Not least my mother, who looked so much like all the others.

'I wish you'd take a cab home,' Linda told her. 'It's not safe walking on your own. Especially now it's getting dark so early.'

She brushed off her friend's concerns, said she wasn't prepared to live her life looking over her shoulder.

Then the corpses of three more women were discovered. One near Lord's Cricket Ground in St John's Wood. One in the ponds on Hampstead Heath. And another in a pool of blood at the recreation grounds all the way over in Totteridge.

The police didn't reveal the exact details at the time, common practice in these sorts of cases, as I now know. There was one little snippet that leaked out though, the footprints found at several of the crime scenes. Prints not from shoes but bare feet. Though that wasn't all he left.

The woman found at the ponds was Brenda Marsh, a sixteen-year-old runaway from Brixton who'd been missing for three weeks. She'd had rocks lodged in her throat and vaginal cavity, to weigh her down in the water, according to speculation I've read since. A sign that the perpetrator was perfecting his process, that he had no remorse for his actions, the criminologists say.

'Who would do something like that?' I remember my mother asking Matty, flicking a quick glance in my direction.

'Quite something, isn't it?' he replied.

Did he sound proud, or is my memory toying with me again?

He'd just given me the birthday surprise he and my mother had been whispering about. Not a bike but a little white mouse I called Snowy. Eleven years old and highly original.

It tickled its way up my arm, down my sweater, coming out the other end into my waiting hand. Matty watched me, a smile dancing on his lips.

'I used to have a mouse when I was a kid,' he said. 'Teeny tiny bones.'

My mother gave him a funny look, told me to put Snowy down while I blew out my candles.

'Your mam's right,' Matty said. 'You don't want to set fire to the wee guy. Now make a wish, pumpkin.'

As police divers combed the canal, he tied a bandana around my eyes.

'You ever played Blind Man's Buff?'

The bandana was knotted too tightly. It smelled funny; sickly sweet like the perfume they sold at Superdrug for a fiver.

I tried to loosen it.

'Uh-uh. No peeking!'

He spun me around, faster and faster, then let go.

'Right, now find us!'

I was dizzy, stumbled, banged my shin hard against the table leg.

'You hurt her!'

'Jesus, Ams. You're acting like I did it on purpose.'

I was tugging at the bandana. Sparks danced in front of my eyes it was on so tightly.

I felt my mother's fingers working at the back of my head.

'This was a stupid game to play.'

'Lighten up, Ams. Let's have some fun.'

'I'm okay,' I said, shrugging my mother off. 'Matty's right, this is fun. Spin me again.'

This time when I banged my knee, I kept the *ows* to myself.

Later that night, I heard them talking. I was lying awake, high on sugar and unable to sleep. I thought about getting up, seeing if they'd let me sit with them a while. It was my birthday after all. But their voices gave me pause.

Matty was calm like always, but I could tell my mother was winding him up. When he was annoyed, he became quiet; as though reining himself in. The way a parent might speak to a recalcitrant toddler. Patient, extra reasonable. Trying not to blow.

So instead of joining them, I eavesdropped, annoyed she was goading him. That she had been all day.

No wonder he's getting fed up with us, I thought, which straight away sent my mind to my father, to where he was now. To trying to understand why he'd left us.

'You know how I feel about marriage,' Matty was saying.

'I'm thirty already. My mother's really on my case. I need to show her—'

'I didn't realise it was your mother I was dating.'

'You love me, don't you?'

'Of course I love you. I've proved that, haven't I?'

'So, what's the problem? Have you any idea what it's like for me? What people must think?'

'And that's a reason to get married? Because of what people think? I thought you were better than that, Amelia-Rose.'

Amelia-Rose? That was a first.

I heard the pad of his feet moving down the hallway followed by the front door clicking. No slam. No shouting. Just gone.

And then my mother hurling something at the wall. Crying. Her bedroom door banging shut.

TWELVE

We're tramping about on Parliament Hill. I don't know why I never moved away from the area, only that I couldn't. My guilt is a ghost I can't lay to rest.

'What did we do, Sophie?' my mother asks, Bambi eyes brimming. 'All those women. That poor little girl . . .'

'How could we have known? He fooled everyone.'

'Did he, though? Or was the man we knew, the man he was?'

It always comes back to this. What we should have done. How did we not realise we were living with a monster? Which morphs quickly into, *Was* he a monster?

Did Matty really kill all those women, or did they lock up the wrong guy? The twist in the tale, the serpent's bite.

And if he is innocent, what does that make me? Guilty. Shameful. A latter-day Judas. Take your pick, they'd all apply.

I long to know the truth, but if I did, would it set me free? Or bury me deeper?

My therapist asks me that question a lot. I've never been able to give her an answer.

'I don't know who Matty is any more,' I've told her, how

many times? 'I don't know who I am any more either. It's like getting halfway through a book only to find what you thought was chick lit is actually a horror novel.'

Janice will lean forward at this point, hands clasped in her lap, head cocked like a bird. This softly spoken woman with wispy tendrils escaping from her bun whom I see every week and who is both an anchor and no help at all.

'This isn't his story, Sophie,' she says. 'It's yours. You get to write your own ending, not him.'

I pick at my nails, always bleeding slightly around the edges.

'You're wrong,' I say. 'It's his story. It always has been.'

She remonstrates of course, dresses up the same arguments in different coats. But she can never persuade me. Just as the newspapers and book agents who continue to approach me all these years later, have never managed to persuade me to sell my account. My 'side', they call it.

'We want to title it *The Serial Killer's Daughter: My Life with Matty Melgren*,' I was told by a particularly determined tabloid journalist.

'I wasn't his daughter,' I said. 'Matty wasn't my dad.'

'Close enough though.'

'DNA would disagree.'

I shut the guy down, but he was right of course, and that's the problem, the reason Matty's conviction has been so difficult for me to deal with. He wasn't just my mother's boyfriend. He was also the closest thing I had to a father.

It's why I can't walk away from what happened to those women, can't shrug it off as having nothing to do with me. I'm infected by what he did or didn't do just as if I shared his blood.

The path curves around and the capital's showcase comes into view, the hard edges softened by the mist. An enchanted castle rising through the clouds. The London Eye, Canary Wharf, the dome of St Paul's where we watched Charles and Diana get married the day Sheryl North's body was found.

I inhale deeply, focus on the now, the way I've been taught. The cool, crisp air, the smell of earth and autumn. Birdsong and leaves on the turn, the sun shining through them, setting them ablaze. Part red, part green as though brushed with blood.

My heart rate returns to a normal rhythm. I walk in the direction of Parliament Hill Fields, Buster trotting at my side, wonky hips tipping him left and right.

We pass another dog walker, exchange a perfunctory 'Morning'. Keep going. Along the path, past the café, the playground.

Ahead is the running track. There's no one on it today and yet I see two people. A woman, in her twenties. Dark curls. Slim. A man with hair the colour of gold.

The temperature drops. The hairs on my neck stand up one by one in a Mexican wave.

I pat my flank, quicken my pace.

'Let's go,' I tell Buster.

Twenty years and I've never made it to the running track.

THIRTEEN

This morning, police announced they are hunting a single perpetrator believed to be responsible for the deaths of at least six women in the last three months. Meanwhile, the number of women going missing from North London is growing steadily, with two more disappearances added to the list this week.

Andrew Mulveny has the story . . .

Angry residents are demanding more is done to stop the killings. One woman who lives in Highgate near the woods where the second victim was discovered says she's terrified to go out.

'It's got to the point where I'm scared to leave the house,' she told the reporter, and she's not the only one.

North London based minicab firms have reported a forty-five per cent increase in bookings by women since July, while sales of panic buttons in the area have risen threefold.

Police say the victims are similar in appearance: young, slim women in their late teens or early twenties with curly brown hair, between five foot two and five foot five. Although they have stressed that all women should be extra vigilant regardless of their appearance.

Scotland Yard says it believes a single psychopathic killer is responsible for the crimes. However, as Detective Inspector Harry Connor, who is heading up the investigation, told a press conference this morning:

'It would be improper from an investigative perspective to become tunnel visioned and exclude the possibility of a copycat or multiple offenders.'

Andrew Mulveny, Channel 3 news, Lond—

My mother came into the living room, saw what was on, and killed the TV.

'I've told you, I don't want you watching that.'

Her jaw was clenched. For a moment she could have been Nanna G telling me to chew with my mouth shut.

'I think you should get a new job,' I said, eyes fixed on the now black television screen, picking at my nails.

'Why would I do that?'

'So you can work somewhere closer to home. I mean, with all this going on . . .'

She wet her lips, tilted her head the way a sparrow will listen for rain.

'I know it's scary, what's going on. But don't you think you're overreacting a bit?'

'It's dark when you walk home. Please, Mummy. It's not safe.'

'It's perfectly safe, sweetie. There are always plenty of people around.'

There weren't though. Her route was quite deserted in places. I told her as much, but she shrugged it off, called me her Little Miss Worry-Wart.

'Will you at least straighten your hair?'

She laughed.

'Can you imagine what Matty would say about that?'

I could. According to him, her hair was her best feature. *Don't ever change it, Ams.*

I looked at my mother, took in the dip of her head, the way she was rubbing the back of her neck.

'You're scared too, aren't you?'

She started to answer but the phone cut her off.

'Hello? . . . Oh, hey, Matty.'

They were talking again, the argument I'd overheard the night of my birthday consigned to the dustbin of their not always romantic history.

'The honeymoon phase doesn't last for ever, Am,' Linda told her.

The fairy-tale part may be over, she added, but that didn't mean the relationship was. She went on to use a strange and somewhat muddled metaphor of resuscitation and drowning.

'She's a dark one,' my mother said one time, adding with a laugh that's what she liked about her. 'It's edge that makes a person interesting.'

I mulled over Linda's advice, reasoned it might be a good thing that Matty and my mother were less lovey-dovey. A sign they were comfortable being themselves. That they were entering a deeper, more meaningful stage. I was reading a lot of Judy Blume back then. *Just Seventeen* too.

My mother cupped her hand over the receiver.

'Matty's suggesting lunch. You up for that?'

'Pizza Hut?'

'Sure.'

I responded with a thumbs-up.

At the restaurant Matty polished off a Super Supreme with extra beef, pepperoni and ham followed by an ice cream sundae.

'You're going to explode,' I said in admiration. 'You been running a marathon or something?'

'Sophie!'

'What?'

'It's not for you to—'

Matty ignored her, tilted his head at me.

'Meanwhile, you've eaten nothing, sweetheart. What's up?'

My mother answered for me, an annoying habit made all the more so by the fact she had conniptions any time I interrupted her.

'She's stressing about the murders.'

'That true, pumpkin?'

'The victims look like Mum. What if—'

I broke off, unable to finish the sentence. Last thing I wanted was to start crying at the table.

They exchanged a private look.

'And you're worried that—'

'He might hurt her.'

Matty shook his head, smiled kindly.

'These women get into risky situations, Soph. Walking about on their own at night. That's what puts them in danger, not the way they look.'

'You're blaming them? The guy's a nut job. A total psycho, they said on TV.'

'That's enough,' my mother exclaimed, as if I'd used a swear word.

I looked at her.

'What's wrong with "psycho"?'

Matty took a deep breath, paired his silverware neatly on the plate and dabbed his mouth with a napkin.

'I promise you've nothing to be afraid of. Your mam's safe. He's not coming after her.'

At the time, I found his words soothing. Trusted him in the unquestioning way only children can.

I have plenty of questions now though. In particular, how was he able to guarantee our safety with such confidence?

The obvious answer haunts me.

And why it didn't occur to me then.

Extract from the *Herald Gazette*

New Documentary Shows Change in Monster Melgren's Voice When Asked About His Victims

A new docuseries – *Sessions with a Psycho* – will feature televised conversations with serial murderer Matty Melgren from inside Battlemouth Prison where he is serving a life sentence with no parole.

The programme marks the fifteen-year anniversary of his conviction for the murders of nine women in North London and an eight-year-old girl in Brownstone, Ireland in the early 1980s.

In a trailer for the programme, Melgren says:

'It's important people hear my side of the story. I've been painted as this monster, an evil being with terrible urges I can't control. But that's not who I am.

'I'm a regular guy, locked up for crimes I didn't commit. Imagine how that feels, spending your life behind bars even though you didn't do anything wrong.'

In another trailer, the interviewer tells the camera:

'When I asked him about the murders, Matty's tone changed. It became deeper, noticeably lower-pitched. He began speaking more slowly too, more deliberately. The way you do when speaking to a person you find attractive. When you're turned on.'

The series is directed by Emmy winner Henry Salinger, who also directed *My Name is Matty*, a feature film starring Jeffrey Dean Morgan, who had to dye his hair blonde for the role of Melgren.

Extract from the *Tribune*

'When I asked him about the murders, Matty's tone changed. It became deeper ... He began speaking more slowly too ... The way you do when speaking to a person you find attractive. When you're turned on,' says Tom Richardson, the interviewer in a new docuseries about serial killer, Matty Melgren.

Did it though? Really? Or is this just yet another example of someone attributing more to Melgren than is really there? Of casting him in the role of an archetypal villain. And is doing so, perpetuating another form of villainy?

As so often happens in programmes of this sort concerning Melgren, the interviewer paints him as the 'impossible-to-understand killer' owing to the simple fact of his good looks and intelligence. The only reasonable answer to – How could someone so apparently normal be guilty of such heinous crimes? – being to rip off the mask and reveal the monster beneath. And this is where the problem lies.

In the same way juries so often fail to convict handsome, well-educated young men of rape because they don't want to 'ruin their lives', there is something profoundly perverse about feeling the need to portray Melgren as some kind of anti-hero.

Claiming his voice changed when talking about the women he brutally murdered plays directly into this unfortunate trope and effectively lionises a man who is frankly little more than mediocre.

FOURTEEN

'I have so many questions. It haunts me not knowing what happened to her, if she might still be alive . . .'

Olivia Paul's mother was on television last night, yet another documentary about Matty. It's been twenty years since his conviction, yet the public's fascination with him hasn't waned. They're still greedy for details, intrigued by the man behind the mask.

How could someone so apparently normal be so evil? they ask. What drove a seemingly well-adjusted, smart and handsome man to rape and murder? How was he able to hide his true self for so long?

I'm intrigued too, though for different reasons. Intrigued to know why, when. If . . .

Over the years, the internet has become both my kindest friend and my cruellest foe. It offers rays of hope that quickly fade; nuggets of information that turn out to be false leads or wild fantasy. A suggestion he was framed (that one surfaces a lot). That the evidence against him was fabricated. That another serial killer he never met has it in for him.

A preponderance of police reports, trial transcripts, photographs. Witness statements, interviews with fellow inmates, forum threads. So many threads.

A rabbit hole of information and misinformation that I dive down regardless, an addict in need of a fix, much the same as the addiction they say drove Matty. Highs that could never live up to the thrill of his first kill, and yet which he was compelled to seek out again and again until he was caught.

I still struggle to believe it though; the gentle-eyed man I loved, stalking women, cutting them up. Hankering after his next hit. Yet other people describe it so clearly, seem to understand him so well.

Richard Klein, the FBI criminologist, described him as 'a shadow; a creature of the night leaving no trail'.

The press dubbed him the Shadow after that. I imagine the name would have rather appealed to Matty. Image always was important to him and the Klein moniker was certainly more dramatic than the anodyne 'North London Killer', which everyone called him at first.

Over the years I've read a library of profiling books. Klein, Ruskin and Doyle piled up on my nightstand, in a desperate bid to understand him. To get inside his head as if that'll finally shine a torch on the truth. Why, when, if.

The internet calls to me most though. *La Belle Dame sans Merci.* The temptress I can't resist, offering a treasure trove of information at my fingertips. The hope of new evidence. The punch-the-air excitement when I think I've finally caught hold of a clue, swiftly followed by gut sinking disappointment when it turns out to be another dead end.

I don't have friends any more; no one I can call for a chat or a gossip. No one who wants to hear the honest answer to, 'How are you doing?' Janice doesn't count. She's paid to listen.

No one wanted anything to do with me after Matty was arrested, although the papers were constantly printing quotes from, 'a source close to Matty's daughter . . .'

Never mind that I wasn't his daughter. That I hadn't spoken to anyone. That there were no sources close to me.

When I first came to London, I longed to be accepted, after his arrest I just wanted to be left alone. I found I didn't have anything in common with the girls who'd once been my friends. They were interested in clothes and boys. I knew where those interests could lead. When I heard them whispering about so and so's smile, all I could think was that Matty had a nice smile too.

Twenty years on, I still keep to myself. I date a little, but nothing ever lasts and nothing is ever serious. Buster's the only one who knows my secrets and whilst I know he'll keep them, his advice isn't worth much, though his cuddles are gold.

'We were too trusting,' my mother says. 'That was the problem.'

'Not any more,' I tell her.

The pendulum has swung the other way. I no longer trust anyone.

Trust is about allowing yourself to be vulnerable. Having faith the person you open your heart to won't maul it to shreds.

How can I do that after what happened? How can I even trust myself?

FIFTEEN

'You've got to trust him,' Linda told my mother. 'Stop questioning the poor guy all the time.'

We didn't see Matty the whole of that December. He'd gone to visit his parents in Brownstone, he said, a small village in County Wicklow, Ireland.

It's completely cut off. The sort of place you can go days without bumping into another living soul.

'Sounds lovely,' my mother answered when he mentioned he was going. 'All that peace and quiet. What do you say, Soph?'

He didn't take the hint.

From the little he told us about them, we figured Matty's folks must be hard up. From the great deal my mother told Linda, that's why he hadn't asked us to join him.

She was over at our place again. She helped herself to another Walker's shortbread, dunked it in her tea. Five years in the UK, and I still didn't understand the British obsession with soggy cookies.

'Could be Matty's embarrassed about his family's financial situation. Maybe that's why he didn't ask you to go with.'

'He thinks I'd judge him?' my mother replied, horrified.

Linda pulled a face that involved tucking her chin into her neck and scrunching up her nose. The sort of expression Nanna G would have warned would get stuck that way if the wind changed.

'I'm sure he knows deep down you wouldn't. But think how he dresses. The cufflinks, the jackets, the perfect hair . . .'

'What are you saying?'

Linda shrugged.

'That image is obviously important to him.'

'So?'

'So, he wants the world to view him a certain way. If you saw what he came from—'

'I might think less of him?'

'He might think so.'

'That's ridiculous.'

'Doesn't mean I'm wrong.'

My mother fiddled with her crucifix, worried at her lower lip.

'Do you think that's why he still hasn't asked me to marry him?'

'Goodness only knows what goes on inside a man's head, Am.'

I sat staring out of the picture window, watching the snow fall; heard the click of Linda's lighter, the long exhalation following her first drag.

I glanced at my mother, no doubt what she was thinking.

Grandad used to have a sixty-a-day habit. He only quit after part of his lung had to be removed. *The operation mellowed him,* she told me one time. *You wouldn't guess it now, but he had quite the temper on him back in the day. Lashed out like a whip if his pride was hurt. Bit like you* . . .

The comparison wasn't meant as a compliment.

'Those things will kill you,' she said, watching Linda through disapproving eyes.

'We all got to go sometime, Am.'

She blew out a perfect smoke ring.

'You look like Rizzo in *Grease*,' I told her.

'You wouldn't be so admiring if you could see her insides,' my mother replied tartly.

Linda scoffed, shook her head.

'You're in a nice mood tonight, Amelia-Rose.'

'I'm sorry. It's this business with Matty. And the weather. Sophie's school's been shut nearly a week already because of the snow.'

I puffed on the windowpane, drew a smiley face in the condensation. Told her that was fine by me.

'You'll have to get your mum to take you to Parliament Hill, Soph. Go sledging.'

'Can we, Mum?'

'Not in these storms.'

'They're saying it hasn't been this cold since the turn of the century,' her turncoat friend replied.

'The whole country's at a standstill. What's wrong with the British? Haven't they heard of snowploughs?'

'Sledging'll warm us up,' I said, steering the conversation back to where I wanted it.

'I said no, Sophie.'

'Linda's right. You are in a foul mood,' I muttered.

'What did you say to me?'

'That Linda's right. It would be fun.'

She looked at me a moment, eyes narrowed, then went back to angsting about Matty's silence.

'Three weeks he hasn't called. Not even on Christmas Day. Sophie was crying her heart out.'

Absolutely no regard for my pride.

'Was not,' I glowered.

They weren't listening though.

'It's not the 1950s, Am. You can call him, you know?'

'He didn't leave a number.'

'Really? Well, have you tried getting it off the operator?'

'She can't. She doesn't even know what Matty's parents are called,' I said with a degree of vengeance.

'Who's "she"?' my mother snapped. 'The cat's mother?'

I made a show of looking at my bum.

'No tail . . .'

'Go to your room.'

'What? I was only—'

'Now!'

I stomped off, slammed my door. Sat with my back pressed up against it, arms hugged around my knees. I planned how to punish her when she knocked, knowing it wouldn't take long before she was along to apologise. But she didn't come.

No wonder Matty hasn't phoned, I thought. Who'd want to phone *her*?

I opened the door a crack to see what was going on. The scene was exactly as I'd left it. Her and Linda still gassing on the couch, working their way through a packet of Maryland cookies now the shortbreads were finished.

'He must be seeing someone else. It's the only thing that makes sense.'

My abdominals tightened. I felt a sudden burning behind my eyes.

Was she right? Had Matty left us? Disappeared like my dad? Would I ever see him again?

Linda answered in a weary voice that suggested it wasn't the first time she'd given this speech.

'Chrissake, Am. The guy loves you. Just give him some space.'

I jumped on it, anything that meant Matty would be back.

My mother was always on my case. I hated it, felt suffocated. Maybe he felt the same way.

It would explain why he'd gone to Ireland, why he hadn't phoned. He needed room to breathe. To put some distance between him and my mother second guessing him all the time. Banging on about marriage, questioning every little thing he said and did.

I resolved then and there that if only he'd come back I'd make things easier for him. Stick up for him, show I was on his side. Same as he always did for me.

You're my best girl, he used to tell me. *A chip off the old block*, whatever that meant.

I asked him once, but he just laughed, told me to speak to my mother.

'Please God, bring him home,' I whispered now, eyes clenched in concentrated prayer. 'If you do, I promise I'll never let Mummy be mean to him again.'

Is that where it started? Me turning a blind eye. Refusing to believe he could ever be in the wrong. Or had I been doing it long before that? Had my mother too?

Janice has a saying; *Your gut knows before your head.*

Did my mother's gut know what he was? That he wasn't as perfect as he seemed? Is that why she was always doubting him? Always asking questions?

Or was it something worse? Did her constant nagging hem him in? Make him feel angry, frustrated?

Drive him to kill women who looked just like her?

SIXTEEN

January 1982. With no fresh murders reported since the previous September, the tension which had gripped our leafy corner of the world began to dissipate. A breath long held, finally released.

The apparent hiatus in the killings has led some to speculate whether the offender may have been imprisoned for another crime. Or perhaps even committed suicide – the *Post* wrote in one of its leaders.

The dreaded 11+ high school exams were approaching. We'd been told to read the papers every day, ideally a selection of titles from varying political standpoints. Even better if we could compare tabloids with broadsheets, our form teacher, Mrs Coates advised us – always one for extra homework.

Miss Bacon was thankfully long gone, along with my American accent and inability to fit in. I was delighted, a little sorry, and relieved about each of those thing in that order. I'd tried to convince myself I didn't need friends, but as my mother said, no one is an island. Somewhat ironic coming from her, but that didn't mean she wasn't right.

I've never been more conscious of how I was standing or

what I was doing with my hands as I was when I had no friends. Nor has a school noticeboard ever been more interesting.

Now though, I had people to talk to, to sit with at lunch, even to walk home with. And while Sally Sniders, the erstwhile freckled ringleader, was still a stone on an otherwise smooth road, I had at least learned to kick her to the kerb.

My mother was always going on about how you can't tell what a person's really like till you've walked in their shoes.

'Maybe you should try doing it with Sally,' she suggested adding that bullying came from a place of weakness rather than strength.

'I suspect she's insecure. Making you feel small to big herself up.'

When she was out of the room, Matty told me, forget this girl's shoes. *What you want to do is crush her.*

'Show you're stronger than she is. She'll leave you alone then.'

I liked his approach better than my mother's. I also liked the idea of punching Sally in the face, though things hadn't gone so well the last time I'd taken it to the mattresses. I explained my predicament.

'You ever heard of that saying; Sticks and stones can break your bones?'

'. . . but words will never hurt you.'

He nodded. *That's the one.*

'It's backwards though. Take it from me, the right words can destroy a person.'

Echoes of Nanna G in my grandfather's accent.

I spent the rest of the evening trying to identify the right words to destroy Sally.

Next day, she started up in her usual friendly manner the second I stepped into class.

'Well, if it isn't Miss USA.'

The chatter stilled, everyone tuning in for the morning show.

I looked her up and down like Clint Eastwood in *Hang 'Em High*, Matty's favourite movie. ('I used to watch it with my dad too.')

'You can make fun of my accent all you like, Sally Sniders, but it won't stop you being fat and ugly.'

That got some laughs. The circle closed in.

Sniders spluttered.

'Well, at least I like talk properly.'

'Like, do you?'

More laughs, glorious mutterings of 'Good one, Sophie.'

It went on in that vein until Sniders recognised she was beat. When there was no one around, she said she wanted to be friends and did I want to go to her house after school for tea?

I wasn't keen on spending any more time with the girl than was strictly necessary, but I'd been taught never to turn down an apology. So I thanked her and accepted her invitation graciously.

'I guess I could come over . . .'

That afternoon, she gifted me a sticker book and a *Jackie* magazine. I accepted those graciously too.

By the time we were in Mrs Coates' form, I hadn't punched anyone for years and was even spelling 'colour' with a 'u'. But not everything was changed for the better.

'What does your daddy do?' was a recurring question to which I had no answer. While the ritual of making Father's

Day cards in Art was an activity I dreaded every time June rolled around.

But Miss Blythe, Sophie doesn't have a dad . . .

Yes, I do. Else how would I have been born?

Not having a father was one thing. Having a mother came with its own bank of problems.

Mine wasn't like the other mums. She didn't bake cupcakes or attend coffee mornings. Her job meant she couldn't come to school shows or help out at fundraisers. My classmates' mothers were homemakers who went to the theatre and out to dinner with their husbands in the evening. My mother worked in an accountancy office and spent the evenings reading in bed.

When you're eleven, being different isn't a good thing.

'Your ma's a wonderful woman, Sophie Brennan,' Matty told me one time when I'd gone moaning about her to him. 'Makes the best apple crumble I've ever tasted. Pretty good at Gin Rummy too,' he added when I looked less than impressed.

'Can't be that good. I always beat her.'

'Only because she lets you.'

I shuffled around, looked at my feet.

'I just wish she could be more like everyone else.'

'Have you ever considered perhaps they'd do well to try and be more like her?'

I told him, not really. No.

'How many of your friends' pampered mammies do you think could put food on the table and raise their kids by themselves the way she has?' he asked. 'How many of them have her determination? Even half her imagination?'

'I just wish—'

He put a hand on my shoulder.

'You'll see things differently when you're older.'

'Maybe,' I answered. But I doubted I would.

Then while he was in Ireland, something happened to make his prediction come true.

Lucy Allen, a girl from school who lived close by, turned up one Saturday afternoon full of tears. *Like her face was melting*, my mother said afterwards.

'Have you seen Mozart?' she sobbed.

Mozart was her dachshund, an old guy with a limp and a lung condition that made him wheeze like a chain-smoker.

'We were in the park and I lost him. My parents'll kill me if I go home without him.'

My mother came up behind me, already shrugging on her coat.

'We'll help you look,' she said. 'Go get your shoes on, Sophie.'

Lucy sniffled.

'I don't know where . . .'

'You're not going to find him crying in our doorway, that's for sure. Come on.'

We searched for hours; the light fading, trees becoming silhouettes against the greying sky.

Lucy threw her hands up.

'I give up. It's hopeless. We're never going to find him.'

My mother wasn't having any of it.

'Giving up's not an option. Imagine how scared the poor thing must be in the dark on his own.'

I noticed then how dark it was, how few people were about. Matty's voice in my head. *Easy prey.*

'Maybe we should go back,' I told my mother, her curly hair bouncing in the wind. 'It's not safe out here.'

'It's perfectly safe. Do you think I'd let anything happen to you?'

'I mean . . . what if . . .'

I couldn't bring myself to mention the killer directly. I had no problem bringing him up at home with the doors and windows shut, but out here it felt like a summoning spell. Talking of the devil.

My mother was less superstitious.

'Being a Nervous Nellie isn't going to help anyone. Now think, Lucy. If you were Mozart, what would you be doing right now?'

'Looking for food, knowing him.'

A light went on in my mother's eyes. She started marching in the direction of the café, leaving us to scamper after her.

'Recognise anyone?'

The dachshund was sitting by the café door waiting for someone to open up and let him in.

'Your mother's the best,' Lucy told me as we walked home, Mozart hoppitying at her heels.

'Yeah, the café was a good call.'

She shook her head, put a hand on my arm to make me look at her.

'Not just the café. I don't know anyone else who'd have spent a whole afternoon looking for someone else's dog.'

'She didn't mind,' I said.

'Exactly,' Lucy replied.

SEVENTEEN

'I don't mind what papers you read, but you need to be able to talk fluently about what's going on in the world. Have an opinion on the news of the day,' Mrs Coates had told us as we packed up our desks for the Christmas holidays and again while we re-loaded them with books on our return.

That's possibly when my interest in the murders really took off. No more bodies had been found since the previous autumn, but journalists continued to talk about the Shadow as if he were still active.

Apart from the three days Mark Thatcher went missing in the Sahara, news was slow at the beginning of '82. Speculating about the killer gave them something to fill their columns with and me something to fill my head. Whereas before I'd only caught the odd headline or feature on TV, now I could quote whole theories, dates and statistics.

'Did you know women are three times more likely to be killed by a partner than a stranger?' I told my mother shortly after the Mozart incident, three and a half weeks after Matty's desertion. 'And a third of them tried to leave their partners before they were killed.'

'That's terrible.'

I nodded. Yes.

'Do you think it happens the other way round too?'

'What do you mean?' she asked.

'Women killing their husbands.'

She pushed her porridge away.

'Can we change the subject, Soph? It's a bit early in the morning for all this.'

It wasn't too early for the breakfast news though.

Police investigating the execution style murder of six women in the past seven months have confirmed there is a pattern to the crimes suggestive of a sole perpetrator. These motiveless random killings by an offender stalking victims in a series of separate attacks are known as 'serial murder', a new term coined by the FBI.

We heard about police upping patrols around North London, and Scotland Yard leaving 'no stone unturned' in their hunt for the murderer. Again, I begged my mother to change her hairstyle, wear heels to give her some height. Again, she refused to 'humour' me.

There's a limit to how much you can write about something that's no longer happening. With no new killings, the amount of newsprint devoted to the Shadow began to dwindle, other world events taking over the pages.

Erika Roe streaking across the pitch during the England–Australia rugby union match. Madness getting into the Top Ten. The Queen opening the Barbican Centre.

In other words, life fell back in line. I stopped seeing lurkers around every corner. Stopped listening to Des Banister, our creepy downstairs neighbour, coming home at all hours and running his engine under my window. Stopped wondering quite so much if there was a reason the Shadow's victims looked so much like my mother.

The weather lifted and the snow began to thaw. The pigeon-coloured sky giving way to crystalline blue and bright winter sunshine.

'Pathetic fallacy,' my mother called it, her mood lifting too as she began to get used to Matty's absence. 'Put it in your "New Words Book", Soph. It'll impress the examiners.'

I secretly hated these faceless people on whose whims my future seemed to hang. And I hated having to do the 11+, was convinced I was going to crash and burn. My friends were all taking it too, but the stakes were higher for me.

To get a place at the prestigious local private high school, with its trips abroad and top of the range science labs, I'd need a bursary – a sort of scholarship where the fees were largely waived. No way we could have afforded it on what my mother earned otherwise.

'It's a total long shot,' I said.

'To give you the best shot,' she replied.

Her education had been cut off by pregnancy. *I never had the chance to make something of myself.* And, in the way so many parents want for their children what they never had for themselves, she was determined I should have *The best schooling possible so you can do whatever you want without having to change who you are.*

'So bright,' my teachers told her. 'Works so hard. A brilliant future ahead of her.'

I just had to get through the wretched tests first, every day mapped out on the revision timetable I stuck on my bedroom wall. Every day crossed off when it was done.

I didn't want to talk about studying now though, didn't want my mother to talk about it either. *Let's just enjoy our walk.*

We were stamping about on Parliament Hill. I was trying to persuade her to get me a kite.

'This is the perfect place to fly it,' I said. 'The open space. How high up we are.'

'If I recall, the last one I bought you got tangled in a tree.'

'Well, I'm older now. I know what I'm doing.'

She laughed.

'The two don't always go together.'

We stopped at the café, bought hot chocolate. Sat on benches blowing steam off the top, watching the world go by.

I let out a puff of air, the condensation swirling in front of my mouth.

'Like a dragon,' I said.

'I love you,' she replied.

I smiled into my coat collar, couldn't remember when she'd last said it. Couldn't remember when I'd last said it to her either come to that.

We sat awhile pressed together against the cold. For the first time in a long time, neither of us mentioned Matty. A man and woman swinging a little girl by the arms gave me a twinge, but only for a moment and then it was gone.

I slipped a hand into my mother's.

'I love you too,' I told her.

A spaniel raced past, ears flapping, a pain au chocolat in its jaws. Then an old guy in a Barbour and flat cap giving chase.

'Come back, you swine! That's my breakfast.'

My mother caught my eye, the corners of her mouth twitching. We both cracked up, not because it was that funny so much as it felt good to laugh together.

She put an arm around me, pulled me close.

'We're okay,' she whispered.

'Yes,' I said.

The red light was blinking on the answerphone when we got home. My mother hit 'Play' at the same time as suggesting Scrabble, 'Or maybe a movie.'

The voice coming out of the machine guillotined her sentence—

It's Matty. I'm back.

EIGHTEEN

I'm back . . .

We hadn't heard from Matty once. No phone calls, no Christmas card. Nothing.

A vanishing. Gone without a trace. Just like Olivia Paul, whose mother was on *The Outlook Show* again that night appealing for information about her daughter.

By the time we listened to his answerphone message, something in my mother had disappeared too. The despair that had plagued those first weeks of his absence had gradually eased and in its place came a sort of acceptance.

She stopped tormenting herself with what Matty might be up to, stopped bringing his name into every conversation. Began to move on without realising that's what she was doing.

She'd even started mentioning a man from work, a boring sounding accountant called Barry. Repeating anecdotes he'd told her which she seemed to find hilarious, though I told her I couldn't see why. Matty was much funnier and, unlike this Barry guy, he never stooped to dad jokes.

I missed him; thought about him every morning when I

woke up and every night as I drifted off to sleep. I agonised that I'd never see him again, that I'd forget the sound of his voice the way I'd forgotten my father's.

Even so, something had shifted in me too. The blame I felt towards my mother for driving him away softened. My anger at her subsiding, despite the gaping hole of his absence.

She'd been moody with him, often unfair. Though he could be moody too, I realised. He cancelled plans at the last minute or else didn't show up at all. And when he did spend time with us it was often as though part of him wasn't there.

'In your own world again,' my mother would say.

'What's that?'

It made me laugh though I'm not sure it was meant to. Matty would look surprised for a moment then laugh too as if only just getting a punchline.

I'd been given a diary for Christmas, had ambitions of being the next Adrian Mole. Wrote in it religiously for five days.

Okay, mum can be difficult. But that's not a reason to walk out on your family. You don't not call. You don't not give them a way to call you.

And then the words echoed out of the answerphone – *I'm back.*

Straight away everything changed. Life was going to return to normal. Everything was going to be okay.

Disappointment, the cruel child of hope. Perhaps if I'd been less quick to believe things were looking up, I'd have been better prepared for their trip south.

In that moment though, we both believed. Both grinned from ear to ear at the thought of seeing Matty again.

'Let's go and surprise him,' my mother said. A hot flush of pink on each cheek.

All this time and we'd never been to Matty's place. He either came around to ours or else we went out together. Turned out he didn't live far away, a terraced house near Hampstead Road Lock.

My mother kept her finger too long on the doorbell, hit the knocker too.

'Give him a chance,' I said.

Already I was hyper aware of anything she might do to piss him off. Whatever happened, we couldn't lose him again.

The spy hole went momentarily dark. We heard him turn the bottom lock, pull back the security chain.

He opened up dressed like a catalogue model; white collared shirt beneath a baby blue V-neck sweater. Brown trousers with crisp creases down each leg.

'My two favourite ladies. What a nice surprise!'

He glanced over his shoulder, hand resting on the door jamb. Blocking our path.

My mother peered past him into the hallway.

'Aren't you going to ask us in?'

'It's a bit of a bombsite,' he warned with a laugh. I'd missed the sound of it, the way it made his eyes crinkle. 'But if you don't mind mess, be my guests.' He stepped aside, made a sweeping gesture with his arm. 'Welcome to Casa Melgren.'

My mother wrinkled her nose.

'What's that smell?'

'Drains are blocked. Awful hard to find a plumber right now, so it is.'

'Speak to Des. Maybe he can help.'

Matty winked at me, pulled a zombie face. Des the Undead, we called him privately. My mother didn't approve. *It's not his fault. He's just a bit socially awkward, that's all.*

I giggled, slipped my hand in his, the way I'd done with her in the park. His hand was bigger, it swallowed mine whole.

'I'm glad you're back,' I told him.

'Me too, pumpkin.'

He pulled me close, kissed the top of my head. Any lingering resentment I'd had about how he'd abandoned us melted away. Matty belonged with us, the missing jigsaw piece.

My mother was less forgiving.

'Glad I'm back?' he whispered in her ear.

A kid who knows they've been bad. *Do you still love me?*

She shrugged him off.

'Six weeks. They don't have phones in Ireland?'

'Not this winter, they don't.'

She cocked an eyebrow, gave him a sceptical look.

'The storms were terrible. Worst snow in a hundred years, guy at the post office said. The lines went down as soon as I got there. I felt terrible, knew how you'd be feeling. You must have thought I'd forgotten about you. And then when you didn't hear from me over Christmas . . .' He shook his head. 'I'm so sorry, Ams.'

She shrugged.

'I figured it was the weather.'

'I knew you would.'

I glanced at him. If he realised he'd just contradicted himself, it didn't show.

'You weren't exaggerating!' I exclaimed, delighted. 'What a tip!'

My mother went red.

'Sophie!'

'What? You said it smelled.'

Matty chuckled.

'Kid's got a point. The state of the place. It's practically a crime scene.'

I noticed then that he always backed me up, even when it wasn't in his interests to do so. A sign of his love, I thought at the time. Later it occurred to me there might have been a different reason. By that time my trust was less easily bought.

He was right about it being like a crime scene though. There were crumpled clothes strewn over the couch. Empty champagne bottles. And a leash. Leather handle, heavy silver chain.

I picked it up, examined it.

'You've got a dog?'

He took the leash from me gently, glanced at my mother.

'Now how'd that get here?'

In my stomach, a sherbet fizz. I did a happy dance, grin so wide the corners of my mouth practically touched my ears.

'Oh my God, Matty! Is it for us? You got us a puppy? For Christmas?'

I tried to spot a hiding black nose, made clucking noises to draw it out. Matty laughed, shook his head.

'Sorry, pumpkin. Lead belongs to my ma's beagle. Cute hoor, that fella. Turned my back for a second and he pinched my dinner. Ma thought it was mighty craic. Can't say I shared the joke.'

Matty was notoriously proprietorial about his food. Allowing me to steal even a French fry off his plate was a massive concession.

'Now how about some drinks for you ladies? I've got squash, Coke—'

'Since when do you smoke?' my mother interrupted, picking up a half empty packet of Marlboros.

He rotated his shoulder slightly, cricked his neck.

'They're a good ice breaker. Loosen people up.'

'Your patients?' I clarified.

He smiled.

'Who else?'

My mother just stood there looking like she was trying to work out a tricky maths sum. Matty began tidying up. I used the opportunity to poke around.

'Binoculars. Cool!'

They were hanging over a chair. I tried them out. The lenses weren't in focus though, set up to watch things close up rather than far away.

Matty 'stole' my nose along with the field glasses, tucked them away in a drawer.

'Can we get some, Mum? I can be Harriet the Spy.'

A character in the book I was reading.

'Mum?'

She was appraising something in her palm, a strange expression on her face. I became very aware of the pulse beating in my neck, the soft crackle of static in the air.

'What's up, Ams?'

Matty's words were light enough, but there was unease

beneath the surface. The same tone a kid gets when it knows a telling off's coming.

My mother opened her hand slowly like the reveal in a magic trick. In it, a small object, round and gold. An earring. She glanced at the empty champagne bottles, the crumpled clothes.

'Have you had a woman here, Matty?'

Her voice was tight, eyes pinched to slits.

I felt the heat spread to my cheeks, a pit opening in my belly. Matty would never cheat on us. Would he?

He laughed, called her a silly bunny.

'Is that what you really think?'

'I know this isn't my earring.'

The heat receded as I put it together.

'It's a present for Mum, right? Since you didn't get us that puppy.'

'I had a slightly different gift in mind for your mother,' he said with a flirty look thrown her way, and not returned. 'Talking of presents . . .' He rummaged in a sports bag, pulled out a Rubik's Cube. 'Catch.'

He chucked it at me before I could react, hit me smack in the face.

'Sorry, pumpkin. You all right?'

My eye was throbbing but I told him, yes I was fine.

'Sure? It looks red.'

'It's not like you did it on purpose.'

'I'm still waiting to hear where that earring came from,' my mother interrupted, voice hammer hard.

'My ma's place. Same as the leash.'

'A lot of things of hers seem to have walked into your suit-case. Have you even been in Ireland?'

'Of course I've been in Ireland.'

'With no working phone and an apartment here full of champagne bottles.'

'I like to treat myself. You got a problem with that, Amelia-Rose?'

Her shoulders slumped. She took a step towards him, palms open.

'Just tell me the truth, Matty.'

'That is the truth.'

'You really expect me to believe you've been drinking cham-pagne by yourself and accidentally put your mother's earring in your luggage?'

'I don't *expect* you to believe anything. Though I do wonder, why are you here given you clearly have such a low opinion of me.'

'He was so resentful,' she told me years later, 'I almost bought it.'

From the blog *MattyMania.com*

Matty Melgren is INNOCENT!!

Need convincing? Get this—

Before his arrest, Melgren helped police close in on Clarence Walsh, the Night Strangler who had previously used Matty's services as a bereavement counsellor following the sudden death of his daughter, Deirdre, in a fire at their home.

Even more interesting, the two men were looking for work in Boston, MA at the same time in the 70s before coming to London in the 1980s. Though it's not known whether their paths ever crossed there.

What is known is that Walsh had a fixation about feet – just like the Shadow.

Proof that the police got the wrong guy? That maybe he was framed?

It's definitely possible . . .

5 comments

Brenda725

Could it be he was setting Walsh up as a patsy? Sign of guilt rather than innocence??

Chocoholic1975

Matty and the Night Strangler met in the 1970s. Maybe they were in cahoots . . .

SueinLondon

Who set that fire? That's what I'd like to know

Angiesmum

This is one of those cases we'll never really get answers to

TommyB

I don't get this thing about feet . . .

NINETEEN

'It's not possible,' my mother told Linda. 'There's no other explanation for how he got all that stuff.'

It made no difference what Matty or anyone else said, she just couldn't accept he didn't have another girlfriend stashed away.

Listening to her going on at him made me want to punch the wall, but looking back through adult eyes, I can see she could never have given him the benefit of the doubt. Not with her Bible-before-bed upbringing and the monochrome sense of how to behave drummed into her by Grandad and Nanna G. A fact her critics, so adamant she must have known about Matty's extracurricular activities, would do well to remember.

If anything, it was me who turned a blind eye.

'Can't you lay off him? Trust him for once?'

You'd have never known it to listen to her, but ever since his disappearance over Christmas, she was nervous of pushing him away again. I worried about the same thing.

Having him back reinforced how much I'd missed him, spotlit how empty life had been without him. How he'd turned our house into a home. Made our family whole.

Things began to shift between the three of us like the continental drift I was learning about at school. I moved closer to Matty and further away from my mother, the hot chocolate moment on the bench long forgotten.

Perhaps it was my hormones kicking in, the inevitable breaking away that signals the first step towards adulthood. Or perhaps I was simply trying to make Matty stay. *I'm on your side. Don't leave again.*

I started confiding in him, an unconscious attempt to draw him to me. Creating a bond through the sharing of secrets. An alliance that isolated my mother and established us as an independent unit.

I had my first crush. Joey Peterson, smart and cute and no idea I existed.

'He sits in front of me in maths class. I spend the whole time just staring at the back of his head. Don't say anything to Mum though. You know what she's like.'

Matty tapped the side of his nose.

'Scouts' honour.'

I imagined confiding in Linda. No way she'd have been that cool.

Do you think your mother never had a crush on anyone? You should talk to her.

Yeah right.

'You're a guy. What do I do? Should I say something?'

Matty shook his head. *Mm-mm.*

'Definitely not.'

'But—'

He leaned back against the couch, left ankle over his right knee.

'Men are hunters, pumpkin. They like to catch their prey. It takes all the fun away if you hand them their meat on a plate.' He spoke slowly so it'd sink in. 'If you want this boy to like you, he needs to think you're not into him.'

I gave him an 'Are you nuts?' look; an expression I'd been perfecting for a while, along with the sardonic eye roll.

He smiled, cocked a brow.

'Trust me. Guys like a challenge.'

My mother was being a challenge, but I suspected not in the way Matty was recommending. I'd eavesdropped on a phone call between the two of them a few nights earlier, a habit of a lifetime I saw no reason to give up.

'I just don't understand,' she'd said. 'Why are you being like this?'

'Being like what?'

'Distant.'

'I'm not being distant. It's all in your head.'

'You didn't come over last weekend.'

'I told you, I was working.'

'The weekend before, you cancelled on us.'

'You think I wanted to? I've been up to my ears the last few weeks. Work's crazy.'

'And yet you're always sleeping when I call. It's just like back in—'

'You need to get a grip, Ams. You're being ridiculous.'

'You never phone.'

He sighed heavily. Exasperated.

'You're always phoning me, hardly gives me a chance to call you.'

It was no different when he came over.

'I got us a treat,' he'd said the other evening, pulling a bottle of Laurent-Perrier out from behind his back with a flourish. *Ta-da!*

'You ever had pink champagne, Ams?'

My mother narrowed her eyes at him the way she did when she suspected I was fibbing about having done my homework.

'Not Laurent-Perrier, I haven't. It's over *fifty pounds* a bottle.'

'Should be rather special then, eh?'

'Is this what you drink with *her*?'

'There is no *her*. Christ!'

She flinched. She had a thing about blaspheming, as he well knew.

It went on and on, the walls slowly closing in. What was happening to my mother? Where was the woman of the bed picnics and sea glass hunts? The person who eschewed bedtimes and twirled to *Sergeant Pepper*? How had she lost her sense of fun around a man as fun as Matty? Become so buttoned up?

I could see he was getting fed up too, his whole demeanour changing. His movements became slower, as though he were sleepwalking, his shoulders stooped. And even though he always seemed to be napping, there were dark shadows under his eyes. His skin was pale and puffy.

'What's your problem? Why can't you have any faith in him?' I demanded.

They'd had yet another row. My mother was sitting at the

kitchen table, nursing a glass of Chardonnay. Not a natural drinker, she'd added a splash of orange juice to sweeten it.

She slid her fingers up and down the stem of the glass.

'I don't expect you to understand.'

'I understand you're going to drive him away. Just like you did with Dad.'

Her face tightened on its frame.

'Go to your room, Sophie.'

'For God's—'

'I said, go to your room. And don't you dare take the Lord's name in vain.'

Anger flashed through me, white and hot.

'Maybe you don't love him any more, but I do. He's the closest thing I have to a father.'

'Well, he's not your father. And he's not my husband either.'

'Easy to see why.'

She flushed.

'Your room. Now. I'm not telling you again.'

The chasm created by Matty's absence had been filled with his return. But the crack spreading between me and my mother was gaping wide.

TWENTY

The rows carried on into the spring. The threat of war loomed large, both literally and metaphorically. When I think back to that time, the two are conflated in my mind. My mother attacking Matty. Margaret Thatcher readying to attack Argentina.

And in North London, more women about to die.

At school I was distracted; couldn't focus, handed homework in late, became overly familiar with the detention room.

Mrs Coates asked me to stay behind after class, 'For a little word, please.'

'Is something upsetting you?' she asked, not unkindly.

'No.'

I was well past the age of opening up to a teacher.

'Are you sure?' She cocked her head, black eyes blinking behind her glasses. 'It's not like you to get in trouble, Sophie. And your grades are slipping. All these Bs.'

I assured her I was fine, that'd I'd try harder.

She gave me a long look. I shifted uncomfortably.

'It's tough being eleven. I'm not so old I don't remember how it feels.'

That surprised me. She seemed ancient to us, in the way all adults do when you're a kid.

Matty was different, a Peter Pan. His sense of fun. The way he horsed around. My mother hated it. Our Prisoner Game especially, anything that didn't involve her.

'That's enough. Go tidy your room, Sophie. It's a pigsty.'

'It's my room.'

'In my house.'

'The landlord's actually. And it's a flat.'

Later she started on Matty. I was half asleep, their voices rousing me.

'It's amber, thought it'd bring out the colour of your eyes.'

'No box?'

'Didn't come with a box.'

A moment's silence, louder than words.

'It's hers, isn't it?'

'What?'

'You think I've forgotten the earring?'

'Jesus, Ams. I told you—'

'I know what you told me. And I know what I told you.'

'I was just trying to do something nice. But if you don't want the fecking necklace, don't have it.'

'Mrs Cohen sees you, you know? Coming home at all hours.'

Mrs Cohen was Matty's curtain twitching neighbour. We'd met her the day we stopped by on his return from Ireland. Mrs Matzo Ball Soup, my mother called her afterwards, on account of her Yiddish accent, stronger even than the gefilte fish balls she knocked on the door insisting we try. *My bubala's recipe. All the way from Hungary.*

'Mrs Cohen has early onset Alzheimer's. She doesn't know what she's seeing.'

'Is what we have together not enough for you? Is that what all this is about? Why you've been so . . .' She grappled for the word, left it hanging.

Matty didn't answer straight away.

I tiptoed to the door, opened it just enough to see into the hallway.

'I never told you . . .'

He sounded so flat, so unlike himself. My mother dropped her shoulders. Through the gap, I watched her put a hand on his arm, move closer.

'Never told me what?'

Another pause, the sort you don't rush to fill.

'My father isn't my father.'

'What do you mean?'

'My ma had a one-night stand. Some random buck. Didn't even know his last name.'

Matty wasn't a churchgoer like my mother and Nanna G, but I could hear the disgust in his voice. The dark depth of his shame.

'All those years I was calling that man "Dad". Only that's not what he was.'

'He brought you up. Loved you. That's what makes him your dad, not whether he shares your blood.'

'Maybe,' Matty scoffed. 'But what does it make her?'

TWENTY-ONE

'What does it make us?'

I'm on Parliament Hill, talking to my mother while Buster snoofles about among the fallen leaves. When I was a child, I used to think autumn leaves were the souls trees shed at the end of each year, that spring was a sort of resurrection. Back in Newton, I was brought up on the Bible, Sunday School and grace before meals. Not surprising I suppose that my imagination got a little warped.

Look at them waving their bones, my mother used to say.

It did nothing to dispel the image of them as dead beings. Nor did the gnarly branch that tap-tapped at my window every night. I used to bury my head under the duvet, imagine it calling to me—

Let me in . . .

That was before Matty came along. With him around, I was less afraid of the night. When he told me to trust him, that he wouldn't let anything bad happen to me, I believed him.

'Shows she needs a father,' Nanna G told my mother. 'It's about time that young man of yours put a ring on your finger, Amelia-Rose. Made an honest woman out of you.'

'I don't need a man to make me honest, Mom.'

'See now, that's why you're not married. Sass is very unbe-coming.'

Society and its infernal preoccupation with appearance. Without it, things would have been much less easy for Matty.

'What does it make us?' my mother asks again.

'Stupid,' I tell her. 'That's what.'

For allowing ourselves be taken in by him. For deluding our-selves. For ignoring what was right under our noses.

'If he really did those things . . .'

As always a weight settles on my shoulders. 'If', the most loaded word in the English language.

What if Matty is innocent?

What if they got the wrong guy?

What if I made the biggest mistake of my life?

If, if, if . . .

'They blame us, you know?' my mother says. 'The families.'

Such resignation in her voice, so much pain. Part of her for so long, I can't remember what she sounded like without it.

'It's understandable,' I say. 'Wouldn't you blame us too?'

'Yes,' she says. 'I would. I do.'

I think of the victims. Of the children who've grown up without mummies to tuck them in at night or Band-Aid up skinned knees. Of the fathers who never got to walk their daughters down the aisle. Of the mothers who never give up hope that one day their little girls will show up at the door.

They hold us responsible. I see it in their eyes when they're interviewed on TV. The way their expressions change whenever our names are brought up. The tightening around their mouths, the muscles moving in their jaws.

My mouth tightens when I think of them too. My throat, my abdominals.

Plenty of other killers have lived apparently normal lives; going to church, doing the school run, sitting by the pool on family holidays. Duping the women who loved them.

It doesn't make it easier though. If anything, it makes me feel worse for being tricked too.

'He did those things,' I tell my mother now, trying to convince myself as much as her. 'It's on him, not us.'

'Doesn't mean we're not guilty. If he did what they say.'

If . . .

'Because?'

'Because we ignored what he was doing. Which means we effectively killed them too. They'd be alive if we'd acted differently.'

My mind goes to the pearl-handled penknife in my dresser drawer. Same place my mother kept the picture of the little girl who died, and the pin-pricked photo of my father.

Matty was more of a dad to me than Jame Brennan ever was. Jame, no 's'. An affectation to make him sound special. I laughed when I watched *Silence of the Lambs*. My father had the same name as Buffalo Bill. Jame Gumb. What is it about me and serial killers?

As usual, my mother echoes my thoughts.

'Matty was a father to you, right from the start.'

I wipe my eyes on my sweater cuff. I don't want anyone out here to see me crying. I have some pride.

'He came to all my school shows,' I say.

I could add, 'unlike you', but I don't. He took time off work to be there. Sat in the front row with his ridiculous Nikon around his neck.

'God, I was embarrassed. The size of that thing. The way he used to fiddle about with the lens, adjusting it to get the shot just right.'

She smiles. Her eyes are misty.

'Him and his photographs.'

'Remember all those pictures he used to take of you when you weren't looking? How mad you used to get. *You've got my bad side!*'

'Never mind all the randoms in the park.'

'Human safari, isn't that what he called it?'

'People in the Wild.'

'Yes, that was it.'

For a moment we're reminiscing about a regular Joe we both loved. The person who made our lives whole.

But Matty wasn't a regular Joe. And while he made our lives whole, he ripped others apart.

If . . .

'We should head back,' I answer. 'It's getting chilly.'

A man walks past in a deerstalker hat, gives me a funny look. *Let them look*, Matty would have said. *Screw 'em.*

TWENTY-TWO

'Screw 'em. Why do you care what anyone thinks?'

I'd been telling Matty I'd die if anyone found out about my crush on Joey Peterson.

It was only the two of us at home. My mother was out at a work drinks party, a send-off for one of the partners at the accountancy firm where she worked in the secretarial pool. Matty was babysitting, a rare occurrence since it was usually the two of them that went out together.

'How do I look?' she asked before she left, doing a little spin in the middle of the living room, a self-conscious spot of colour on each cheek.

She was wearing a new dress, a red off-the-shoulder number with a big bow on the neckline. We'd bought it together at Wallis the previous weekend. Matty was supposed to have come with us but hadn't shown up. Overslept, he claimed, even though we hadn't set out till well after lunch. *Didn't want to get dragged round the shops, more like*, my mother said.

He sucked his teeth, rubbed his chin with the side of his thumb.

'You look beautiful, obviously. But . . . I don't know . . .'

Her face fell. She smoothed down the skirt, re-examined through fresh eyes the outfit she'd been so pleased with.

'What's wrong with it?'

Matty shrugged.

'I just wonder if it strikes the right note for a hooley with your boss. Do you think you might be more comfortable in something a little less . . . showy?'

'I've got a black tunic, I could try that, I suppose. It's a bit frumpy, but—'

Matty nodded.

'Yes. Good idea.'

The news was playing in the background, the TV on low while we waited for *Only Fools and Horses* to come on. My mother thought it was 'stupid', but Del Boy always set Matty and me off. The blow-up doll episode especially.

Police expressed grave concern today for the safety of two young women from North London who haven't been seen since April. They are asking anyone who may have seen them to come forward and are urging women to be vigilant when they go out at night.

'*Travel home with a friend if you can,*' Detective Inspector Harry Connor of Scotland Yard advised. '*Try to avoid isolated areas. If you feel threatened, call 999.*'

'Do you think it's him?' I asked Matty.

He just shrugged, told me I had nothing to be afraid of.

My mother came back into the room wearing a black dress. She was right, it was frumpy, the sort of thing Nancy Reagan might wear to a funeral.

'I don't know about this. What do you think, Matty?'

He pulled his eyes away from the screen.

'What's that?'

'The dress. Is this one better?'

'Aye,' he answered, straight back to the TV. 'Much.'

'I liked the red dress,' I told him after she'd left.

'Me too. She should have more confidence in herself.'

'But you said—'

'Fancy a pizza? We could order in.'

'Mum made a casserole.'

'It'll keep.'

I smiled.

'Yeah, all right then.'

He grinned, gave me a mock salute.

'Grand. Back in a tick, comrade.'

He reappeared as I was doing my probability homework at the kitchen table.

Joanna has ten apples. One has a worm in it. What's the probability of her picking the rotten fruit?

'Pizza'll be here in half an hour.'

I glanced up, the word 'Great' drying on my lips. Matty was standing in front of me, stark naked. I felt my face heat up, didn't know where to look.

'You've got no clothes on,' I stammered as if he wasn't aware he was parading around the flat in his birthday suit.

He sauntered over, plonked down in the seat next to me, helped himself to a pear from the bowl.

My stomach tightened. My face burned harder.

'Why aren't you—'

'I took a shower,' he said. 'Couldn't find a towel.'

'They're in the bathroom.'

I stared at the table. Anywhere that meant I didn't have to look at him.

'I can't use those. They're yours and your mam's.'

'Get one from the laundry closet then.'

'Can you show me where it is?'

I pointed, without raising my head.

Matty laughed.

'Gee, Soph. I didn't take you for such a prude.'

'Gee', like he was a character out of *The Brady Bunch*.

'Haven't you ever seen a man naked?'

I shook my head, no. My tummy felt wriggly, alive with maggots. A pulse beat hard in my neck.

'You're making kind of a big deal out of it, don't you think?'

He was so relaxed. Maybe I was overreacting. My mother walked around in her underwear sometimes. Was this really so different?

And yet still the maggots squirmed.

'You reckon your friends' dads never go about in the buff?'

'I don't know. Maybe.'

'Of course they do, you wee daftie. Well, I'm dry now so you can get off the stage.'

I never told my mother about that night, and by the time the news about the next murder broke, I'd pushed the memory down so far it withered and died.

That evening though, it was all I could think about. My brain saying one thing, my body another. As much as I'd been looking forward to pizza, when it arrived I couldn't manage a mouthful.

Meanwhile Matty was ravenous, gobbled the whole thing.

TWENTY-THREE

I push my toast away, unable to swallow a bite. It sticks in my throat, chokes me. I sip my coffee, the scalding liquid washing it down.

'Tuesday. Four thirty.'

I say the words out loud. The sound beating a rhythm in my mouth, a death march.

'I have to go, don't I?' I asked Janice yesterday, the solidity of the phone comforting in my hand. Grounding.

She gave me her personal phone number a while back. *For emergencies.* I know what that means. The scars on my wrist are hieroglyphics. A language even my mother never learned to write.

The day I went too far. Step away from the edge. Mind the gap.

The abyss hasn't been calling to me, but I'm pretty sure the prospect of seeing Matty counts as an emergency. 'A trigger', Janice might say.

'I have to go, don't I?'

'What do you think?' she asked, her voice always so even and measured.

She has an annoying way of responding with questions rather than answers.

'I know I don't *want* to go.'

'What we want and what we need are often different things.'

I rubbed my lips together, didn't reply.

'Sophie, are you still there?'

'Yes.'

I sounded like a child. Sulky, the sort of tone my mother used to tell me off for using. *No one likes a Moody Martha.* She liked alliteration. Moody Martha. Nervous Ninny. Worry Wart . . .

'I know you think it'll be good for me,' I said. 'Healing or whatever. But it could just as well have the opposite effect. All these years. Seeing him again might be the final nail.'

'We've talked about this. The only way to deal with a trauma is to face up to it. And what happened to you was a trauma, Sophie. Matty's conviction. Your mother's . . .'

I squeezed my eyes shut, inhaled deeply through my nose.

'What I'm saying is you're a victim too.'

'Not like those women.'

'No. But still a victim. You need to confront the man, move past your guilt.'

I scoffed in a way Nanna G would certainly have called 'unlady-like'.

'He's hardly going to admit to everything after so long.'

I imagined Janice shrugging, saw in my mind's eye the trademark downturn at the corners of her mouth that always accompanies it.

'You don't know what he might admit now he's dying.'

'That's assuming he really did those things.' Still I can't put

Matty's name and 'murder' aloud in the same sentence. 'What if he really is innocent? What if I believe him? That's not going to help me move past my guilt, is it?'

Janice sighed down the line.

'No. But at least once you know the truth you can start to deal with it head-on. Stop with the "What ifs".'

'I have to go.'

A statement this time, not a question.

'Yes, you do.'

If we'd been together in her consulting room – beige walls, cream furniture, white curtains; a study in blandness – she'd have reached over, put a hand on mine. I usually hate being touched, but I don't mind when Janice does it. I like the feeling it produces, the sense of connectedness. Of being mothered.

I hang up. In my chest a sudden yawning ache for my real mother. My mother before Matty, before everything started to go wrong. The yearning has been coming more frequently recently. It's why I've been talking to her so much, I think.

Buster watches me from his basket, gets up heavily, pads over. I stroke his flank as he rests his head in my lap, the warm wetness of his jowls snug against my thigh.

'Good boy,' I tell him.

I may have rescued him from the pound, but the truth is he rescued me too. I can't lie in bed all day feeling sorry for myself any more. I have to go to the park whether it's sunny or not. Have to feed him, attend to his needs. And in taking care of him, I end up taking of myself too.

I look at the date circled on the wall calendar. Red biro, like a sick joke. Today everything is putting me in mind of blood and death. Matty's little gift.

'Tuesday. Four thirty,' I whisper again.

I put my head in my hands.

'Christ.'

There's a hangover pummelling my eye sockets, my limbs are lead. I went at the bottle pretty hard last night, not that it helped. It never does, but I do it anyway. The definition of madness they say; repeating the same mistakes over and over and expecting a different outcome.

Buster noses my thigh, lets out an indignant *woof*.

Get a move on, he's saying, pointing with his nose at the leash hanging on the hook by the sink. *Walkies time.*

I tell him to keep his fur on, heave myself up.

I stroke his big head; careful to avoid his bad ear. Part of it was ripped off in a fight with another dog before I got him. A pit bull who wasn't treated any better than he was.

The bastards who owned Buster didn't get it treated, probably reckoned it made him look fiercer with part of his ear missing. That more people would put money on him that way.

We both have our scars, I think, which straightaway conjures another thought. The images of the body they pulled out of the river. The photos I've tormented myself with online. Bruises. Bloating. Blank blue eyes.

'What made us different?' I asked my mother once. 'Why didn't Matty kill us too?'

She looked at me so sadly, the whole world on her back.

'He did kill us,' she said.

I didn't understand her then.

But I do now.

TWENTY-FOUR

'I don't know what to do. It's killing me.'

Things still weren't good between my mother and Matty. Everything she said seemed to goad him. I worried constantly that they'd split up, that he'd disappear off again. Leave me alone with her.

Perhaps I'd have felt differently if he'd been off with me too. But it was business as usual with us. Matty and Pumpkin against the world. It was a line he actually used, as if we were father and daughter. One time he even referred to me in that way to an ice-cream seller, a slip-up I didn't correct. *A scoop of vanilla for ma'wean.*

I think our closeness made it worse for my mother; highlighted that the problem was with her, something she was doing wrong.

I just wish I knew what.

September 24th. I was having some kids from my new senior school over for my birthday. Just girls, although I'd have quite liked to invite a few boys too. I was at that age where I wanted them around but was too shy to ask.

It was Matty's idea to throw a party.

'We should celebrate. Leave it to me.'

Two more bodies had just been discovered in a refuse disposal site in Islington, strangled with their own underwear and posed in the shape of a crucifix beneath the trash. One of the women, a runaway from Birmingham, had been partially decapitated by a shovel a workman had been using to clear the garbage. The other was a family courts barrister in her first year of tenancy.

I didn't connect the timings until years later, long after he'd been incarcerated. Though as Janice says, 'It could have been a coincidence. Easy with hindsight to see patterns that were never really there.'

My mother was creaming butter and sugar, the radio on in the background.

Detective Inspector Harry Connor, the Senior Investigating Officer in charge of the North London murders case, has issued an impassioned plea to the killer to give himself up.

'Clearly you have a problem. It can't be easy for you. Please get in touch. We can deal with this together. Let me help you.'

Matty scoffed, gave his head a little shake.

'Do you think that shite ever works?'

'Does seem a bit clutching at straws.' She glanced in my direction, lowered her voice. 'Got to try though, haven't they? There's women in my office refusing to go out at night.'

'Whole capital's having a cack attack, so it is. No one's safe. Talking of which, will I put that new lock on your front door now?'

My mother shook her head.

'It's okay. Des did it already.'

A darkness passed over Matty's face.

'When was this?'

'The other day. I bumped into him downstairs, mentioned it was sticking. He offered to help.'

'I bet he did.'

'What's that supposed to mean?'

'Only that the fella has a massive hard-on for you.'

'That's disgusting.'

He shrugged.

'Just stating facts, Ams.'

'Being ridiculous more like.'

He wasn't though, and she knew it. She'd have to have been blind not to notice how into her our neighbour was. She only had to say 'Hi' and old Brown Teeth would colour up like a moulding beetroot.

Matty rubbed at his shoulders, blew his lips.

'Cruel warm,' he said. 'Could do with a breeze.'

An Indian Summer, he called it. Hot enough for shorts and T-shirts during the day, cold enough for a fire at night.

He said that too, another connection I only spotted with hindsight.

'We should light a fire tonight, Ams. Cosy up.'

I remember him saying it because it was the most loving he'd sounded for a while. And also because some perverse part of me was jealous.

My friends began to arrive, a bubbly mass of ra-ra skirts and denim cut-offs.

'Your dad's gorgeous,' one girl whispered.

'He's not my dad.'

'Really? His eyes are just like yours.'

'I've got a game planned for you, ladies,' Matty called. 'Come on outside. It's going to be deadly!'

We shared a garden with Des Banister, but we were the only ones who used it.

'Worried the daylight will kill him,' Matty joked one time, capering about making claws with his hands. 'Save me. Not the light . . .'

'That's not nice,' my mother rebuked. 'It's not his fault he's—'

I finished the sentence for her.

'Totally weird?'

Matty laughed, gave me a high-five. *Nice one, pumpkin.*

My mother put a slide in when we'd first moved to London. If you stood at the top you could see the trees on Parliament Hill, and a splash of reddish brown in the distance which was the running track.

'The slide is base,' Matty told my friends now, giving it a pat. 'You have forty seconds to hide, then I hunt you down.'

With anyone else, the game would have been lame. We were in high school, a bit old for Forty Forty Home. But Matty put magic in it. That, and all my friends were blatantly crushing on him.

'Who's ready for cake?' my mother trilled. Plastered-on smile, plate raised high like she was a waiter in a fancy restaurant. She even had a tea towel over her arm. On each cheek, a tongue-pink blush.

I knew she was shy of my friends, worried they'd think she was hick. *Do they know we get help with the school fees? What cars do their mothers drive? Did they all go to university?*

I should have empathised more. Instead, I felt a prickle of irritation, as if her discomfort would infect me, tar me by association.

Why couldn't she be fun like Matty? Easy-going. Why did she always have to hang back from the other mums? Was it really so hard to join in with them, chat a little, go for coffee?

As she held the cake aloft, all pleased and proud, I wanted to die. It was a misshapen pancake, one side risen while the other side slept.

My friends' mothers bought them birthday cakes from Sherrard's in Hampstead Village, beautiful creations with piped pink icing and vanilla frosting. This cake looked like it belonged in a charity shop.

My friends glanced at each other, smirking. Embarrassment lit my face.

I scowled at my mother.

'Not now. We're playing.'

She crumpled.

'But everyone'll be leaving soon.'

I shrugged.

'So we'll have cake when they've gone.'

'I've spent all afternoon making it.'

There was a moment's stand-off. I was starting to feel guilty, about to relent, when Matty called—

'I'm counting, girls!'

There were shrieks of delight as they raced off. I hid too, but this time I didn't shriek. I'd been cruel and I knew it.

From my hiding spot I watched Matty, hands over his eyes, counting to forty, skipping numbers as he went. My mother still on the stoop, trying to act as though she wasn't hurt.

And spying out of the window, eyes trained on her, our neighbour Des Banister. Face obscured in shadow, drinking her in.

Extract from an interview with Matty Melgren
and *On The Sofa* presenter, Rob Hill

MATTY MELGREN

Of course, it makes me angry. How would you feel if you'd been
banged up for something you didn't do? If you had to spend
the rest of your life looking at the same four walls, paying for
crimes some other fella committed?

I'm treated like some kind of monster though all I did my
whole life was try and help people. I was a bereavement counsellor, for goodness' sake. Does wanting to guide people through
loss and despair sound like something a killer would do?

So yes, I get mad when I think about the unfairness of it all,
of how I'm wasting my life away stuck in here. My only hope
is justice will prevail in the end. That people will finally realise
they got the wrong guy.

ROB HILL

To be clear, you're saying you're not guilty?

MATTY MELGREN

I'm absolutely not guilty. I mean, have I made bad choices in
my life? Aye, course I have, same as anyone. I didn't always

treat my girlfriend well. Stole comics when I was a kid, cut school. But guilty of murder? Christ, no, nothing like that.

ROB HILL

So, what do you think happened to those women?

MATTY MELGREN

You know what I think happened. I've said it very many times. In fact, I'm fairly sure your man tried to kill my girlfriend too.

ROB HILL

The police ruled him out, you know that.

MATTY MELGREN

Easy to rule someone out when you haven't properly ruled them in to start with. And let's be honest, no one's ever got to the bottom of what really happened the night of the fire . . .

TWENTY-FIVE

The heat woke me, my dream of Christmas in Lapland turning into the Sahara. I tussled about, tangled in my duvet. Hair plastered to my head.

Silence amplified my heartbeat, my rasping breath. I couldn't take in enough air, started to cough. My head was cotton wool. Behind my eyes, a dull stabbing pain. It was still dark; the clock face hidden in the gloom. Furniture reduced to hazy outlines. The room roasting despite the cool night.

Was I brewing a fever? Getting sick?

I touched a hand to my forehead the way my mother might. *Cool as a cuke, Soph.*

So, why so hot? So parched?

Sleep muddled, I stumbled out of bed to the door. My kingdom for a glass of water.

I'm not sure what hit me first. The heat. The smoke. The licking flames.

I couldn't move, my feet welded to the floor. Imprisoned in my bones. Muscles turned to ice.

I screamed, I think. Called out. For Matty. Always him.

My voice was stifled, as though I were being smothered. As though it didn't belong to me. My mother heard though, came running, bedroom door swinging.

'Sophie, what's— Oh, God!'

We were both coughing then, claws in our throats. Eyes streaming as we blinked to clear our vision, to take in what was happening. Around my ribs, a pressure band, tighter by the second.

'Too much smoke,' my mother spluttered. 'Need to open a window.'

My eyes liquefied, tears turning to acid. In my nostrils, an acrid stench. And from the kitchen, bright flickering tongues.

'It's locked,' I heard my mother say, sounding very far away.

She was by the window tugging at the frame, head turning wildly from one side to the other. A tree tossing in a storm. Then, dropping to her knees, crawling towards me. Without thinking, I did the same. Reached out to her through the impenetrable shroud of thickening smoke.

'We need to get out. Stay low.'

'Where's Mat—'

'Hold onto me.'

I could just about grab a hand. Sweat ran down my back, dripped into my eyes.

'Where's—'

She took off her robe, balled it up.

'Hold this against your mouth. It'll keep the worst out.'

I wanted to tell her I was scared, that I was sorry about the birthday cake. Instead, I started to cry.

'We're going to be okay. You hear?'

I nodded, sniffed up my snot and tears. Wanting to believe her. Wanting to look brave.

'Ready?' *Cough.* 'Okay. Keep to the wall.' *Cough.* 'Don't let go . . .'

We couldn't have been more than thirty feet from the front door, but it took us a lifetime to reach it. The smoke and heat making us slow, our heads hot and heavy. Slithering on our bellies like snakes.

Three feet, two, one . . .

My mother reached up, rattled the handle.

'My God, Jesus—'

I'll never forget how she looked at me then. Her eyes never looked so big, her face so pale.

'The deadlock's on. Where's the key?'

Why wasn't it in the door? We always kept it there at night. *In case there's a fire and we need to get out . . .*

She felt for the cupboard, worked her hands along the hooks. Shook her head.

'No.'

Her voice dripped with fear. I turned away to hide my tears. In my peripheral vision, an orange glow.

She banged on the door. Yelled for help that didn't come.

We were too high up to jump out of a window, too weak to break down the door. The flames were sneaking along the wall. We were trapped. No way out.

A lurking thing crept out of the shadows, a presence I now think of as my wolf.

Resistance is futile. Matty's favourite show.

And then—

'It's here!' I brandished the key, our salvation. 'It was hiding under the mat.'

I'm not sure what made me look there.

'God,' my mother said later, 'watching out for us.'

I gave it to her, hands shaking too much to use it myself.

Time moved in slow motion. Her putting it in the lock, turning it, us getting out. The delicious rush of clean air filling my lungs, the sweet relief of escape.

We stumbled down the stairs to the door of the building, clinging to each other, a pair of shipwreck survivors.

Des Banister opened his front door, poked his comb-over out.

'What's going on?' he asked, looking my mother up and down. Part curiosity, part leer.

'Fire,' she wheezed, standing there in her nightshirt, too much in shock to be aware of her state of undress.

The blood drained from Des' face.

'Fire?'

He rushed out of his flat without a backward glance, tore through the main door. From inside his apartment, the sound of barking.

'Your dog!' I called after him as we trooped blinking out of the building. To our eyes, the lamplit night was searchlight bright.

From down the street came the wail of an approaching siren. A flash of blue dancing over the tarmac. Curtains parting in neighbouring windows.

'There's a dog in there,' I shouted to the firemen as they stormed into the building. 'You've got to help it.'

I'd told Des five times. Tried to go back inside myself when he wouldn't.

My mother held me tightly.

'It's not safe,' she said.

I started to cry, couldn't help it. That bastard. Who leaves a dog to die?

'Looks like the oven had been left on with the door open,' a fireman told my mother while the others were inside, making our apartment safe again. 'The heat must have melted the knobs and temperature dials. Set fire to a tea towel. Frankly, you ladies were lucky. It could have been a lot worse.'

My mother shook her head, confused.

'But I didn't use the oven tonight.'

'Just be careful,' the fireman replied. 'There's nothing wrong with leaving an oven on so long as the door's shut. Even a crack can cause a fire.'

My mother just nodded, still puzzling out how it could have been left on when we'd only had salad for dinner.

I turned to her.

'What happened to Matty?'

'Who's Matty?' the fireman asked.

'My boyfriend.'

'He's up there?'

She shook her head.

'Said he was going to run home for a sweater. But . . .'

'He didn't come back?'

'Got tired I guess.'

The conversation moved on.

'You said you couldn't get the windows open?'

'I must have locked them. I don't remember.'

I asked why she hadn't just used the key, a question only now occurring to me. Like the door, she always kept it in the lock.

She rubbed the base of her neck, brows drawn together.

'It wasn't there . . .'

'Did you look behind the radiator? Maybe it fell.'

Outdoors and out of danger, my brain was finally working again.

'I couldn't find it. I suppose I was panicking.'

She addressed the fireman rather than me. A child explaining itself to a teacher.

'It's understandable,' he said. 'Under the circumstances.'

The next day I heard her on the phone to Matty, his voice echoing out of speaker phone while she scrubbed at the soot-stained walls. *It's going to take weeks to get this place back to normal.*

'They said we could have died if she hadn't woken up.'

'They're right. If the fire hadn't got you, the smoke inhalation would have. Really Ams, leaving the oven on? I have to say, I'm a bit surprised at that.'

Strangely, my mother and I only talked about the incident one other time, not long after Matty was sent down.

'I never understood it,' she slurred.

She was slumped on the couch sipping gin, half-cut. Staring into the bottom of her glass, the days of sweetening wine with OJ far behind her.

'Understood what?' I prompted.

She was always starting sentences mid-thought when she'd been drinking.

'The oven.' She was frustrated, as if it were my fault I didn't understand what she was trying to say. 'I know I didn't use it that night. Or lock those windows. I never did. That high up and looking out onto the street, they were hardly a security risk.'

'But they were a way to call for help.'

'Exactly,' she said.

TWENTY-SIX

There are kids in my neighbour's garden.

'Help,' they scream.

The screams of a game. Screams of fear sound different. Lower pitched.

I wonder if the women Matty killed screamed; the women they say he killed. What they thought in those last moments, the prayers and final regrets that tumbled through their heads.

Did they plead? Beg for mercy? Or did fear rip out their tongues?

My brain's a one-way train today, the date circled on my calendar, the signal master. I rub a palm across my eyes, inhale deeply. In for five, out for five, the way Janice has taught me.

'Be fully present in the moment. Let your breathing ground you.'

I wander over to the window in need of distraction, look out over next-door's garden, cradling my coffee mug, the steam rising warm against my face.

There are two of them playing out there, a boy and a girl.

Can't be more than eight, the age I was when I first met Matty.

My neighbour's grandchildren. Blonde hair, chubby cheeks. Coats flapping open, gloves dangling from string poking out of their sleeves. Chasing each other between the trees. Laughing.

'They're angelic,' I told her once, snared by the unspoilt innocence of their youth. 'So cute.'

She chuckled.

'I love them to bits but don't be fooled, Sophie. Looks can be deceptive.'

No need to tell me that, not that she meant anything by it. I've never spoken publicly about my relationship with Matty. Never let journalists take my photo or shared my story with anyone other than Janice. Even then there are parts she doesn't know. Parts I'm too ashamed to reveal.

'Survivor's guilt,' she calls it.

She's wrong though, it's not that. I don't feel guilty he didn't kill me. I feel guilty about what I did. And for not doing it sooner. You see why I'm so messed up.

In the early days, when we were getting to know each other, Janice suggested I give myself a voice. Publish my own account of what happened. She thought it would be freeing, 'therapeutic', to let people hear my perspective, to express myself.

I never have done though, never felt I deserved to have a voice.

How could I not have known? Why didn't I see what was happening? What if I'd acted sooner?

I take another sip of coffee, attempting to wash away last night's excesses, to soothe my thumping head.

Tuesday. Four thirty.

Tomorrow and tomorrow creeps in this petty pace.

'Remember that drive?' I ask my mother.

'You thought Matty tried to kill you. Refused to get in a car with him ever again.'

'Can you blame me?'

'I blame myself, for not seeing things as they really were.'

'What is the way they really were?'

'I don't know,' she says, voice coffin heavy.

I hear the rattle of cubes in her glass. By the afternoon, she never bothered with ice.

'Was that drive before or after the fire?' I ask.

'After, I think. I'm not sure. My memories are all jumbled up.'

'Mine too,' I tell her. 'A jigsaw I can't fit together.'

I'd been doing a jigsaw that morning. Parliament Hill broken into a thousand pieces, a birthday present from Grandad and Nanna G. *To improve patience and concentration*, she'd written in the card, her penmanship perfect, unlike mine which has always been an illegible scrawl.

'Just what you always wanted, eh Soph?' Matty teased as I tore off the wrapping.

The pieces were so small it had taken me over an hour just to do the corners.

'How about taking a break, pumpkin? Come for a drive with me, leave your mother to her funny Sad Tent book.'

'Marquis de Sade,' my mother corrected with an exaggerated eye roll. 'And it's not funny, it's a classic.'

She was always reading 'classics', nine times out of ten with a pen in her hand to underline key passages.

'Tent, marquee. What's the difference?'

'You might know if you ever picked up anything longer than a newspaper.'

'Yeah, all right. Let's go,' I told Matty. 'It's a bit stuffy in here.'

He laughed.

'Scat the pair of you,' my mother said.

'Where to?' I asked, settling into the passenger seat.

I didn't buckle up. It wasn't yet law to wear seat belts.

Matty started the ignition, revved twice.

'Would you listen to her roar? Ready for some fun, Soph?'

I started to answer, some quip about this being a Mini not a Ferrari, when he tore away from the curb, accelerating down the hill at such speed my stomach was left at the top, my body flung smack into the dash.

'Jesus, Matty! What the hell!'

It was like he didn't hear me. His eyes were glazed, fixed dead ahead. His hands rigid on the wheel. Faster and faster we went, the speedometer arcing around like a pole-vaulting Olympian.

'Slow down!'

I clung to the door handle; my knuckles bone white, my spine pinned to the seat as though bound by invisible ropes. In my ears, the thunderclap of my heart.

Matty flicked me a quick look, the corners of his mouth twitching upwards.

'Not scared are you, pumpkin?'

A challenge not a question. Before I could answer, he was jerking the wheel sharply to the left and then back to the right, sending the car drunkenly from one side of the road to the other, throwing me with it.

'It's rollercoaster time!'

'Look out!'

A little old woman with a cane was hobbling along a pedestrian crossing – three, two, one metres from the bonnet. She glanced up, mouth slackening. Frozen to the spot.

Matty didn't brake, just spun the car in a hundred-and-eighty-degree turn, slamming my head into the door. The impact reverberated through my skull, spots dancing in front of my eyes. My very brain seemed to throb.

'Missed her!' Matty said, triumphant, never mind the oncoming traffic now ploughing straight towards us. A twenty-tonne lorry blasting its horn.

'Oh God!'

We'd learned about momentum in physics; velocity, mass and unstoppable force. We were going at fifty miles an hour, but in a fight between us and the truck, Matty and I would be the ones ending up as ketchup.

On instinct, I raised my arms to shield my face, squeezed my eyes shut. There was a vulpine cry, high-pitched and animal. From me, I realised.

My mouth was dust, my skin soaked in sweat. The air thick with the sickly-sweet smell of petrol.

'You can open your eyes now.'

The lorry had gone, the car slowed to normal speed. And yet I couldn't stop shaking.

Matty glanced at me, his pupils expanding to fill his irises. Then, with an almost imperceptible nod, he pulled the car over to the side of the road and killed the engine.

'You're not crying are you, pumpkin?'

'What the hell's wrong with you? Why would you—'

'It was just a game, Soph.'

But I was already getting out of the car.

'Where are you going?'

'You think I'm letting you drive me home?'

He beat me back, tried to make out everything was hunky-dory when I got there.

'The wanderer returns . . .'

My mother took in my tear-stained face, fired Matty a questioning look.

'What's wrong, honey?' She touched a hand to my forehead. 'Are you okay?'

'No, I'm not okay. Matty just tried to kill me.'

'Tried to kill you?'

Her voice had gone very quiet.

'Drove like a maniac. Did his best to crash the car. Literally fifty miles an hour in a thirty zone. Directly into the path of a truck.'

She straightened up, glowered at Matty. Jaw so tight it changed the shape of her face.

'What were you thinking?'

I'd assumed she'd tell me I was overreacting. That she'd taken my side so quickly had the strange effect of making me feel worse rather than better.

'Come on now, Soph,' Matty said, all butter-wouldn't-melt. 'I was only mucking about. I thought we were having fun.'

My mother responded before I could.

'Fun?' she spat.

'Why are you making such a big deal out of this?'

147

'Seriously?'

He shook his head, eyes shuttered as though she were the unreasonable one.

'You need to lighten up, Ams. Jesus.'

'Don't "Jesus" me. And don't you dare tell me to lighten up like I don't—'

He made puppy eyes, hung his head. A sudden costume change.

'I'm sorry, pumpkin. You know I'd never hurt you, right?'

He was funny and charming the rest of the day; helping me with my puzzle, going out for Rocky Road. That night, a new Post-it note went up: *The key to change is to let go of fear.*

FOR THE ATTENTION OF DETECTIVE INSPECTOR HARRY CONNOR

THIS IS THE ONE YOU FEAR.

HARRY CONNOR ASKED ME TO "GET IN TOUCH", SO I HAVE. MAYBE I'LL WRITE AGAIN, WE'LL SEE . . .

I AM THE KILLER OF SHERYL NORTH. TO PROVE IT, HERE IS A BLOODSTAINED PIECE OF HER SHIRT. I AM THE SAME MAN WHO DID THE GIRLS AT THE WOODS AND THE RUBBISH TIP.

TO PROVE I KILLED THEM I SHALL DISCLOSE SOME DETAILS ONLY THE POLICE AND I KNOW:

1. UNDERWEAR TIED ROUND SHERYL NORTH'S NECK: PINK WITH BLUE POLKA DOTS
2. THE LAST GIRL WAS FOUND ON HER BACK WITH HER LEGS SPREAD OPEN
3. I DID THE SAME THING TO THE ONES AT THE DUMP AS ALL THE REST

HAPLESS HARRY SAID I HAVE A "PROBLEM". BUT HARRY, I THINK YOU'RE THE ONE WITH THE PROBLEM, NOT ME. AND I'M NOT GOING ANYWHERE.

PS HAVE YOU FOUND THE GIRL FROM HOLMES ROAD YET? SHE WAS INTO KINKY SEX AND HAD A LOOSE TONGUE – WHICH YOU'LL DISCOVER IF YOU FIND HER . . .

DESPITE WHAT YOU'RE SAYING, I'M NOT SICK. I'M NOT INSANE. BUT NONE OF THAT WILL STOP THE GAME.

YOURS TRULY

TWENTY-SEVEN

Police investigating the murders of seven women in North London over the past fifteen months were confronted this morning with what they describe as 'a new and morbid challenge' by a person purporting to be the killer.

A cryptic note was sent to the Tribune *newspaper marked 'For the attention of Harry Connor', taunting the Detective Inspector heading up the manhunt, and bragging about a possible eighth victim.*

A blurred carbon copy of a document typed in block capitals, it is, police say, impossible to trace back to its source. However, the envelope it arrived in also contained a bloody swatch of cloth which the writer claimed was torn from the shirt of Sheryl North, an eighteen-year-old homeless woman whose naked body was discovered back in July last year on a canal towpath near Hampstead Road Lock, in Camden, North London.

Opening with the chilling line: 'This is the one you fear. I am the killer of Sheryl North. To prove it, here is a bloodstained piece of her shirt. I am the same man who did the girls at the woods and the rubbish tip' – the writer goes on to reveal details about the murders that only the perpetrator would know and addresses DI Connor directly, before

taunting him with the possibility of another, as yet undiscovered victim
'from Holmes Road'.

We were all on the couch waiting for *Dynasty* to start, my mother's feet in Matty's lap while he painted her toenails. He was in a great mood, telling us some story about a guy at work, really hamming up his accent.

He broke off when the news about the killer's note came on.

'What do you think of that?' he asked my mother, eyebrow tilted upwards.

'Like the Zodiac,' she replied.

Matty scoffed, shook his head.

'The Zodiac was indiscriminate. Used a gun. This guy's more . . . skilful.'

'You mean evil,' I said.

'I guarantee your man doesn't see himself that way.'

'How can he not?'

'Everyone's the star of their own movie, pumpkin. He'll have his reasons for doing what he does.' He glanced at my mother, making sure he had an audience. 'Those reasons will make sense to him even if no one else has the imagination to understand them.'

'There's no good reason for killing people.'

He shrugged.

'Like I said, he has his reasons. What do you think, Ams?'

'I think you probably know more about this sort of thing than us. And that I'd rather not talk about it so soon after supper.'

'Matty's a bereavement counsellor. What's that have to do with murderers?'

He gave me an arch look.

'You'd be surprised what you can learn about a person when they're grieving. All the shutters open wide.'

'People talk about killing when they're grieving?'

'Aye, sometimes. But not just then. You wouldn't believe how commonplace violent fantasies are.'

My mother shook her head at him, gave him a, *That's enough* look.

'All I'm saying is things are really going to ramp up now.'

My eyes darted over to my mother, to her dark hair and curls.

'What makes you say that?'

He leaned forward, articulated each word as if he were giving dictation.

'Because he's started playing to the crowd.'

'Are you listening to me? I said stop, Matty.'

Dynasty came on, Alexis Carrington taking over the screen.

'Such a bitch,' I muttered appreciatively.

'I don't like that language, Sophie.'

Matty chuckled.

'But I guarantee she likes that reaction.' He yawned widely, stretched. 'I might do a chocolate run. Anyone else fancy a treat?'

'There are some Cornettos in the freezer, I think.'

He put on an Italian accent, sang the jingle from the advert.

I chucked a cushion at him.

'You're terrible.'

'So's your aim.'

The atmosphere wasn't perfect, but it was definitely an improvement on the previous evening.

'If you're not interested in marriage, perhaps we should call it quits,' my mother had told Matty in no uncertain terms.

I was on my bed reading *Just Seventeen*. They were in the hallway, her shouting a foil to Matty's calm. It always went that way when they argued. She lost her temper, he kept his cool.

'If that's really what you want.'

'I know I don't want a man who can't commit after nearly four years.'

'Haven't I committed in other ways?'

'Not with a ring, you haven't.'

'I'm sorry you feel that way.'

'You're sorry I feel that way? Just get out.'

The old sinking sensation in my stomach returned, the sicky feeling that always accompanied it.

I heard the front door click shut. Something being thrown at a wall. The sound of china smashing. Not long afterwards the bell rang.

My shoulders loosened, the tightness in my chest released.

I peeked out. Watched as my mother gave her reflection a quick check in the hall mirror before opening the front door.

'Oh, Des. It's you.'

Her body sagged.

'I erm . . . just wanted to make sure you were okay. I heard rowing and um . . .' He cleared his throat, a death rattle of shifting phlegm. 'I always thought you were too good for him.'

'It was kind of you to look in. But I'm fine.'

She moved to close the door. A black army boot blocked it.

'I could stay a bit if you like. Make you a tea or—'

'That's really ki—' She broke off, straightening up the way a drooping plant will after it's been watered. 'Matty? You're back.'

'You're my soul mate, Ams. None of it means anything without you.'

Des took a step forward, blocked his way.

'Now look here, pal. I don't mean to stick my beak in—'

'Then don't,' Matty replied with an expression like he'd just walked in dog mess.

My mother fell into his arms.

'I'm sorry.'

'Me too, sweetheart.'

Old Brown Teeth took one disgusted look at them both then crawled back under his rock.

'No Matty?' I asked the next morning.

My mother popped a slice of Hovis into the toaster for me, flicked on the kettle.

'It was his turn at the crisis centre last night. He couldn't let them down.'

'He's a good man, Mum.'

She smiled.

'I know. I need to stop focusing on the bad.'

What I'd give to be able to go back in time and tell her she was wrong. That the 'bad' is exactly what she should have been focusing on.

Extract from the *Tribune*

On The Hunt For a 'Bad Man'

Scotland Yard today confirmed that the body of a nurse from the Royal Free Hospital has been found in an area of disused railway near Archway Road, North London.

The young woman, identified as Farah Lawson, shared a house with three other women in Holmes Road, Kentish Town.

A week ago, the editor of the *Tribune* newspaper received a cryptic note from a person claiming to be responsible for the series of murders that have taken place in North London over the past fifteen months. In it, the chilling words:

'HAVE YOU FOUND THE GIRL FROM HOLMES ROAD YET?'

Fear has gripped North Londoners since July last year, with young women being abducted off the streets by a single perpetrator who leaves behind no clues as to his identity, despite reassurances from Detective Inspector Harry Connor that:

'This is a bad and dangerous man, but everything he does brings us closer to catching him. With each crime he commits, he tells us a little more about himself.

'His victim choice, the way he kills, his post-mortem activity – all these are calling cards that will lead us to his door.'

So far though, no one knows where that door is. Meanwhile, Farah Lawson's mother, Mel, has released photographs of her daughter to the media in the hope a possible witness will recognise her and come forward.

'Farah saw the best in everyone. She was a gentle soul who spent her life helping others. It breaks my heart that her last moments were so brutal.'

TWENTY-EIGHT

I look at the photo of Farah Lawson, the Shadow's eighth murder victim. The CPS displayed it on an easel at Matty's trial. A picture taken at a dinner with friends, fellow nurses from the hospital where she worked. *She was the kindest person*, they said. *Nothing was ever too much trouble. Her whole life ahead of her.*

The prosecutor used their words during the court case, an over-emotive line of argument that prejudiced the jury against Matty according to many of his advocates. People who, unlike me, have refused ever to countenance his guilt.

'Her whole life ahead of her,' Tristan Ambrose QC told the court. 'Until the defendant so cruelly ripped it from her.'

Matty's barrister objected, argued the phraseology was 'prejudicial and irrelevant'.

It's relevant to me though. The life she could have had, the part I might have played in her losing it.

I didn't go to the trial, nor did my mother. I wonder now if it would have been better or worse if we had. Reading through the transcripts is one thing, but they don't show how Matty reacted to the evidence against him.

Did he really seem rapt when the post-mortem images were presented, as some journalists suggested? Was the smile he's supposed to have flashed to the gallery every morning actually born out of nerves rather than hubris, as it was portrayed in the red tops?

He may have worn a mask with us, but five years is a long time. Long enough to learn a person's tells, the micro expressions that speak to their true feelings.

What might his face have told me if I'd watched it in court? What clues might his eyes have revealed? What hidden truth might I have divined from them?

The journalists who did follow the trial, analysing every detail as it unfolded in the Old Bailey day after day, all reported the same thing. Matty looking confident and relaxed, joking with his lawyers, smiling at the crowd.

And it was quite a crowd. So big, there wasn't room for them all in court. Women lined up for hours in the cold to get a seat in the gallery. Hundreds of them, infatuated with his good looks, despite the constant stream of grim photos and crime scene evidence.

There are court drawings of them twirling their hair around their fingers and fluttering their lashes at Matty. TV clips of fresh-faced teens unable to believe he was guilty.

'I'm not afraid of him,' one woman told the cameras, a petite curly-haired brunette. 5'3. Just his type. 'He doesn't look like the sort to kill somebody.'

I trace Farah Lawson's face with my fingertip. She seemed so grown up to me back then, but now I can see she was barely an adult.

'What he did to her,' her mother told a *Newsnight* interviewer. 'My baby girl, thrown out like rubbish. Left for the rats.'

I pick up another article and another. So many clippings; yellowed over the years, the newsprint faded and smudged.

Janice thinks I've got rid of them. I promised her I have.

'Self-destructive,' she calls my obsession with the past, the way I pore over it. The way I won't let it go. She doesn't understand though. I can't turn my back on what happened until I know for sure what he did. If he did it.

I didn't go to his trial, so now I must weigh up the evidence for myself. And in some ways, I'm the only one who can judge. After all, I knew him in a way a jury never could. Yet all these years of searching for answers, and I'm still no clearer than I was at the start.

We are our memories. I forget who said that, but it resonates all the same. If I can't trust my memory, how can I trust myself?

Another article, the second letter sent to the *Tribune*, featured on their front page. I read it again, even though I could recite it by heart I've read it so often. And even though there's nothing new in it, a shiver tiptoes down my spine. A ghost walking over my grave.

Enough, I tell myself.

I put the clippings away. Snap the box shut.

It was Matty's idea to collect them. A sign of his innocence or his guilt? A double bluff? A boast?

Whatever his reason, my mother wasn't keen.

'Bit morbid, isn't it?'

The same way I'd described her box of childhood treasures. The little animal bones.

160

I tried explaining it was my way of getting a handle on what was happening. Ever since he'd started up again, I'd worried the killer would come after her. Not that she'd give me any airtime on that score, or consider changing her route home from work.

'Some things you can never get a handle on,' she told me, giving the clippings box a sidelong look. 'And others it's best not to understand.'

'Why?'

'Because understanding is a step towards condoning.'

I'd read something similar in the paper the day before.

'Maybe Sophie will find something the police have missed,' Matty said, giving me a wink to show he was on my side. 'They're not exactly making much headway, are they?'

'I imagine they know more than they're letting on,' she answered coolly. 'And if he's not careful, that's what's going to trip him up.'

'I wouldn't be so sure. It's been a year and a half, and still no arrests.'

'Cockiness comes before a fall, that's all I'm saying.'

I sensed the tension, changed the subject.

'Are you coming to see *E.T.* with me and Mum tonight? It's about this alien who moves in with a human family. Supposed to be brilliant.'

'Sorry, pumpkin. I can't. It's my turn at the crisis centre.'

Next day the story broke. The editor at the *Tribune* had received a second letter.

TWENTY-NINE

My mother was driving me to school. The end of January now, two months since the editor from the *Tribune* had received the Shadow's second letter.

Every morning we'd get up in the dark, scrape ice off the windshield, run the heater on high. Frankly it wasn't much better than Massachusetts, though at least here, the breath didn't freeze in front of your face. Burn as you sucked it in.

My mother buckled up. *It's the law now.*

'How about some music?'

'Sure.'

'Our House' pumped from the speakers. I tapped my fingers to the beat.

'Madness?'

'What?'

'The band. That's their name, right?'

'Yeah. They're from Camden, you know?'

My mother smiled.

'Practically neighbours.' She listened a moment. 'The words are kind of sad. Nostalgic.'

'Only because you're old. At your age, everything in the past seems better.'

'I'm not using a stair lift yet, thank you very much.'

She was the same age I am now. She was right, it's not old. But I feel ancient. And not everything in the past does seem better to me. It's not such a foreign country, nor do they do things so differently there. Violence, rage, self-delusion. Nothing of substance has changed in the passing decades. People are still killing each other, stealing, lying to the folk they're supposed to love.

The tune faded away, the beeps marking the hour.

The time is eight o'clock. This is the news . . .

My fingers froze on the dial as I went to switch stations.

Edwin Burke, editor of the Tribune *newspaper, informed police yesterday that he has received another carbon copy note from a person claiming to be the killer of eight women in North London dating from July 1981.*

Just three lines long and typed in block capitals, the note addressed to Mr Burke and marked for the attention of Detective Inspector Harry Connor who is heading up the serial murder investigation read:

HAVE YOU FOUND LYDIA DEVAL YET? NOTHING IN THE PAPERS . . .

Scotland Yard has since confirmed that an au pair of that name has been missing since October last year.

October 1982. Not long after the fire and that rollercoaster drive. Matty had been moody for weeks afterwards. He cancelled arrangements or else forgot them altogether – my school Prize Giving included.

I'd been nervous, worried about silly things like stumbling

on the stage or forgetting to say 'thank you' for the trophy. My mother seemed nervous too, fussing about with my hair and the stupid dress I didn't want to wear. My table manners may have improved slightly since leaving Goddard Street, but I still couldn't see the point of skirts.

She stood back, appraised me with a tilted head.

'You've grown. Do you think it's too short?'

'Trousers go down to the ankle.'

A deep breath, a long sigh.

'It'll have to do.' She glanced at her reflection, teeth worrying at her lower lip. 'I wonder what the other moms will be wearing. Ralph Lauren at ten paces, I expect.'

Another sigh followed by a shy smile.

'You look beautiful, sweetheart.'

She checked her watch, forehead creasing into a frown.

'Where on earth's Matty got to? He was supposed to be here forty minutes ago.'

She paced about, gave it another ten.

'We can't wait any longer, we're late as it is.'

All the way she was flipping out about where he was, watching for him on the road.

'Maybe he misunderstood, thought we were meeting there.'

He wasn't at the school though, didn't show up all morning.

'No Matty?' one girl whispered as we sat on the benches waiting to be called up. The girl from my party who'd said he was gorgeous.

'I'd have thought he'd be in the front row with that camera of his,' another chipped in.

I put on a face I didn't feel.

'He'll be here.'

Turned out I did stumble going up on the stage, too busy looking for him in the crowd to pay attention where I was going. Matty wasn't my father, but he was my family. I wanted him watching me, cheering me on.

'Why didn't he come?' I asked my mother afterwards.

'I don't know,' she said, voice pensive. 'Something must be wrong.'

He didn't call, didn't pick up his phone when my mother called him. We went around to his place, but he didn't come to the door. Days passed without a word, no 'sorry', no explanation.

Then finally on Friday evening he showed up with a bottle of champagne. *The good stuff.*

'Bit of bubbly,' he said in a pleased-with-himself voice.

Had he got the date wrong?

'What are we celebrating?' my mother asked, testing.

'Do we need an excuse for champagne?'

She slammed the door in his face.

'What have I done now?'

'The worst thing is, he doesn't even know,' she told me.

She was wrong though. If what we found out later was true, forgetting my Prize Giving wasn't remotely the worst thing he'd done.

MISSING

LYDIA DEVAL

White, female

Missing since 13th October 1982

Height: 5 ft 2in

Weight: 7 stone (approx. 98 lbs)

Eyes: Brown

Hair: Brown, curly, shoulder length

Age: 20 years

Lydia was last seen wearing a yellow sweater and blue denim mini skirt in Crouch End at 11.30pm on 13th October. She never made it home and hasn't been seen or heard from since. Foul play is suspected.

IF YOU HAVE SEEN LYDIA –

OR ANYONE CLOSELY RESEMBLING HER –

PLEASE CALL 999 IMMEDIATELY.

THIRTY

The police never found Lydia Deval, a Madonna-mad au pair from Rouen who'd come to the UK to polish her English and dance the nights away under the London lights. The family she worked for in Belsize Park, two stops away on the Tube from us, assumed she'd disappeared off in search of adventure when she failed to return home the night of her murder. Two days later they'd engaged a new nanny. Only their little boy cried for Lydia.

To this day, no one knows for sure what happened to her or whether she was even a victim of the Shadow. Although all the hallmarks were apparently there, thousands of people disappeared from the capital every year. Lydia Deval could have been a murder victim. Or just another missing person case.

'It's the not knowing, that makes her death so hard to deal with,' her sister, Chloe told the *Post*.

'Lydia fitted what they say is Melgren's victim type. But unless he confesses, we'll never know if he actually killed her.

'My mother went to her grave not knowing what had happened to her. While all I know is, the last time I spoke to my

VICTORIA SELMAN

sister I said things I shouldn't have. Now I'll never get the chance to put it right, to tell her I'm sorry. That I loved her.

'Melgren's victims are dead. But their families are still alive to feel pain and loss. Felled doing the most mundane tasks. Watching TV, drying the dishes . . . You're never prepared for what might trip you up.'

She went on to beg Matty to admit the truth and reveal what he'd done with Lydia, along with the names of his other victims. The scores of missing women, who like her had never been found but whom police suspect he killed.

'If you have an ounce of humanity, tell us,' she pleaded.

But to this day, he's proclaimed his innocence to anyone who'll listen. My pain isn't the same as Lydia's sister's, but like her I yearn for the truth. And I too feel the constant pull of quicksand, the suffocation of uncertainty.

Is Matty the Shadow? Did he kill those women? How many other lives did he take?

'There's been another one.'

Matty let himself into our flat, a bag of bagels in his hand, newspaper under his arm.

My mother was sitting at the kitchen table sipping her morning coffee. Her 'fix'. *I can't do a thing till I've had it.* After Matty's arrest, the coffee went by the wayside. By then, she had other fixes she couldn't do without.

He slapped the paper down on the table.

'Seen this?'

He tapped at the headline with his index finger.

Shadow Latest: Another woman killed and discarded like litter.

'Good God.' She held his eyes, inhaled deeply. 'How many is that now?'

It was rhetorical, but Matty answered without missing a beat. 'Nine.'

'Keeping track, are you?' I teased.

'Nice pun, pumpkin.'

I was confused, asked what he meant.

My mother read aloud. Keeping me from the news was a losing battle.

'Residents today will be shocked to learn that the body of Gemma Nicholls, a seventeen-year-old woman believed to be yet another victim of the killer nicknamed the Shadow, has been discovered discarded in bushes by the running track in Parliament Hill.' She inhaled deeply, shook her head. 'I was by the running track on Friday. To think . . .'

Matty gave her a pointed look.

'I told you the park wasn't safe.'

'But—'

'Trust me, Ams. Last time I was there, I saw a bunch of kids shooting up.'

I rolled my eyes. He was always making out things were more dangerous than they really were. That I'd get attacked riding my bike in the street. Mugged if I walked home in the dark. Cut up into little pieces if I ventured down an alleyway on my own. *The world's not what you think it is, pumpkin. You never know where there's a predator lurking.*

'It says here that a jogger claimed he'd seen the body but didn't report it because at the time he thought it was a mannequin,' my mother said.

Matty snorted.

'You're joking.'

She glanced at me. *Did he really just say that?*

'You think it's funny? The poor girl was only seventeen.'

'I'm sorry. It's horrible.'

'Utterly twisted.'

She carried on reading, her lips moving in the way of a silent prayer.

'Asphyxiated,' she whispered. 'Slashed across the buttocks.'

'Out alone at night,' Matty said. 'Why do they keep doing it?'

'Women should be able to go out at night without getting killed,' I retorted.

My mother glanced up from the paper, a thin line etched between her eyebrows.

'Doesn't say anything here about her being out alone.'

Matty shrugged.

'They basically all are, aren't they?'

I shook my head.

'How do y—'

My mother knocked over her coffee mug, a brown river drowning the paper.

'Dammit, it's gone everywhere.'

Matty grabbed the paper towels.

'Makes you wonder,' she said as he mopped up.

'Wonder what?'

'All this time and he still hasn't slipped up.'

'Quite something, isn't it?' Matty agreed.

THIRTY-ONE

'Where are those men taking Des?'

My mother was at the sink rinsing the breakfast plates.

'What men?'

'Out there. Look.'

She came to join me at the window where I was watching a bizarre scene unfold on the street below.

'They're putting him in that Honda.'

There were two men in suits, one with his hand resting on the door frame of an open passenger door, the other pushing Des inside by the head.

'He'll want to wash his hands,' I muttered.

'There's no need to be unkind, Sophie.' Then more thoughtfully, 'What is going on?' She tilted her head, tapped her forefinger against her lips. 'Something's off. Maybe we should call the police.'

It didn't occur to either of us that they *were* the police.

I opened the window. Every night my mother triple checked they were unlocked before going to bed, the fire branded on both our brains.

'What are you doing? It's freezing.'

'Shh, I'm trying to listen.'

'Always eavesdropping,' she tutted.

She didn't argue though.

'What about Bailey?' we heard Des ask, his not so dulcet tones rising up from the pavement.

'Who's Bailey?' one of the suits replied.

'My dog.'

He pronounced it, 'ma dorg', his Scottish accent thicker than the disgusting blood sausage he'd gifted us at Christmas.

'He'll be okay,' the other man assured him.

I glanced at my mother.

'Should we offer to look after Bailey while he's gone? It's the right thing to do. Neighbourly,' I added for good measure, throwing her own expressions back at her.

'It sounds like those men are going to take care of him.'

'We don't know that.'

'There's nothing to suggest they won't, and how do you think Des would react if he thought we'd been spying on him?'

'But—'

'But nothing. Go brush your teeth. You're going to be late for school.'

Sometimes it's easier to get your own way by letting the other person think they've got theirs.

I grabbed my satchel and, when her back was turned, pinched a few slices of ham from the fridge, which I posted through Des' letter box on my way out.

The news broke that afternoon. I was walking up South End Road, past the ponds, in the direction of the overground with Bea Ruthers, a girl from my class. We weren't friends, but Matty had convinced my mother it wasn't safe for me to walk home alone, even though I was twelve years old and it was broad daylight.

A crowd was gathered round the newsstand outside the train station.

'What's going on?'

A few bodies shifted, giving me a glimpse of the words on the sandwich board—

SHADOW LATEST:
MAN ARRESTED

'I don't believe it!'

'About time,' Bea said.

'Do you have any money for a paper?' I asked.

'Have you seen how long that queue is? I'm not waiting in that.'

'Don't you want to know who they've arrested?'

'It'll be on the telly. Come on, let's go.'

'The line's moving. It won't take—'

But she was already marching off, pigtails swinging. I hovered a moment, trying to get a glimpse of a newspaper, but the only thing visible was the headline. The same words as on the billboard.

Back home, I threw myself onto the couch and was just reaching for the TV remote when I heard Bailey's whining downstairs.

Was Des still not home? The poor animal must be starving.

The ham was all gone. I posted a peanut butter sandwich through the letter box then returned to the TV.

'A thirty-seven-year-old man was arrested at seven o'clock this morning at his home in Parliament Hill in connection with the murders of nine women in North London,' Detective Inspector Connor was telling a news conference.

'This follows a call to the tip line by a witness who claims to have seen the suspect by the bushes near the running track at the time of Gemma Nicholls' murder.

'The man is currently in custody and being questioned about the murders. We will not be releasing the name of the police station where he is being held or of the man himself.

'At this point, he has not been charged. No incriminating evidence has been found in his home, though investigating officers did discover a stash of fetish pornography and a collection of high-heeled women's shoes. As yet, we haven't been able to confirm whether any of them belonged to the murdered women.'

When I look back now, I can't understand why I didn't make the connection. It was all there, the time of the arrest, the location, what I'd seen out of the window. And yet for some reason, I didn't join the dots.

Was I simply blinded by that naive belief that bad things happen to other people? Or was there something more innately wrong with me that meant I missed what was in front of my eyes?

Janice and I have debated it ad nauseam. I'm inclined towards the latter. I was an ostrich, up to my neck in sand.

After all, look how long it took me to connect the dots with Matty.

THIRTY-TWO

My mother didn't make the connection with Des either. Ironic, given how quickly she pointed the finger at Matty only a short while later.

He came over the night Des was arrested, bringing a bulging sack of Chinese food from Singapore Garden.

'What's the news?' I asked.

Chinese was our go-to meal whenever we were celebrating.

'Just a good day,' he smiled. 'Bit of a breakthrough on a case I've been working on.'

My mother came over, a big smile on her face.

'What a treat!'

A delicious waft of spring rolls and Peking duck rose up from the bag.

'What's the case?' she asked.

'I wish I could tell you, but . . .'

She'd heard that before, put her hands up in mock surrender.

'Yeah, yeah . . . confidential.'

Matty kissed her nose.

'Did you get seaweed?' I asked.

VICTORIA SELMAN

'Got the whole menu pretty much.'

'Forgot the plum sauce though,' I said rummaging in the bags.

He helped me look, found the pot stuffed at the bottom.

'You malign me, madam.'

He put me in a headlock, the opening move in the Prisoner Game.

'Stop!'

'Let me hear you beg.'

My mother watched, an odd expression on her face.

'She's a bit old for that, Matty.'

'She's too old when she can get away.'

But he let me go.

We ate in front of the TV, watched the latest on the arrest, which was basically just a re-hash of everything we already knew.

'I don't get it,' I said.

'Don't get what, pumpkin?'

'There have been thousands of calls to the tip line. What's so special about this one?'

Matty glanced at my mother the way he always did when he had a story to tell.

'I hear it was a witness, who called it in.'

'Really?' she said.

'Mm-hm.'

He bit the end off a spring roll, wolfed the thing down in two bites. I helped myself to one before he gobbled the lot.

'So? Plenty of people have claimed to have seen things.'

'I heard this guy was different.'

'Different how?'

'He was able to describe what the girl was wearing.'

'That doesn't make sense. I thought she was found naked.'

'Aye. Afterwards.' He drew the word out, laid heavy emphasis on it. 'The witness saw her before she was killed. Described exactly the clothes she was last seen in. That's how the police know he was genuine rather than another one of these kooks after their five minutes of fame.'

'Where did you hear all this?' my mother asked.

'Lad at the clinic. Mate of someone on the investigation team, I think.'

'Surely that sort of thing's confidential,' she said, harking back to their earlier conversation.

He shrugged.

'Only telling you what I know.'

He took a piece of prawn toast, offered the carton around. Chinese was the only food he ever shared, and then only after he'd loaded up his plate first.

'Shall we watch *In-Depth*? Might be something about it on that.'

We were treated to yet another airing of Harry Connor's statement about the arrest followed by an interview with Fiona Jensen, the effortlessly glamorous news anchor, and Andrew Wilson, a professor of criminology at York University.

'It's national television. You'd think the fella might have trimmed his nasal hair,' Matty muttered.

My mother scowled at him, told him to be quiet, she was trying to listen.

'Whilst not a smoking gun, the shoe collection is interesting,' Professor Wilson responded when Fiona mentioned the stilettos found in the suspect's home.

She raised an eyebrow, asked him to please expand on that.

'We know matching footprints have been found at a number of the disposal sites. So at some point during the commissioning of the murders, the perpetrator removes his shoes.'

'To avoid getting blood on them?'

'It's possible. But I expect it has more to do with enhancing his physical connection to the victims. An indication of partialism, perhaps. Or more specially, podophilia.'

'Podophilia?'

'Sexual arousal derived from the feet. A foot fetish, if you like.'

Fiona processed that, asked what else the professor could tell 'our audience' about the offender.

'He has an innate drive to kill, one that won't go away.'

'What does that mean?'

'That he won't stop until he's caught. He may be able to suppress his urges for a time. But they always return. And when they do, he is compelled to act.'

My skin goose fleshed. I glanced over at my mother and Matty to see if they'd had the same reaction, but whereas she was sitting there, arms wrapped around herself as though cold, he was drinking it in. Every now and then he'd give a little nod as if Professor Wilson were giving a speech he himself had written.

I supposed it was because of his job, he'd studied psychology, understood these things. They probably weren't as shocking to him as they were to us.

'What can you tell us about the perpetrator's mindset?' the newscaster asked. 'His psyche.'

Wilson interlaced his fingers, mirroring her body language. Establishing rapport, Matty told us.

'He's obsessed with the need for control. That's shown by the way he's been toying with the police and how he discards his victims. He's enjoying the power he has over them. Exhibiting his control. Game playing.'

Matty scoffed.

'He needs a degree for that?'

'Shh,' my mother said.

'What sort of person are we talking about?' Fiona asked.

'Someone who might have difficulty forming relationships with women. That could be why he targets lone women. Having said that, they could simply be easy targets. Which means any woman in the wrong place at the wrong time could become his prey.'

I glanced at my mother, hoped she was taking this in.

'We're talking about a loner, then, professor? A person without much confidence or success with women?'

'Probably, although we mustn't exclude the possibility he's leading a double life. A supposedly devoted husband or father.'

'Game's up,' Matty said, letting out a fake sigh. 'May as well admit it now . . .'

My mother shot him a dirty look.

'That's not funny, Matty.'

I've thought a lot about his remark since then. Would he really have made it if he was guilty? Drawn attention to himself like that?

Or was it what Professor Wilson said? Was he playing games?

Though another question haunts me more: why were we so quick to dismiss what he said?

THIRTY-THREE

Des Banister arrived home in the early hours. I was lying awake dwelling on what Professor Wilson had said about the killer. Trying to wrap my head around the idea he was someone's brother, boyfriend, father. That there was a person out there who loved him. Who kissed him goodnight, brought him soup when he was sick.

It made no sense to me. How could you love a man who murdered stranger after stranger they'd never met? How could the people close to him not realise what he was doing? Did not realising make them somehow complicit?

The same questions were posed to Jerome Brudos' wife after his arrest a little over a decade earlier. *Didn't you ever wonder what he was getting up to in his garage? Why he wouldn't let you in without using the intercom?*

In time, my mother and I would be asked those questions too. *How could you not have known? Surely you could tell something was up? Did you really not suspect anything?*

The sound of an engine idling outside our building cut through my musings. Des' voice echoing around the empty street—

'This ain't over.' And then, 'My dog had better be okay.'

Maybe he did love Bailey, after all.

I slipped out of bed, pulled apart the slats on my blinds. He was getting out of the same Honda Accord I'd spotted that morning. I was used to hearing him coming home late at night, often drunk, judging by the way he crashed about downstairs. But this was the first time I'd seen him being given a lift, by men in suits no less.

I still didn't put it together though, not even when I heard the news the following day.

My mother was at the breakfast table sipping her coffee while I chowed down on a bowl of Cheerios. She'd long ago given up trying to force-feed me Weetabix.

The radio was on, as I imagine it was in most houses in North London that morning. Much had been made of the police's narrow time window, the thirty-six hours they can hold a suspect without charging them.

'After that, it's put up or shut up,' Matty had said last night.

The custody clock was ticking, he explained. It wouldn't be long before they confirmed whether they'd caught the killer who'd been terrorising our community for the better part of two years.

A piece of cereal went down the wrong way making me cough.

'Shh,' my mother tutted, turning up the volume.

Yesterday, police arrested a man in Parliament Hill in connection with the brutal murders of eight women in North London. It follows one of the largest police operations in recent UK history. The hunt for the killer was launched in July 1981 after the body of a homeless woman was discovered on a towpath at Hampstead Road Lock.

An appeal for tips has led to over 10,000 calls to the police hotline. And it was one of these calls that led to the arrest of a suspect yesterday.

We looked at each other, frozen as if someone had hit 'pause'.

Had the man been charged? Were they about to reveal the name?

The man in question has since been released in the early hours of this morning with police saying they don't have enough evidence to hold him.

'Shit,' my mother whispered, my mother who never swore.

Scotland Yard has refused to comment on reports that the person they arrested is an odd-jobs man or that he has previously been arrested for soliciting.

She switched the radio off, tipped out her coffee mug into the sink.

'All these people out looking for him, the whole city on alert. And yet he still slips through the net. Keeps on killing.'

'How does he do it?'

She ran a hand through her hair. There were strands of grey I'd never noticed before.

'Who knows?' she sighed. 'Makes you wonder, though, doesn't it?'

'Wonder what?'

'Will the police ever catch a break?'

I thought about what Professor Wilson had said.

'Not unless he slips up.'

Little did we know, he was about to do just that.

And that in slipping, we'd slip too.

From the website *Morbidophile.com*

Shining a Light on the Shadow

Morbidophile is a true crime website created by Emma G. Lowery. Using investigative research, it provides an in-depth examination of true crime cases from around the world.

* 4 min read

The 'Shadow Murders' of at least nine women and one child in the early '80s, is one of the UK's most gruesome crimes. In 1983, Matty Melgren, a bereavement counsellor from North London where the victims were killed, was convicted of their brutal slayings.

He is now serving a life sentence at Battlemouth Prison with no chance of parole. But is he really the Shadow? Or was he set up by his girlfriend's neighbour, as he's always claimed?

And if so, was this neighbour, Des Banister – a pornography obsessed shoe fetishist – in fact the true culprit?

Matty Melgren came to the police's attention after a student claimed to have been approached in suspicious circumstances by an Irish man claiming to be a bereavement counsellor less than an hour before another woman was abducted and murdered from the same location.

She described the man as having blonde wavy hair (like Melgren's) and driving a Mini Cooper (the same type of car Melgren owned).

But why would a serial killer give real details about himself? And would he not don a disguise given he had police on his tail?

Is it possible that instead, Des Banister who lived in the flat below Melgren's girlfriend and had recently been rejected by her, sought revenge by setting up her boyfriend – a man he saw as his love rival?

Might he have put on a fake accent when he approached his victims? Even worn a wig and rented a Mini just like the one Matty owned? And is it possible he targeted women who looked just like the one he could never have?

In so doing, did he set in motion the UK's most terrible case of mistaken identity, resulting in an innocent man being locked up for a crime he didn't commit?

Article Rating: ****

THIRTY-FOUR

I don't suppose I'd have remembered the incident if it hadn't been for the post I stumbled upon during one of my late-night tumbles down the rabbit hole.

The blogger's name was Emma Lowery. She used a middle initial, hoping perhaps that it would give her gravitas. I've noticed American politicians do the same thing. If an English politician did that, they'd be mocked mercilessly. The British invented the class system, but they don't take kindly to airs and graces.

I'm digressing.

Point is, Emma Lowery presented an argument about Des which I'd come across several times before. The internet is the perfect mouthpiece for conspiracy theories.

Des wasn't the only person people claimed had set Matty up. There are whole threads devoted to the question of whether the Night Strangler framed him up as payback for him helping police catch him. Never mind that the police have gone on record saying Matty wasn't consulted about the Night Strangler before or after his arrest.

So, Emma Lowery's argument about Des was nothing new,

but she did raise something no one else had. A motive. The fact Des was obsessed with my mother, that she'd rejected him.

As far as I know, he never asked her out directly. Frankly, I doubt he'd have had the guts. But that doesn't mean she didn't reject him. And that he didn't blame Matty for her lack of interest in him.

My mother was always on my case about not speaking ill of people, but I'm not going to pretend I liked the man just because of what happened to him. Or that I didn't see what I saw.

I almost bought his act about being worried about Bailey, went so far as to question whether I'd misjudged him. Then one day, coming home from school, I saw him through the window, hitting the poor animal about the head with a rolled-up newspaper, calling him names. All for 'shiteing' on his carpet.

Liking dogs doesn't make you a good person. As Nanna G was forever saying, Hitler liked dogs. But in my experience, no decent person is ever cruel to one. My mother could tell me I was wrong about Des Banister all she liked, but I had him pegged.

Matty didn't think much of him either, though I suspect that was about his male ego as much as anything else.

'There's a cold wind blows every time that fella walks past,' he said one time.

My mother shook her head, put on her exasperated face.

'What's he ever done to you?'

'I'm simply calling a spade a spade, that's all.'

'Well, Des isn't a spade. He's a human being.'

'Is he though?'

The three of us were walking on Parliament Hill, a Sunday afternoon in late August.

'Need to make the most of the sunshine,' Matty had said. 'Summer'll be over before we know it.'

He was right, both literally and metaphorically.

'Anyone for a 99?'

He bought us cornets from an ice cream van, led us over to a bench by the running track – opposite it the bushes where Gemma Nicholls' body had been found. The back of my neck prickled.

'Can we find somewhere else?'

'Good idea,' my mother agreed.

Matty looked at us like we were a couple of clowns.

'You're not scared of ghosts, surely?' he said, sitting himself down; arm stretched along the back of the bench, right ankle crossed over his left knee. 'Can't avoid this place for ever, ladies.'

It was typical Matty. He had a way of making you feel you were blowing things out of proportion, that your instincts were skewed.

We bumped into Des Banister on our way home. Bailey was with him, sniffing in the bushes around the track. Des was trying to pull him away, but the animal had picked up a scent, wouldn't be deterred.

He spotted my mother, smiled brownly.

'Hullo, Amelia-Rose.'

He always called her by her full name, pronounced it as if he were savouring a delicacy.

Matty and I may as well not have been there, but to be fair, we didn't exactly say 'hi' to him either.

My mother was wearing an off-the-shoulder white sundress

that highlighted her tan and delicate collar bones. Des looked her over, wet his lips. Struggled for something to say before coming up with the winner:

'All right?'

She smiled as if she was actually pleased to see him.

'Well, thanks. How are you?'

'No bad.' He shuffled his feet, played with the loose change in his pocket. 'If you need any jobs done or anything, I'm, you know, happy to help.'

Matty snorted, muttered under his breath. *What a muppet.*

Our neighbour's lips twitched in response, but he kept it to himself.

'That's very kind of you, Des,' my mother said. Then touching Matty lightly on his arm, 'But this one's pretty good with his hands.'

They exchanged a flirty glance.

'Oh, okay. But even so, if you . . .'

'You heard her, bucko. She doesn't need your help.'

Des' neck marbled.

'Right. Well, I'll see you about Amelia-Rose . . .'

He retreated, tail between his legs just like Bailey, now being dragged out of the bushes at speed.

'As if you'd be interested in a miserable little pox like him.'

Matty said it loud enough for Des to hear. So he could hear, I suspect. Our neighbour turned around, face burning, but again said nothing.

My mother giggled. Discomfort, but he couldn't have known that.

Two days later, the sketch came out.

Last Seen with the Shadow?

POLICE URGE YOUNG WOMEN TO BE "ON THEIR GUARD"
By Rita Palmer
Crime Correspondent

Another woman has gone missing from North London this week following a series of murders in the area dating from 1981.

Kelly Hope, a nineteen-year-old biology student, was last seen in Kilburn on Saturday night. A witness overheard her talking with a man with an Irish accent (wearing a blue cashmere V-neck sweater and dark brown trousers) who claimed to be searching for his lost dog.

Although Miss Hope's body has not been found, she hasn't returned to the flat she shares with two other women, nor has she called home. Both these things are apparently 'out of character' according to her mother, care home nurse, Carol Hope (39).

A second woman, who wishes not to be named,

came forward yesterday. She told police that she was also approached in Kilburn by a smartly dressed blonde man holding a dog lead and claiming to be searching for a beagle who'd apparently slipped his collar whilst tied up outside a shop.

She said he seemed distraught and so when he asked if she'd drive around with him to try and find his missing pet, she agreed.

'He said he was a bereavement counsellor. He seemed nice, quite charming actually. But as we reached his car, a dark coloured Mini Cooper, blue I think it was, I got a funny feeling and told him I had to go. I don't know what it was. I just got spooked, I guess.'

She and the other witness have since worked with a police sketch artist who has produced the composite printed above.

Scotland Yard says the man is in his mid to late thirties, approximately 5'10" and weighs around twelve stone. He has wavy blonde hair and green eyes.

Detective Inspector Harry Connor, heading up the investigation, has asked the public to call the tip line printed below if they recognise the man, and has urged the public to be vigilant.

'Young women especially, should be on their guard.'

THIRTY-FIVE

'You're back early.'

My mother, home before me for once, was at the stove making her famous Napolitana sauce. A top-secret recipe handed down through the generations.

I grabbed a handful of cookies from the tin and picked up the newspaper clipping lying on the side.

'What's this?'

She just shook her head to show she didn't want to discuss it.

Another woman has gone missing from North London this week following a series of murders in the area dating from 1981 . . .

It was an article and a composite sketch of a man, possibly the Shadow, cut from the *Post*. There were pencil markings along the edges where a margin had been ruled before the paper was snipped. Beneath the sketch, someone had written: RING ANY BELLS? A small rip where the biro had stabbed through the page.

The hairs on my neck danced.

'Who's this from? They think we know him?'

'I don't know what they think.'

She wouldn't look at me though.

If the latest victim was the Shadow's work, it would bring his body count to ten. Many of the women killed on our doorstep or in places we liked to go.

Hampstead Road Lock canal was a short walk from our apartment. I passed the running track every day on my way to school. Marine Ices, Matty's favourite ice-cream parlour, was at Chalk Farm. Highgate Woods where I'd been for a friend's birthday.

I couldn't shake the idea I might have come across the victims at some point. On the high street. In line at the supermarket. Waiting for the Tube. Women who were alive one minute – laughing, buying groceries, watching TV. Watching news of the missing persons on TV, no idea they were next.

'I'm scared,' I'd told Matty ages ago.

The killings had only just started, but already I was making connections between the victims' appearance and my mother's.

'Don't be scared, pumpkin. Nothing's going to happen to you. Trust me.'

'You can't know that.'

He kissed the top of my head.

'Yes, I can.'

'How?'

'Just do.'

I lowered the clipping now.

'Where d'you get it?'

My mother shrugged, added herbs to the pan. Still wouldn't look at me.

'Why are you being so secretive? Just tell me.'

She sighed, turned down the heat.

'It was on the mat when I got home.'

I'm not much good at maths, but some sums even I can do.

'Des,' I said. 'Has to be. No one else could have got upstairs. What the hell's he playing at?'

My mother went all lemon-lipped. Told me to mind my language.

'Does it ring any bells?' I asked after a quick back and forth as to whether 'hell' seriously counted as a cuss word.

'The sketch isn't exactly detailed.'

I reread the article. Bereavement counsellor. Irish. Blonde hair. Green eyes. Mini . . .

'He's implying it's Matty, isn't he? What a shit!'

'Sophie!'

I held my hands up.

'Come on, even you have to admit it's a cheap shot.'

'Why would Des want us to think Matty's the Shadow?'

'You saw how he was in the park. He hates him, wants you all to himself.'

'You're being ridiculous. I mean—'

But Des had snared my interest, even if he was a miserable gobshite as Matty was so fond of saying.

'There are similarities though. The Irish accent, the Mini . . .'

'The guy probably put on an accent, I know I would in his shoes. And anyway, Matty's Mini isn't blue.'

'He has a blue cashmere V-neck though. It's practically his trademark.'

'Along with how many other people?'

I didn't think for a minute the man in the sketch was really

Matty, but there was a perverse pleasure in teasing myself with the possibility that it might be. Rollercoaster Syndrome, Janice calls it.

'The woman could have remembered the car colour wrong. She said it was dark, like Matty's. And the make is the same.'

My mother started chopping peppers with far more force than necessary.

'Minis are about the most popular car in London, Sophie.'

'He said he was a bereavement counsellor.'

'Do you seriously think the killer would give away real details about himself?'

Twenty years later, people are still asking the same question.

THIRTY-SIX

My mother made out she didn't believe the sketch was Matty but she had doubts, whatever she said to me.

Ironic to think now that it all started with her. A seed of mistrust that settled in my gut, grew into a tree. Cast my world in shade.

Matty was my hero, the father I'd never had. I loved him all the way to my bones, which has always been the problem of course. Why what I did was so terrible, why the guilt cuts so deep.

'To dispel the shadows,' Janice says, 'you have to first turn on the light.'

It's taken years of therapy to acknowledge my feelings, to face up to the secret truth I could scarcely admit to myself. My mother kissed me better when I got hurt, put food on the table, tucked me in every night. Yet the person I loved most was a monster, a man who butchered strangers. One of them a child, the same age as me when we met.

'Did you really not suspect anything when you saw that sketch?'

My mother won't let it drop, the nagging voice of my conscience.

As I tell Janice, I wouldn't have been able to point out the similarities if I'd thought for a moment it could really be him. If I'd thought that, I'd have searched for discrepancies – *Same way you did, Mum.*

'You could indulge in the fantasy that the sketch was Matty because you were so sure it wasn't. And that's what makes it hard to deal with. You felt tricked. Your notion of safety was compromised. It made you aware of your vulnerability, forced you to question everything you believed in.'

My mouth is dry. I can only nod.

My mother was different. After Matty was arrested, I came to realise she'd suspected him as soon as she read the article. It made me wonder whether a part of her had always felt something was amiss. Why else would she be so quick to think the worst?

I outlined the similarities between Matty and the witness accounts because I didn't believe it was him. She dismissed them because she believed it was.

He was supposed to come over the night the clipping appeared on our doormat. Instead, he called just as my mother was preparing to serve up supper. She put the phone on speaker to free up her hands.

'Let me guess, you're running late.'

'Actually, I'm not going to be able to make it over at all. They need me at the crisis centre, one of the other fellas is sick as a small hospital, so he reckons.'

'That's a shame. I made—'

'Don't be like that.'

'I'm not being like anything. I just—'

'These people have no one else to turn to. I'm their last hope, Ams.'

'I don't know why you're so upset,' I said when she'd hung up. 'It's not like he's never cancelled before.'

'I know,' she said, grating Parmesan into a bowl with extra vigour. 'I wouldn't have minded showing him that sketch, is all.'

She didn't just want to show him the sketch though. She wanted to see how he reacted to it too.

'All this food,' she said. 'I'll see if Linda wants to join us.'

Even I knew inviting Linda over had nothing to do with the amount she'd cooked.

It didn't take long before they were talking about the article. My mother fixating on the similarities between Matty and the guy the witnesses had described.

I gave her a look. *You've changed your tune.*

She played with her food, worried at her lower lip.

'It's weird, that's all. Same car, same nationality, same job even.'

'He'll be delighted to hear you say that, Am. *Hey honey, you sound just like that psycho.*'

'I wasn't planning on bringing it up.'

'Yeah, probably not the best pillow talk.'

My mother didn't answer, just twirled a curl around her finger. Stared into her plate. Linda brought her face to my mother's level, held her eyes.

'You don't really think—'

'No, of course not,' she answered quickly. 'It is strange though. All these things in common.'

197

Linda straightened up, shovelled in a mouthful. Spoke through it in a way that would have got me sent away from the table.

'Because Matty Melgren, your handsome, charming boyfriend who drags halfway across town just to buy your daughter ice cream, is actually a woman-hating serial killer. Yep, that makes sense.'

'Des thinks so,' I said. 'Look.'

I showed her the note. Linda shook her head, let her breath out slowly through her nose.

'No wonder you're in a tizz, Am. What a shitty—'

'He was probably just looking out for us . . .'

'Yeah, wasn't thinking about his penis at all.'

'Linda!'

I stifled a laugh. My mother was thirty-two, but her prudishness was pure Nanna.

'I know you like to give everyone the benefit of the doubt, but in this case, Des Banister is just an opportunist prick.'

'Some thick bollocks,' I piped up.

Linda laughed, deep and throaty.

'What's that now, Soph?'

'It's what Matty calls him. Amongst other things.'

She laughed again.

'Thick bollocks. Ha! I'm going to use that one.'

'He can't really be a bereavement counsellor, can he?' my mother asked. 'The killer, I mean . . .'

Such hope in her voice, a child wanting to be reassured, *See, no monsters under the bed.*

'Would you give out identifying details in that situation?'

'But why give any at all?'

Linda shrugged, loaded up her fork.

'He's obviously into game playing, like Professor Whatshis-name on the telly said.'

My mother mumbled something.

'You what now?'

'Matty has a dog leash.'

'So?'

I knew what she was getting at though, the memory coming at me like a bullet in the dark.

'Sophie found this leash at his place. His mother's beagle's, he said. But he never mentioned his mother had a dog before. I mean, don't you find that strange?'

'Does he know everything about you?'

'No, but . . .'

'But what?'

'He dinged a car the other day, didn't leave a note or any-thing. And then when we were undercharged at the Italian on Saturday night, he kept schtum. "Lucky us", is what he said.'

'Goodness, I never realised you were dating such a gangster.'

'I'm serious . . .'

Linda reached across the table, laid a hand on my mother's, gave it a squeeze.

'So am I. You know Matty. What a good guy he is. Don't let Thick Bollocks get in your head. He doesn't deserve a second thought.'

She was right, but it didn't matter. Listening to my mother, a window of doubt opened up inside me.

One I would never quite close.

THIRTY-SEVEN

We were studying *Othello* in English the day the sketch came out. I had to write an essay on that famous jealousy quote for homework – 'It is the green-eyed monster which doth mock the meat it feeds on.' *Do you agree? Give examples from the text to illustrate your argument.*

Jealousy isn't the only monster that mocks its meal though. Doubt is a demon too, grinding up your insides, leaving behind nothing but an empty shell.

At least, that's how it began to seem to me. How I felt. How I feel.

Consumed. Hollow. Distrustful of everyone, including myself.

My box of newspaper clippings is open in front of me. In the background, some computer-generated music on Capital FM. Not my taste, but anything to block out the never-ending soundtrack of my black thoughts.

Buster snores in his basket, legs twitching as he dreams. I watch him a moment, envious of his quiet ease. Then I turn back to the box, pick out the next page.

My eyes are blurry with tears. They make the headlines swim. So many headlines.

THREE MORE BODIES TAKES THE TOTAL TO FIVE

ANOTHER WOMAN FOUND DEAD

A KILLER MURDERING AT AN UNPRECEDENTED RATE

THE MOST BRAZEN SERIAL KILLER IN BRITISH CRIMINAL HISTORY

A MADMAN GRIPPED BY MURDER LUST

HE KILLS THEM, MUTIILATES THEM, THEN DUMPS THEM IN THE DARK

SEIZED BY FEAR, NORTH LONDON ASKS: "IS THE KILLER A LOCAL?"

And then, two-thirds of the way in, the Matty sketch. The one Des Banister slipped under our door; casting aspersions, scattering the first seeds.

The fact I kept it proves to me that I didn't believe it was Matty. I'd hardly have wanted it as a keepsake if it had been the harbinger I now know it to be. Interesting though that I added nothing new to the box after that.

The newspapers were rife with speculation, whole editorial columns devoted to the witness accounts and what they might mean. And yet my collection stops there. With the sketch of the Shadow. An image I still can't be sure is really the man I loved.

'It's not the man you loved,' Janice says. 'You didn't love a killer. You loved a father figure. A man who took you to the park and bought you ice cream.'

I know what she's getting at, that it's not my fault I loved Matty. That anyone in my place would have felt the same way. That loving him doesn't make me a bad person.

She doesn't understand though. I don't just feel guilty for loving him. I feel guilty that I did what I did *despite* loving him. That our bond wasn't enough to still my hand.

What does that say about me?

Matty may not have been trustworthy. But nor am I.

An old Radiohead tune comes on, something about being your own worst enemy. I haven't heard it in years but it speaks to me as though it's been brought on by telepathy.

I snap the box closed, shut the window on the past. If only it were as easy to shut out the ghosts.

This is where it all started; for me, for him. The sketch. The journey into the never-ending night. The questions, the doubt, the spiralling shame.

'Why do you act like you were responsible for what happened to him?' my mother asks.

Because I was.

I check my watch, not that I need to. I've been conscious of the minutes ticking by ever since I woke up this morning. A clawing sickness in my stomach, my chest weighed down with rocks.

I've been both putting it off and psyching myself up. Hence the box of clippings, the bumpy journey down memory lane. Only now I have another journey to take.

'I don't want to go,' I tell my mother.

My throat is tight. My hands shake.

'What you want isn't always the same as what you need.'

It could be Nanna G talking. Or Janice. In my head, their voices become one.

I sit by Buster's bed a moment, stroking his big head. His eyelids raise, then droop.

God, to be him for a day. To not have to leave my bed.

'The sooner you're gone, the sooner you're back,' my mother says. 'It's time.'

I inhale deeply, in through my nose, out through my mouth. The way I've been taught.

'Okay.'

I put on my shoes, check Buster has clean water, enter 'Battlemouth Prison' into Google Maps.

My fingers are trembling, I have to type the words twice before I hit the right keys. When I swallow nothing passes the obstruction in my throat.

As I start the engine, I can't help wondering if he'll look the same. Those laughing green eyes, that wavy blonde hair.

Stupid, I know.

Just like going to see him.

THIRTY-EIGHT

'What's happened to your hair?' I exclaimed when Matty opened his front door.

'Let's go round and surprise him,' my mother had said.

'Because that worked out so well last time,' I answered, all eye rolls and snark like any other self-respecting almost teen.

I was different with Matty; craved his approval, his attention. We still hugged all the time, although my mother had finally put an end to the Prisoner Game.

'You're too old for all that.'

'He'll be pleased to see us,' she said now as we arrived at his place.

I knew what she was really thinking though. I could tell by the set of her shoulders, the tightness around her mouth.

Still no ring on her finger, still worried he was seeing other women behind her back.

'Don't be ridiculous,' Linda kept telling her. 'He adores you.'

She wouldn't listen though, kept agonising.

'How do I really know he's working late?'

Ironic given what we learned later. Back then I thought she was being crazy. So did Linda.

'You'll drive yourself mad if you keep up with this nonsense,' she told her.

She used the same words whenever my mother brought up the similarities between Matty and the witness descriptions.

'Fastest way to the nut house, Am. You've got to let it drop.'

It had been a week since we'd seen Matty. A week since the sketch had come out.

'Up to my eyeballs,' he said each time she called. 'I'll make it up to you. I promise.'

'You'd think being a counsellor was a nine-to-five job,' she told Linda. 'How much work can he really have on? Or do you think—'

Linda waggled her finger, gave her head a shake.

'*Uh-uh*. Not this again.'

Despite her assurances, my mother wouldn't let it rest and by the following Saturday, she'd decided to take matters into her own hands.

Nice surprise, my ass.

It was eleven thirty in the morning. Matty opened the door rubbing his eyes. They were bleary from sleep. But that's not what snagged my attention.

'What have you done to your hair?' I asked, jaw to the floor. 'It's even darker than Mum's.'

He ran a hand over his scalp, pretended to be confused.

'Christ Almighty, how did that happen?'

'You dyed it?' my mother said, appalled. 'What did you do that for? I loved your hair.'

'Not as much as I love yours.'

Occasionally, she'd talk about getting a Princess Diana do, said a bob would be more manageable, quicker to dry. But Matty always convinced her not to.

'Your hair's your best feature, Ams. Honestly, I just don't think it'd suit you short.'

Since they'd been together she'd always worn it long and curly. Just like the Shadow's victims.

'I don't get it,' she said now. 'You looked so good blonde.'

'Fancied a change, that's all. What do you think?'

'Well, it's certainly different.'

'You didn't want people thinking that witness was talking about you, right?'

I was testing him without realising it. The seeds of doubt starting to sprout.

He just shrugged it off, though. Unflustered as always.

'P'raps I should change my profession too. Bereavement counselling's going to take a hit, I bet.' Then, 'You ladies want to come in, have some tea? I think I've got some KitKats stashed away somewhere.'

He was obsessed with KitKats. Something so satisfying about snapping the fingers apart, he used to say.

We followed him through to the living room. He pushed a cupboard door shut with his toe, stuffed something pink in a drawer.

'What was that?'

'Sorry, I wasn't expecting company.'

It wasn't an answer, but I was quickly distracted by an open sports bag full of tools. Hammers, screwdrivers, so many different types I didn't know the names of them all.

'An axe, cool!'

'Hatchet, actually.'

'What's the difference?'

'You need two hands to use an axe.'

'Put that down, Sophie,' my mother snapped, voice sharp as the blade. 'You'll cut your fingers off.'

Matty laughed.

'Have you any idea how hard it is to cut through bone?'

She didn't laugh back, just shot him one of her disapproving looks.

'What are they all for?' I asked, pulling out another. 'Is this a hacksaw?'

'Sophie, would you please—'

'My ma's been complaining about the cabin. Leaks and the like. I said I'd go over and help fix it up.'

My mother's face fell like a sack of potatoes.

'You're going back to Ireland?'

'Only while the dust settles.'

'What dust?' I asked.

He shrugged, one shoulder.

'Just work stuff . . . Now, how about those KitKats?'

THIRTY-NINE

I was walking back from South End Green, the smell of hot fries and battered cod wafting out of the carrier bag swinging in my hand.

My mother was working late at the office, some last-minute accountancy crisis, whatever that meant. She'd left a note to say she wouldn't be home for supper, told me to help myself to some cash from the drawer in her nightstand: *Get yourself a pizza or fish and fries. A KitKat too if you like xx*

The mention of KitKats straight away made me think of Matty. He'd been in Ireland two weeks already. Like last time, he hadn't called once.

'The lines are probably down again,' Linda told my mother, who was kibbitzing on about his lack of contact, his failure to commit.

'In September?'

'I don't know, Am.'

She was a good friend, but everyone's patience wears thin eventually.

I took the long way home, avoiding the park. I'd been giving it a wide berth ever since Gemma Nicholls' body had been found by the running track. I don't suppose I was the only one doing that.

'Why take risks?' Matty always said. 'Better safe than sorry.' And other times more darkly, 'Predators aren't Disney villains. You can't spot them by their horns.'

I was feeling particularly skittish that evening. Detective Inspector Connor had been on television again. We'd been allowed to watch the news during Form Time on the basis it was important to 'be informed and have views on current affairs'.

'We've been charting the abduction and body disposal sites in order to identify where the killer is likely to be based,' the DI had said. 'This is predicated on the theory that an offender's early crimes are committed in areas they're familiar with. In this case, we believe the perpetrator may reside in or near to Camden.'

A killer targeting women who looked like my mother. And who lived in our district. Neither fact was particularly comforting.

'The police are managing us,' Bea said as we'd walked home together after school, the sky already darkening. 'Feeding us titbits to make it look like they know what they're doing. Like they're on top of things. Nine women are dead though. How on top of it can they really be?'

Her father was a journalist with one of the nationals. She said he knew about these things, that he wasn't fooled by what he called the police's 'party tricks'.

'It's not just about managing the public though. They're

sending a message to the perpetrator too. We're coming for you.'

She threw around words like 'perpetrator' a lot, 'MO' and 'signature' too. Showing off, I thought at the time whilst also being a little in awe of her insider knowledge.

Looking back though, I suspect she picked up most of the lingo off *Cagney and Lacey*. Probably knew as little as the rest of us. Strange to think now, it was me not her with the insider knowledge. That the killer was someone I played Ludo with, someone who dragged all the way to Golders Green just to buy me Rocky Road.

'Our net is closing in,' DI Connor told the cameras.

'He would say that,' Bea said with maddening nose-in-the-air superiority. 'Just think, we might know him,' she added. 'The butcher. The postman. The neighbour who comes round to borrow sugar. You never know what secrets people are hiding . . .'

I kicked a stone into the road.

'I think I'd be able to tell if it was someone I knew.'

'I wouldn't be so sure.'

Her parting shot.

I rounded the corner onto our street, the smell of hot chips rising from the carrier bag. Unable to resist, I dug inside, pulled out a hot handful.

'Hullo, Sophie.'

Des Banister materialised out of nowhere, made me jump. The fries fell into a puddle.

'Jesus, you scared me.'

'Haven't seen Matty about for a bit. Him and your mother broke up, have they?'

A normal person would have apologised.

I felt my hackles rise, the old itch to strike creep into my fists.

'I know it was you who sent that clipping.'

He just shrugged, a thin smile on his nasty lips.

'It didn't work. If anything, they're closer than ever.'

'So where is he then?'

I didn't want to be talking to Des out here in the dark or anywhere else, but I've never been very good at backing down from a fight.

'If you must know, he's helping his folks out in Ireland.'

'Ireland, eh?'

His tone was goading, calling me a liar.

'That's right. Brownstone in County Wicklow.'

'Never heard of it.'

'Yeah well, it's a tiny village. Only a few hundred people live there.'

'And he didn't ask you and your maw to go with him? Doesn't seem very friendly.'

'I can hardly miss school.'

He tutted, took a step closer. His breath smelled like old drains. I stepped back.

'She deserves better. Someone who appreciates her.'

I laughed nastily.

'What, like you?'

Being unkind is the very worst thing you can do, my mother always said.

'Worse than stealing?'

'Worse than anything.'

'I'm sorry. I didn't mean to—'

But he was already scuttling off; head down, shoulders rounded, just like he had when Matty told him to back off that day on Parliament Hill.

I tried to apologise the next morning, steeled myself all night to do it, but there was no answer when I knocked. No dog barking in his flat. No white van parked outside.

We didn't see him again for weeks. And by the time we did, putting things right with Des Banister was the very last thing on my mind.

Extract from *Crime Stories* podcast
with Katie Hardcastle and Louisa Shaw

KATIE HARDCASTLE

It's amazing to me that so many people still think Matty Melgren is innocent.

LOUISA SHAW

To be fair, Katie, most of the prosecution's case was circumstantial. The footprint evidence for example. And don't get me started on that identification circus.

KATIE HARDCASTLE

Okay, I agree that was . . . questionable. But you have to admit, the fact the disappearances stopped right after Melgren was arrested is fairly compelling.

LOUISA SHAW

It might be if it hadn't coincided with a certain other event.

KATIE HARDCASTLE

You're talking about . . .

LOUISA SHAW

You bet I am.

FORTY

I was helping my mother make dinner, a boring radio drama about farming on in the background. An antidote perhaps to Kinnock's leadership election victory speech earlier—

Mrs Thatcher is presiding over and will continue with policies which will bring industrial tragedy to this country . . .

'Goodness' sake. I'm so sick of the Punch and Judy Show.'

Her mood had nothing to do with British politics though.

It had been three weeks since the sketch had been posted through our door, but they still showed it most nights on the news. Two years later, the Night Stalker's sketch would similarly do the rounds.

'They're hoping someone will recognise the Shadow,' Bea said, with that smug know-it-all expression she wore whenever she talked about the murders. 'The police act as if journalists get in their way. But the truth is, they need them. How else do you turn the public into your eyes and ears?'

Her words sounded regurgitated. No doubt it was a re-hash of whatever speech her father had given at the dinner table.

'Surveillance cameras?' I suggested. 'They use them on motorways. Why not regular roads?'

Bea scoffed in a way that would have given Nanna G a run for her money.

'Be practical, Sophie. Have you any idea how much that'd cost?'

'Worth it to save lives, surely?'

I stirred the pasta sauce now while my mother measured out stock, added it to the pot. She was wearing her 'May the Forks Be with You' apron, a present from Matty after he took us to see *Return of the Jedi*. I thought the movie was a sorry waste of two hours of my life and told him so. My mother felt the same way but pretended to have enjoyed it.

The apron was her reward. I told Matty he was a chauvinist. He told me he'd make a lady of me yet.

'Can you grab me the tomato paste?'

I got it from the fridge, handed it over. She squeezed a dollop into the pot.

'Oregano?'

'Here.'

It might have looked all Norman Rockwell on the outside, but beneath the surface the cracks were starting to spread. Zoom in and you'd have seen the tightness in my jaw, my mother's gaze turned inwards.

She fumbled with the lid on the herb jar. It sprang off, a mist of chopped leaves clouding the countertop.

'Goddammit.'

She still swore like an American, and rarely swore at all.

I fetched a cloth. On the cupboard above the sink was a new Post-it note: *Faith moves mountains. Doubt creates them.*

No prizes for guessing what that was about.

'I can't stop thinking about what the witness said,' she'd told Linda a few evenings ago, the two of them loud enough for me to hear from my room. 'It's driving me bananas.'

'You've got to stop this, Am.'

'Easier said than done.'

'You can't seriously think that sweet man's a murderer?'

'No, of course not.'

Her tone and words were out of sync though.

I couldn't help hating her a little. Why couldn't she believe in him? Why did she always have to jump to the worst conclusion?

He was going to come back to London and pick up on her doubt, I could tell. I'd seen the way he'd reacted when she challenged him about all the new things in his flat. How would he feel if she started questioning him over something like this?

I was going to lose him and it would all be her fault.

I was reading *To Kill A Mockingbird*, had just got to the bit where Judge Taylor talks about people seeing what they look for.

Wasn't that exactly what my mother was doing? Seeing the bad in Matty all the time because that's what she was looking for?

'What's wrong with you?' I demanded, gusting into the living room like Storm Beryl which had ruined hundreds of lives the year before. 'Why do you have to ruin the one good thing that's ever happened to us?'

'You want to listen to that daughter of yours, Amelia R,' Linda said.

There's a twisted pleasure in nursing resentment. Wiping up the spilled oregano, I sent my mother sidelong glances hoping she'd notice I was upset and ask what was wrong, only to feel doubly resentful when she didn't. A bit like that day when Matty had ignored me when I'd wanted to watch *Jim'll Fix It*.

A rather dull storyline on the radio about a calf being born was interrupted by a news flash. My mother turned the volume up.

You'll think I'm remembering it wrong, but a shudder passed through me. A prickling sensation, a hundred needle points on my neck. Déjà vu. Though how could I have possibly known what was coming?

Police believe the Shadow may be operating in Ireland too . . .

My mother whispered something.

'What?' I think she said. But it could just as easily have been, 'Why?'

The body of an eight-year-old girl last seen talking to a well-dressed man claiming to be looking for his lost dog has been discovered near the river in Brownstone, County Wicklow.

My mother's face drained white. The pan crashed to the floor, red sauce splashing over the wall. Like blood spatter.

FORTY-ONE

Battlemouth Prison looms up ahead, crouching against the sky-line. Turrets and chimneys and Victorian red brick. The walls sixteen feet thick, impenetrable from inside or out.

Mind you, they said that about the other place too. HMP Huntersville. A Category-A prison in South London. Maximum security, supposedly. Didn't stop the rooftop being breached though, and a certain serial killer getting loose.

The riot began a little after six months into Matty's sentence and took nearly as many weeks to quell. An angry mob fed up with being locked in their cells for twenty-two hours a day, took control of the chapel before spreading out through the jail. It was a violent, bloody affair with officers being beaten by masked inmates wielding sticks and fire extinguishers.

I don't know all the details, only that after order was restored, Matty broke out of his cell. The same cell he'd sat in quietly reading a James Patterson, while his fellow inmates ran amok. Now they were back in their cages, he was out. No one ever discovered how.

The prison counsellor found him propped against the wall

of the canteen when she swung by at 6 a.m. for her morning coffee; his legs stretched out in front of him, crossed over at the ankle. He'd been there all night apparently; a half-eaten Pot Noodle by his side, a book in his lap. Having finished Patterson, he'd moved onto Frederick Forsyth. Edge of the seat stuff, he told the magazine journalist who later interviewed him.

He had the upper hand, the element of surprise. But he didn't lash out at the counsellor. Simply smiled sweetly and wished her good morning. A slim, curly-haired brunette, same as his victims.

The news exploded on a Monday morning. I was on my way to school, saw the headlines on a billboard. My mother was doped up on the couch at home, same as she had been every day since his sentencing. *I just want to die, Soph.*

MELGREN BREAKS OUT

My hands shook as I handed over the change. I sat on the kerb, spread the paper out on my lap.

> *Convicted serial killer, Matty Melgren escaped from his cell at Huntersville prison in Balham, South London late on Saturday night, less than eight months after being handed down three consecutive life sentences.*
>
> *Melgren, responsible for the so-called 'Shadow Murders', eluded guards at the Category-A facility for over twelve hours. A matter of weeks ago, the same facility was overcome by riots in which three correctional officers lost their lives, bludgeoned to death by an angry mob.*

*The Home Secretary is expected to face questions in the
House of Commons today and to launch an urgent inquiry
as to how the serial killer was able to break free.*

Much has been made of the fact that Matty didn't attack the
counsellor who found him, or try to hurt anyone else. That he
just sat there reading his book, waiting to be noticed. Proof,
they say, that the authorities got the wrong guy – a point Matty
was keen to play up in his interview with *Men's Magazine*.

'Why did you do it?' the journalist asked him.

'To show I could,' Matty answered.

'And once out, why didn't you try to escape?'

'Because I'm innocent. Only the guilty need to run.'

'Matty Melgren is clearly a narcissist, keen to demonstrate
his superiority. But would a murderer with a lust for blood
really not kill again when he got the chance?' Louisa Shaw
from the popular podcast *Crime Stories* asked recently.

It's a question I've asked myself too. Another notch of doubt on
my bed post. Another reason to feel guilty about what I'd done.

I draw closer to the prison, the barbed wire coming into view,
seemingly miles of it. A thorny monster snaking around the
prison perimeter. Huge steel gates. A mostly empty car park.

Sweat drips between my shoulder blades, prickles over my
scalp.

I've worn a blazer over a white shirt. Dark jeans, ankle boots.
The bland outfit that speaks nothing to my personal taste is a
shield. It doesn't stop him getting inside my skin though, into
my bones.

I pull out my mobile to phone Janice. I'm a child again needing to hear everything's going to be all right.

But my mother's there before I can dial.

I pull into a space a ways away from the gates, telling myself it'll do me good to stretch my legs before I go in. Get some air.

It's not the real reason though. I'm trying to put this off as long as I can, the same way I walked as slowly as possible into my new school the year we came to London.

'You still have to go,' my mother said. 'No matter how slowly you walk.'

I hear her say something similar now.

'You have to do this. It won't be over until you do.'

I don't get out yet though, just sit there in the deserted car park, gripping the steering wheel, trying not to cry.

'Do you think we were the true target of his rage?' my mother asks, terminology I've come across countless times in criminal profiling books. 'Do you think his victims were stand-ins for us? That we were the ones he really wanted to kill?'

'I don't know. Maybe.'

'Those poor women. If only I . . .'

'It's not your fault,' I tell her. 'He's the one who did this. Not you.'

But did he? whispers the other voice in my head. How can you be sure?

FORTY-TWO

The news was on again. The murder at Brownstone. The eight-year-old who'd been killed on her way to her grandmother's birthday party.

Although Scotland Yard has not yet confirmed whether it believes this crime to be connected to the string of murders in North London, there are certain key similarities between the cases which it says are, 'striking'.

'All those women,' my mother said, pouring a large glass of wine. A new habit. The orange juice gone by the wayside.

'They aren't all women. Niamh Keenan was eight.'

She covered her eyes, ground the balls of her hands into the sockets.

'My God, Jesus.'

'It's not Matty,' I told her. 'You can stop thinking that.'

'I know,' she said, but I could tell she didn't.

Ireland's a big place, but Brownstone isn't. A population of just a few hundred people. A village where people used to leave their doors unlocked and wouldn't hesitate to help out a stranger – until Niamh was attacked.

All these years later, I'm haunted by the birthday party that never happened. The image of Niamh's mother scanning the street; increasingly anxious about where her daughter had got to.

Of her grandmother never blowing out her candles. Of Niamh's present to her (a clay pot she'd made at school) remaining forever in its wrapping.

And Matty in the centre of it all, a spectator to events unfolding. Joining the search for the child. Comforting her parents.

'I met her the other day,' he apparently told them. 'I'd got lost. She told me how to get back to the village. Such a sweet girl. You're in my thoughts.'

Brownstone. Population of 771. A murder committed just weeks after Matty arrived, with 'striking' similarities to the Shadow killings. Killings carried out in North London, 'by a man living in Camden' according to the police, just like Matty. Witness accounts that could have been describing him.

None of that was lost on me. But I knew Matty, knew he'd never hurt a child. I latched onto the smallest things, convincing myself there was nothing to worry about, without actually realising that's what I was trying to do.

He was staying with his parents, wouldn't they notice if he came home with blood on him? He'd recently sprained his index finger playing squash. You can't strangle someone with a finger sprain. Can you?

I'm not sure I actually articulated these thoughts. They were more like spectres dancing at the back of my mind. I didn't voice them, because I didn't need to. That a murder had taken place in his village so soon after he arrived was a coincidence, that's all.

Besides, as I tried to explain to my mother, the profile proved Matty couldn't be involved.

A psychological portrait of the killer had recently been released to the press, put together by some big shot from the FBI's Behavioral Science Unit who'd flown over to the UK to advise Scotland Yard.

Behavioral Science – or B.S. as the wretched Bea called it – was a new discipline. Certain people, including her father she said, reckoned it was a load of 'hocus pocus'. But I loved the idea you could deduce details about a perpetrator from the commissioning of their crime.

A Sherlock Holmes fan, I daydreamed about becoming a famous criminologist when I grew up, cracking cases no one else could. Or maybe I'd write a mystery thriller, make my detective a profiler.

'Bright girl like you; work hard and you can be anything you want,' my teacher said when I mentioned my ambitions.

I suppose I have become a murder specialist of sorts, but not in the way I intended. My academic career didn't go the way I'd intended either, though by the time it went to pot I no longer cared.

'Listen to this,' I'd told my mother, reading from the profile printed on the front page of the paper lying on the coffee table:

'Given the level of overkill, the offender has a violent temper. He is not likely in a relationship, but if he is, it will be an abusive one in which he exerts physical and/or coercive control over his partner such as repeatedly belittling her or monitoring her time and what she wears.

'He has a history of cruelty to animals and possibly arson.

Given the nature of the attacks, he also has trouble relating to women and may appear uncomfortable around them. Likely he is socially awkward, a bit of a loner . . .

'See,' I concluded triumphantly. 'Nothing like Matty. Since when was he ever awkward around anyone?'

'True,' she answered, but her heart wasn't in it.

She topped up her wine glass, sipped it sleepily.

There are things that creep up on you when you're not looking. Getting taller, for instance. Acquiring breasts. Both had taken me by surprise in the last year. I was now nearly five foot one and wearing a training bra.

'Growing up,' Matty said.

I told him to sod off, which he claimed just proved his point.

My mother's drinking crept up on us too. A glass of wine when she came in from work. That glass becoming two. Graduating to gin. With ice, then not bothering with the ice at all. Slowly, slowly, so I didn't realise that what had started off as a habit was becoming a problem, topped off of course by the pills.

'They said the guy from Ireland had light hair,' I said another day. 'Matty's got dark hair now.'

She stared into her glass. Mumbled, 'Mm'. I wasn't sure if she was responding to what I'd said or passing comment on her drink. Either way, it wasn't terribly satisfying.

Later, I went to phone Bea. I was hungry for details about what had happened in Ireland, thought she might know something I didn't, given her father's job. Already I was falling down the rabbit hole, grasping at straws.

An uneasiness was seeping into my veins, although I didn't

acknowledge what was causing it, that my mother's doubts were changing the colour of me, like the celery experiment we did at school. The cells drinking up dyed water, morphing the stick from green to red.

She was on the line when I picked up the phone in my room. It sounded as though she'd been crying.

'I just can't shake the feeling he's involved.'

Chrissake. Not again.

I was replacing the receiver in the cradle when Nanna G's voice on the other end stilled my hand.

'Maybe it's time you called the police . . .' she said.

The beginning of the end. For all of us.

FORTY-THREE

'Maybe it's time you called the police . . .'

I charged out of my room, a tornado of fear and fury.

My mother was curled up on the couch, the phone tucked against her ear. Staring at the wall opposite through blind eyes.

'Don't!' I screamed. 'You can't . . .'

I was trying so hard not to cry, my throat aching with the effort of it.

'I'll call you back, Mom.' She got off the sofa, came over. Her mouth was an 'O', her brows knitted.

'What's wrong, sweetheart?'

I just shook my head, looked down so she wouldn't see the tears brimming.

'You can't,' I repeated in a gulpy sob. 'It's not right. You can't . . .'

She put her arms around me, pulled me in. I pushed her away; wanting the comfort of her closeness, hating myself for needing it.

'Sophie? What's going on?'

'You ruin everything. Take everything good away.'

'What do you mea—'

'I didn't want to leave Massachusetts, to move halfway across the world. But it didn't matter, did it? Because it's what you wanted. Same with my dad. Never mind maybe I still wanted him around. And now Matty. Always thinking the worst of him even if that means driving him away. I stick up for you, but Nanna's right. You *are* selfish.'

She flinched.

'Where's all this coming from?' Then, 'Has something happened at school?'

She reached out to touch my shoulder. I twisted out of the way.

'This isn't about school. It's about Matty. The man you're supposed to be in love with.'

She sighed, looked at the floor, lips mashing together.

'I know I've been stressing, but it's going to be okay, Soph. God would never let anything bad happen to us.'

The pressure ball in my chest expanded to bursting point.

'He'll leave us. Can't you see that?'

She shook her head as though trying to dislodge something stuck.

'What do you—'

'If you go to the police. That'll be it. He'll never forgive you. And nor will I.'

Her expression hardened.

'Were you listening in on my phone calls again? How many times have I told you—'

'Please, Mum. He didn't do this. You know he couldn't have.'

The tears were streaming down my face now, but I was too upset to mind my pride.

'Sophie—'

'I hate Des. It's all his fault. If he hadn't written that shitty note, you'd never be thinking like this. He's just trying to get you to do his dirty work, can't you see? Getting you to snitch on Matty, to turn on him. It's sick. But not half as sick as you falling for it.'

A moment's stand-off and then she nodded, the tiniest dip of the head.

'All right.'

'All right?'

'I won't go to the police.'

I let out a breath, wiped my nose on my cuff.

'Really?'

My mother never backed down on anything. Not with me.

She gave a little laugh, no mirth in it.

'Think how mad he'd be if I'd called the cops on him.'

I smiled through my tears.

'Pretty mad.'

This time when my mother went to kiss me, I let her.

'You should get to bed. It's late. You look exhausted.'

'I'm not,' I said. But I was.

'I love you, Soph,' she whispered.

There was such sadness in it. It turned, 'I love you' into 'I'm sorry'.

I leaned into her, let her put her arms around me. Breathed in her warmth and the sweet smell of wine.

It was only later, lying in bed, that I realised what was still bothering me.

'Think how mad he'd be' wasn't the same as, 'I know he didn't do it'.

FORTY-FOUR

After Niamh Keenan's murder, the killings dominated the news even more than usual. You couldn't go two minutes without hearing the Shadow's name mentioned. Even at school, he was all anyone was talking about. Property prices in the area began to plummet. The price of personal security alarms went up.

'He's going to slip,' DI Connor told a press conference. 'Killers like this always do. It's just a matter of time.'

'He hasn't slipped though,' Bea said, holding court in the common room, milking her father's insider status.

'The eyewitness was a slip-up,' another girl replied. 'You'd think someone would have recognised him from that sketch.'

'Maybe they're scared . . .' A fifth former this time. Conversations about the murders dissolved the usually inviolable year-group lines. 'Or involved,' she added ominously.

The police had just found more body parts ('in an advanced state of decomposition') near Hawley Lock. And although they hadn't been formally connected to the Shadow, more witnesses were coming forward saying they'd seen a man approaching women for directions in King's Cross before Niamh's murder.

'I heard there've been more than five hundred new calls to the tip line since the sketch,' someone else said.

Bea tossed her hair.

'Yeah, but most of them will be cranks after their five minutes.'

More or less what Matty had said. He finally called a few nights after the Brownstone murder. My mother was in the shower, the radio in the bathroom turned up high, competing with the sound of cascading water.

I picked up the phone.

'Hey pumpkin. Is your mam in?'

'She's still at work,' I told him, the lie slipping out.

I don't know what prompted it. Maybe I wanted him to myself. Maybe I was worried if he spoke to her, she'd say something stupid, give away her suspicions about him.

'I miss you,' I said. 'When are you coming home?'

'I miss you too.'

'That's not an answer.'

He laughed.

'When did you get so smart?'

He was teasing, same as always, but he didn't sound quite himself. Absent almost, like a part of him was missing from the conversation.

'Is everything okay?' I asked.

He sighed.

'It's my ma. She's sick. I'm going to have to stay up here a while longer.'

'Sounds like the Shadow might be up there too.'

I was unconsciously testing him again. My mother's doubts infecting me, a cancer slowly growing.

'Better lock my doors then, eh?' he said.

His tone was so relaxed, so jokey, I knew she had it wrong about him.

'The sister was your age, wasn't she?'

His voice had changed, dropped an octave. Suddenly serious.

'Yes,' I whispered.

'That must have frightened you, when you heard.'

An avocado-sized lump formed in my throat. How well he understood me. He was the only person who saw it from my point of view, got so instinctively how I felt.

'It made it real,' I said. 'Does that make sense?'

'Completely.'

And although we were hundreds of miles apart, I could see the expression on his face as he said it. The warmth in his eyes, the love.

My mother came out of the shower, poured herself a glass of wine, filled it right to the top. Her hand shaking as she brought it to her lips.

'It was on the radio just now. They've confirmed Niamh Keenan was killed by the Shadow. There's something he does to all the bodies, apparently. Though they won't say what.'

My body tensed, a suction machine tightening the air around me.

'We know Matty,' I said, eyeballing her. Reminding her of her promise.

'How well do we know him really though? I've never met his parents, his friends. All this time, I've only been to his house twice.'

'We know him,' I repeated.

But this time I sounded less sure.

FORTY-FIVE

I'm shaking as I walk towards the visitor centre, a building just outside the main prison. Squat like a brick outhouse.

Before I left home, I told myself I was doing the right thing. But now I'm not sure.

I didn't come to see Matty after he was charged. No prison visits, no stilted exchanges across bolted down tables in crowded visitor halls. And yet, passing through the gates now, it feels like I've been here before. That a part of me recognises it. A part of me feels I belong.

'Do you have an appointment?' the woman on reception asks. She sounds bored. 'Your visiting order?'

I hand over the form I received in the mail, Matty's details already filled in.

We're in a little office; beige walls, brown carpet tiles. Someone's stuck up a poster of Monet's *Water Lily Pond*, the corners peeling away from the wall. I don't know why, but it makes the room look even bleaker.

The receptionist has split ends. Unfortunate teeth. Oversized glasses.

They don't suit her, I think. Drown her face.

A deflection tactic, Janice would say. Focusing on this woman's appearance so you don't have to focus on yourself. What you're feeling, the spool of thoughts unravelling in your head.

She'd be right.

It's late afternoon; the sun already dipping, starting to wane. I think of what my mother said about the weather that day on Parliament Hill, right before Matty called to say he was back. Only a few months before the next two bodies were discovered; one of them a runaway, her head partly cut off by a workman's shovel.

Pathetic fallacy. Put it in your 'New Words Book'.

It had been such a clear, bright day. A reflection of our mood in that moment perhaps, but not of what was to come.

I give myself a mental shake. Pull it together, Sophie. Jesus.

The past is really closing in today. A skein of crows scenting a kill.

I force myself to focus on the moment, to block out the ghosts. Janice sets me all sorts of meditation and mindfulness exercises. I tell her they help, but the truth is, I never do them. I'm just not into that hippy crap, I'd say if I had the guts. There's so much I don't tell her.

I remind myself to breathe, to take in my surroundings.

The smell of burning dust on the fluorescent light strips. The black blotches of dead flies caught inside the cover. The heating cranked up too high, drying the air. Making it thick and hard to breathe.

I'm sweating even more now, the moisture beading under my arms. I must stink, I think, then immediately rebuke myself.

Why do I care how I smell, how I look? I'm not trying to impress Matty. Am I?

No, of course I'm not. I don't want any chinks in my armour, that's all. And just as I'm dreading seeing what he's become, so too am I dreading him seeing what's become of me.

'Brains like yours, the world's your lobster,' he said after I got my bursary place at the high school. An *Only Fools and Horses* reference my mother didn't get.

He was so proud of me that day, told me I could be anything I wanted. I don't want him to see how far I've fallen. To know I didn't make it to college, that I dropped out of school before even taking my A levels. To guess he's the reason why.

I don't want him to have that power over me. Don't want to give him the satisfaction. And he would be pleased, if he's the psychopath they say he is.

If . . .

Stop it, I tell myself.

Another deep breath, in and out.

There's a radio turned on low. An '80s tune I used to dance to, coming out of the speakers. 'Karma Chameleon'.

Is this karma? I think. Is meeting Matty, seeing what his life has been reduced to, the price I have to pay for what I did?

Through the window, I can see a guard tower. Barbed wire. So many bars.

Matty's grey world. His dues to society. His punishment.

But is it a punishment he deserves?

Or am I the one who should be punished?

From *Wordonthestreet.com*

Did Police Fabricate Evidence Against Matty Melgren?

I've always had questions about Grace Keenan's testimony (her kid sister, Niamh was supposedly killed by Melgren in Ireland).

It made me think of that case where the guy ends up confessing to being involved in a murder he couldn't even remember committing. All because police were able to manipulate his brain and plant false memories.

There's this really creepy thing one of the cops says:

"We're pretty sure you've been through a traumatic experience. One you've blocked out. We'd like to help you remember."

Could it be something similar happened to Grace Keenan, a scared young girl who'd been through a horrifying ordeal? Who maybe identified Matty Melgren because the police effectively coached her to? And because she was so desperate to get justice for her sister – and make up for her terrible mistake?

Links:

https://mattymelgrentestimony.blog/trial-transcript-grace-keenan-part-iii/

https://www.truecrimecasefiles.co.uk/resources/idt-sh/the_ nordic_confessions

FORTY-SIX

At twelve years old, you're not nearly as grown-up as you think you are.

My fear had nothing to do with deep down suspecting Matty though. It's true there were some strange coincidences, though if it hadn't been for my mother, I don't suppose I'd have thought twice about any of them. People have a hard time accepting that, but it's the truth.

Matty was the closest thing I had to a father. I was hardly going to leap to the conclusion he was a serial killer just because he drove the same model of car as the guy in the sketch. Because he happened to have a dog leash at his house. Or because he'd been in the area when Niamh Keenan was murdered.

There was no hard evidence tying him to the crimes. No bloodstained knife in his wardrobe, no body parts under the floorboards. Harper Lee was right, people see what they look for. And none of us is looking for the person we love to be a multiple murderer.

'Human beings are social creatures. We're designed to trust others,' Janice told me during one of our early sessions.

My GP had sent me to her, refused to write out the prescription for Prozac I wanted unless I spoke to a 'professional' first.

'And of course, the people we trust most are our parents,' she said. 'After all, it's their job to look after us, to keep us safe.'

My mother didn't keep me safe, I thought. She brought a monster into our lives, left me alone with him while she went to a party.

I kept that to myself though, said instead:

'I trusted him completely. It makes me feel so stupid.'

She fixed me with her unblinking stare; disquieting at first, but I got used to it.

'You were a child. He was kind to you. Of course you trusted him. You can't blame yourself for that.'

But blame isn't something you can just switch off. It's impervious to argument, however rational.

I was scared, not because I thought Matty was the Shadow, but because I was terrified there was a killer on the loose who might come after us.

Before the murder in Brownstone, the murderer targeted adults. Niamh's death marked a new direction. His tastes had changed. He was interested in kids now. As well as women who looked like my mother.

I stopped complaining about having to walk home from school with Bea. Started thinking maybe Matty wasn't being melodramatic after all. That those rape alarms he'd bought my mother and me weren't actually so stupid.

I switched on the TV one afternoon. North Londoners were being interviewed on the local news.

'Are you more safety conscious since the murders started?'

'Oh yes,' one woman answered, leaning into the microphone. 'I don't travel at night on my own any more. If I meet up with friends, I always call to say I've got home safely afterwards. We're all doing that.'

The public was on high alert, there was increased police presence on the streets. None of it was having an effect though. Bodies were still showing up.

Is 'He' Actually a 'She'? the *Post* asked in one of its editorials. *Is that how the killer keeps slipping through the net? Because we're all looking the wrong way. The ultimate smoke and mirrors trick.*

The idea got picked up by other papers. The *Tribune* interviewed Professor Wilson, the criminologist who'd been on television after the arrest back in March.

'No, I don't believe the offender is a woman,' he told the journalist. 'Female serialists kill for personal gain, money mostly. On top of that, the sexual element in these murders doesn't fit with a woman perpetrator.'

Not that he would be drawn on what the sexual element was. The police had managed to hold that back despite the business about the footprints leaking out.

That he could be a transvestite was another suggestion. Or perhaps he simply used women's clothes as a disguise, one tabloid suggested darkly.

There was also some discussion about whether the perpetrator would have given his real profession when luring victims, whether saying he was a bereavement counsellor was a ruse. The ubiquitous Professor Wilson had explained to an anchor woman that game playing was typical of psychopathic killers like the Shadow – along with a sense of invincibility and superiority.

'He likely gets off on telling his victims his profession,' he said. 'Same as knowing his face will be the last one they see before they die.'

The other theories, the cross-dressing idea in particular, were rather far-fetched though. I don't think anyone really believed any of them. We just wanted answers, were desperate for them. We needed a way to make sense of the madness. To shape some kind of order out of the chaos.

My mother was no different in that respect.

She'd finished speaking on the phone with Matty. I didn't hear what he said, but from her end it was all monosyllables and long silences.

'He says he's coming back to London this week,' she told me, her tone so different from the last time he'd said he was home.

I remembered how she'd told me to grab my coat that day, that we were going to surprise him. The excitement in her voice, the glitter in her eyes. Now those eyes were dull as stones.

'You seem disappointed,' I said.

She didn't answer. On the radio:

Police are re-interviewing Grace Keenan, the twelve-year-old sister of the victim, Niamh . . .

I went to my room to get cracking on my homework. My mother had bought me a desk for my birthday so I no longer had to study at the kitchen table. I took out my books, popped the recording I'd made of *Lucky Star* into the cassette player.

'How can you concentrate with that racket on?' she called from the hallway.

'Madonna's hardly a racket,' I shouted back, but I turned it off.

We had a science test the next day, I wanted to do well, was addicted to good grades.

I emerged ten minutes later, needing the bathroom. My mother was making supper, the phone on speaker.

'I'm falling apart, Lin. And now he's talking about coming back to London. I'm just not sure I can face seeing him.'

'I don't know what else to tell you, Am.'

'I have to call the police. I don't see what choice I've got.'

I sank to my knees, half buried under the weight of it all. Part of me wanting to burst in and remind her of her promise. The other part knowing it was better to hear what I was up against first.

Linda came on again.

'And what if it's *not* him?'

'What if it is and I say nothing?'

A pause, a sigh. A softer tone.

'What's your gut telling you?'

'I don't know.'

Her voice was breaking. Shattered into shards of glass.

'Well, I do. See what happens with that witness before you go doing things you can't take back.'

'But—'

'It'll be okay, Am. Trust me.'

Matty used to say the same thing.

FORTY-SEVEN

Shortly after his return, we met up with Matty at Ferko, a patisserie in Hampstead.

'London's oldest coffee shop,' he informed us, as if he were some kind of tour guide. 'A proper icon. They used to serve tea in real silver teapots back in the day. They don't do that any more but just wait till you clock the cake trolley. The marzipan cookies are to die for.'

My mother's face twitched at the mention of things worth dying for.

Being at Ferko was like slipping behind the Iron Curtain. Dark wood panelling. Studded velvet seats. Marble-topped tables.

'Popular with wartime refugees,' Matty said.

It was easy to see why.

He'd waved us over from a spot by the window, opened his arms wide for a hug. My mother stiffened as he embraced her.

'You okay, Ams?'

She looked away.

'Coming down with something, maybe.'

'Dangerous time of year,' he replied. 'Savage things going round.'

She cleared her throat, made a scooping motion at the back of her skirt as she sat down. Immediately she started fiddling with the silverware, picking at her napkin, scowling.

I gave Matty an extra tight hug to make up for her stinking mood.

'You've got a moustache.'

He gave the ends a twiddle.

'What do you think?'

I wasn't sure.

'You look completely different,' I said.

'Well, I didn't grow it to look the same.'

He kept touching it during the afternoon.

'Still there,' I told him.

A week later he'd shaved it off and started growing a beard. *A new disguise.*

He seemed happy that afternoon; joking, laughing away. But there were dark circles under his eyes, his skin pale and pouchy. And despite his best efforts to jolly her along, my mother was as brittle as a damaged reputation, one of Nanna G's favourite expressions.

A waitress wheeled over a laden trolley. It clattered across the deep red carpet making the plates rattle. She straightened the lace cap on her head, snarled, 'Cake?'

Matty rubbed his hands together, wide grin.

'Ah, quality. I'm starving.'

'You're always starving,' my mother snipped.

I felt my muscles tighten. How could she ruin Matty's

homecoming like this, after everything I'd said? She wasn't even giving him a chance.

'How's your mum?' I asked him, trying to fill the awkward silences she was creating. Deliberately, I suspected.

'My ma? Aye, she's grand. Loved having me home. Full Irish every day for breakfast. Reckon I've put on weight. What do you think, Ams?'

My mother gave a faint shrug, as if a proper one wasn't worth the effort.

'So, she's better then?' I continued, confused.

'Better than what, pumpkin?'

'I thought you said she was sick.'

Not so much as a flicker.

'Aye, she was for a while. But she's okay now.'

'I'm pleased to hear it,' my mother said tightly.

Matty chuckled.

'Not as much as she is.'

'Can we come up to Brownstone with you some time?' I asked.

'You wouldn't be scared?'

'Why would we be scared?' my mother asked, voice icy.

'After what happened. I was there, you know? At the hunt.'

Her eyes flashed.

'Hunt?'

'To find the kid.' He shook his head, breathed in deeply. 'Those poor sods. You never get over the loss of a child. Her ma must be about the same age as you, Ams. Looks a bit like you too actually.'

He took a huge bite out of his éclair, smacked the cream off his lips. My mother eyed him in disgust.

'How can you sit there talking about murder while calmly eating pastries?'

'How else do you suggest I eat them?'

He was trying to lighten the mood. But she didn't show so much as a tooth. He changed tack.

'You don't need to lecture me, Ams. You have no idea what it was like being a part of all that.'

She said nothing, just gave him the bug eye over the top of her teacup.

'I was analysing him,' she told me later, after he'd been charged. 'Searching for a sign. I was sure he'd say something. That I'd be able to tell . . .'

'Tell what?'

'Whether he was involved.'

'And could you?'

'No. In fact, the more I dissected what he said, the less sure I was. I didn't know what to think.'

It was different for me. He was the same Matty he'd always been. The man I loved more than anyone, the closest thing I had to a father. Of course he wasn't a killer.

Until the cardigan.

He was jabbering away.

'. . . you wouldn't believe the amount of journalists up there—' when suddenly he broke off, leaping out of his chair.

A woman from another table was walking past us on her way to the door. Slim, early twenties. Petite. Curly hair worn loose down to her shoulders.

'Excuse me,' Matty said as he leaped up, touching her lightly on the arm. 'I think you forgot your cardigan.'

'My cardigan?'

He nodded, flashed one of his charming smiles.

'It's on the back of your chair.'

She looked over to where he was pointing.

'You must have eagle eyes! It's practically camouflaged.'

He smiled wider.

'Glad to help.'

My mother thawed after that, became quite chatty. It was me who lost my voice.

We were sitting a number of tables away from the curly-haired woman, but Matty had seen everything. Only one thing made sense. He'd been watching her.

A woman; same age, same hairstyle as all the Shadow's adult victims.

If that's all that had happened, I might have persuaded myself it meant nothing. If he hadn't said what he did next.

We were back on the subject of Niamh Keenan. In retrospect, he couldn't stop talking about her. Another sign, I suppose.

'I don't get it,' I said, peeling apart my millefeuille, eating it in creamy layers. Saving the iced topping till last.

'Don't get what, pumpkin?'

'Why the police think the Shadow killed her. She was a kid. The other victims are all grown women.'

Matty helped my mother to more tea, topped up his own cup.

'I expect it's what he did to her toes,' he said.

The pastry lodged in my throat, smothered my voice.

Scotland Yard had never revealed that the Shadow did anything to his victims' toes. Or what had happened to Niamh's.

That was something only the killer would know.

FORTY-EIGHT

I feel the receptionist watching me. Her eyes boring into the back of my neck as a corrections officer with a balding head and a spot of dried ketchup on his lapel leads me into an adjacent room. She'll tell her friends about me later over G&Ts down the pub; all of them craning in, hanging on her words.

'Not what I was expecting,' she might say. Or, 'She looked so normal. Hard to believe she was raised by *him*.'

Does she know Matty? I wonder. Has she ever spoken to him?

Stupid. Why would she? This isn't exactly a holiday camp.

The CO waves a metal detector wand over me, asks me to load my handbag onto a grey tray, the sort you see at airport security. Runs it through an X-ray machine, pulls out a Tampax at the other end, examines it.

'It's not a bomb,' I say, covering my embarrassment.

'You'll have to leave everything behind,' he replies, face impassive. 'Can't take any personal belongings in with you.'

'Not even my phone?'

'No phones allowed.'

'But what if . . .'

I tail off.

'What if, what?'

I grind my thumb into the ball of my hand.

'What if there's a problem?'

'You buzz for the guard.'

'Buzz?'

'This is a closed visit. You'll be separated by glass, have to speak through a phone. He'll be brought along once you arrive.'

I exhale deeply, drop my shoulders, pleased Matty won't be sitting there watching me come in. That I'll have a chance to arrange my face first.

'Right,' I say. 'Okay.'

He laughs, not entirely kindly.

'I take it this is your first prison visit.'

I try to smile.

'Is it that obvious?'

''Tis to me. And you're starting off with Melgren. What are you, a writer or something?'

For a moment I'm surprised he doesn't know, then I'm just relieved. It takes the pressure off, not being under a microscope. Matty's been such a huge part of my life, it's weird to think not everyone knows what we are to each other. What we were.

'We had a bloke up here to see him a few months back; soft hands and shiny shoes. You know the type. Said he was writing Melgren's biography.

'I told him, men like Matty Melgren are better off without a soap box, but he wouldn't listen. Reckoned the public's insatiable when it comes to the Shadow, can't get enough. They want to understand what drove him to do such terrible things, he said. Can't fathom why a man with no history of childhood abuse or neglect would have done what he did.

'Some people are just born bad, I told him. He said he didn't believe that. Reckoned society creates its own monsters. No one's evil when they come out the womb, those were his words. I watched him leave afterwards. Bloke looked like he'd shrunk three inches. Never came back as far as I heard.'

I don't know what to say to this.

'Any cigarettes?' he asks when it's clear I'm not the audience he was hoping for.

I shake my head.

'Food? Drink?'

'No.'

'You'll have to leave your wallet.'

'Right.'

'We've got lockers. Will you be wanting to buy tokens?'

As if I'm going to the fair, as if this is something I'm excited about.

'Tokens? What for?'

'Tea. Coffee,' he says, enunciating each word carefully as though I'm slow, or hard of hearing. 'You can get hot drinks from the vending machine before you go in. But you need tokens.'

'That's okay. I'm not thirsty.'

He shrugs. Suit yourself.

He finds me a locker, stands too close while I place my things inside. My hands are shaking, I tuck my elbows into my sides to steady them. Hope he hasn't noticed.

The metal door clangs as I shut it.

'Right then,' he says, hands on hips. 'Ready?'

'Yes,' I say, although I'm not. I'll never be ready for this.

FORTY-NINE

'Ready?' my mother asked.

I joined her in line at the post office where she was waiting to get airmail stamps. Royal Mail. When we'd first arrived in the UK, I was convinced it was the Queen's personal postal service, set up so Joe Public could send letters to Her Majesty.

My mother suggested stopping off for crêpes on the way home.

'That stand in Hampstead . . .'

I shook my head, told her I wasn't hungry.

'You hardly ate any lunch either. I do hope you're not still dieting.'

She had strong views on how 'growing kids' shouldn't cut back.

I wasn't trying to lose weight though. I just couldn't stomach food. I'd had no appetite ever since that day at the café. Everything wedged in my throat, tasted of cardboard.

She was launching into a speech about how I was beautiful just the way I was, when a rapidly blinking old lady tottered up behind us.

'Amelia-Rose?'

Matty's neighbour, Mrs 'Matzo Ball Soup', with a net shop-ping bag bulging with jars of purple horseradish and Mrs Elswood pickles.

My mother put on her polite smile, asked how she was. The old woman leaned in, lowered her voice to a conspiratorial whisper.

'I had a visit last night . . .'

'What sort of visit?'

'From the police,' she said proudly. 'Late, well after seven. I was already in my robe.'

'What did they want?' I said, folding my arms to hide my shaking hands.

'They were asking about Matty.'

It was as though my intestines were being sliced open. I thought I might be sick. I don't know how my mother felt, only that she'd gone very pale.

'What sort of questions?' she said.

Mrs Cohen set her bag down between her feet, opened her hands wide as if she was weighing fruit.

'It makes no sense.'

'What doesn't?'

There was a note of impatience slipping into my mother's voice, along with something else. Panic perhaps.

'They asked if I'd noticed him coming home late the nights those poor women were killed.' She shook her head, eyes closed. 'Oy, what a business.'

My mother's knuckles had turned white on the handle of her purse. A pulse beat hard at her temple.

'They can't think he . . .'

'Matty? A mensch like that? No, of course not. They were just going through their files, they said. Checking up on men in Camden who live alone. Protocol, they called it.'

My mother had to clear her throat before she could speak.

'And were you able to, um . . .'

The old lady looked confused. She adjusted her glasses as if that would help her hear better.

'Able to what, dear?'

'Confirm his whereabouts,' I clarified over the thud of my tell-tale heart.

She patted my arm. Her nails were painted coral pink, her skin was warm. She wore antique rings, Yardley's Lavender.

Funny the way memory works. I can remember everything about her, the stuffy central heating, the smell of dust burning on the lights. But nothing of what I said next. Only the fire in my stomach, the nausea welling in my throat.

'I couldn't say. Frankly when you get to my age . . .' She trailed off, looked momentarily concerned. 'I told them what a wonderful young man he is, though. Always so polite and helpful, bless his heart. Such a hard worker too, the hours he puts in at that crisis centre. I hope his boss appreciates him.'

'Did you tell them that?' my mother asked.

'Tell them what?'

'About Matty working late.'

'Oh dear, no, I didn't. Do you think I should have?'

'No. I don't think so.'

But she didn't sound sure.

'Do you believe that?' I asked my mother, once we were in

the Volvo on our way home, my heart doing a tap dance inside my chest.

'Believe what?'

'That it was a routine visit.'

She sighed, a heaviness in it.

'Honestly, I don't know what to believe any more.'

We spent the rest of the journey in silence. Me staring out of the window, her staring resolutely ahead.

Later that evening, a deliveryman turned up with a huge bunch of flowers. Twenty-four long-stemmed roses and a card with a picture of a teddy bear holding a heart. On the back, a message from Matty:

You give life meaning. M x

My mother dumped them on the kitchen counter, left them in their wrapping.

By the next morning, the petals had started to brown.

FIFTY

My world collapsed three days after the flowers died. I got a commendation in English and Joey Peterson said he liked my trainers. It should have been a good day.

My mother was waiting for me outside the gates after netball practice. My cheeks rosy from running around the court, spidery tendrils escaping from my ponytail.

I was coming out of school with a bunch of other girls, all of us high on adrenaline and endorphins, making up silly nicknames for each other.

'Lisa Jackson, you can be P.Y.T' – after the Michael Jackson single, 'Pretty Young Thing' that had just hit the charts.

'And Rach can be Crackers.'

'Crackers?'

'Rachel Jacobs. Jacob's Crackers, *duh*.'

'I don't—'

'The cheese biscuits? Keep up, Soph!'

'Like you were doing on the court back there?'

'Ha-ha.'

'I reckon you're going to be picked for the team, Sophie,' Lisa interjected. 'You were on fire today.'

I flushed with pleasure.

'You think?'

'Yes, I think. You've really got your groove back.'

I tried to look nonchalant, turned away so she wouldn't see me smile.

She was right about getting my groove back though. A weight had shifted inside me. Ever since that stupid sketch came out, I'd felt there was cement in my chest. I missed easy goals, dropped balls. Today I'd scored twice, dropped nothing.

It had been three days since we'd run into Mrs Matzo Ball Soup. No one had come knocking on our door or phoned asking questions. Even my mother seemed more at ease. The police had checked Matty out. Clearly there was nothing to worry about. Ireland, the witness accounts, the café even – it meant zilch.

'What was I thinking?' my mother said. 'I feel so stupid.'

'I did try telling you.'

'Can you honestly say you didn't wonder, even a bit?'

'Nope,' I lied.

My friends and I burst out the school doors.

'Isn't that your mum, Sophie? Over by the gates.'

She saw me, gave a little wave. A dayglo orange waterproof over her work clothes.

'See you guys,' I mumbled, hands stuffed deep in my pockets as I walked over to join her, face burning.

The others sauntered off; arms linked, heads bobbing together so you couldn't see where one girl's hair ended and another's started.

'What are you doing here?' I asked my mother, hissing the words.

'I was just passing, thought you might like a ride.'

'Passing? Why aren't you at work?'

She shuffled, tucked a curl behind her ears.

'I left early.'

I thought of the empties in our kitchen bin.

'Oh God, you didn't get fired, did you?'

'No, of course not. Come on, let's get going. I've been freezing my butt off waiting out here for you.'

'No one asked you to,' I muttered.

My friends were halfway down the street but I could still hear them laughing, was convinced they were laughing at us. My mother and I walked to the car in silence. By the time we were inside and out of view, I'd forgiven her. The day had been too good to waste it sulking.

'I scored two goals,' I said. 'I think I might make the team.'

'That's great, sweetheart.'

'And I got a commendation in English. For my essay on betrayal in *Caesar*.'

'Brilliant.'

'Mrs Quinalt says I've got a perceptive eye.'

'That's fantastic.'

It was like talking to a robot.

She pulled up outside the flat and cut the engine but didn't unbuckle.

The old weight settled back in my ribcage.

'What's wrong?' I asked, although a part of me already knew.

The look in her eyes gave it away. It was as though she was struggling to keep her balance. As if she couldn't quite focus. After Matty's conviction, that look was there all the time. Although, of course, that might have been the pills.

She took a deep breath, turned to face me. Time moved in freeze frame. Her mouth opened, lips forming the words. I heard a gasp, realised it was coming from me.

'Sophie, I . . .'

She reached out to touch my hand but I pulled it away.

'Why?' I whispered.

My ears rang. I gripped the door handle, felt the sting of acid in my throat.

'The women,' my mother was saying. Her voice sounded as though it was far away. Underwater. 'The disappearances . . .'

'Is it because . . .'

My mother frowned.

'Because of what?'

I just shook my head, couldn't say it.

I sometimes wonder now what would have happened if she'd forced it out of me. If I'd told her the truth, bridged the gap between us.

It's all moot though. Neither of us opened up to the other. Instead, we drifted out to sea, each on our own leaky raft, bobbing further and further apart.

In the pocket of the passenger door I glimpsed the rape alarm Matty had given my mother. Mine was zipped up in my school bag.

You never know when you might need them. I don't know what I'd do if anything happened to you guys.

Matty who loved us, who wanted to keep us safe. Matty who had just been arrested for serial murder; the most recent victim, a girl half my age whose face was so mangled when the police found her that her own parents couldn't identify her.

A fresh surge of bile rode up my digestive tract. I started shaking.

And then everything went black.

FIFTY-ONE

I sat at the kitchen table with my mother, cradling a cup of overly sweet tea.

'For the shock,' she said. She'd made one for herself as well, but so far hadn't touched it.

Over the top of her head, I could see a photo magnet stuck up on the fridge. *A day to remember*, printed at the bottom in bright colourful letters, the three of us saying, 'Cheese!' at the camera. Me leaning into Matty, my mother shielding her eyes from the sun.

I got up and plucked it off the fridge, brought it back to the table.

'What are you doing with that?'

I shrugged, stared at Matty's face.

'Murder,' my mother said, more to herself than to me. 'I can't get my head around it. All the stuff I was saying before, it just . . .' She shook her head, stared into her tea. 'God, what if he thinks . . . I mean who . . .'

I was only half listening, looking instead into Matty's eyes, thinking back to that day at Brighton Beach. It had been his idea to get the magnet. *A souvenir*, he'd said. *To remind us . . .*

A gaggle of girls giggling past had severed his train of thought. He never said what the magnet was supposed to remind us of.

That we loved each other? I wondered now. That life was good once?

Had he planned the whole thing? Was our life together just a cover, an elaborate ruse to make him look normal, to hide who he really was? Were we simply pawns protecting the King? Or was it real? Did he love us? Was this all a terrible mistake?

I'd been so certain that day in the café, but now, searching his eyes so like mine, for some hidden truth, I wasn't sure of anything any more.

How could that man with his arm around me, who sat up with me after a nightmare and went out of his way to buy my favourite ice cream, be the same monster who choked those women to death, tied bows round their necks with their own underwear? How could that smile I knew so well have lured women to their deaths? How could the fingers that played 'This Little Piggy' with my toes be the same fingers that had strangled a child?

I ground my knuckles into my forehead, clenched my eyes. Tried to shut out the horror of it all, the gnawing guilt.

My mother reached over, touched my arm, squeezed it gently.

'It'll be all right,' she said. 'I know it's hard to believe now, but—'

I shrugged her off, curled back my lips.

'How can you possibly say that?'

'I just mean—'

'What *do* you mean, Mum? The other day you were telling Linda you were going to the police. Now you're telling me you can't believe he's a killer. Do you have any idea what it's been like to live with you? This constant see-sawing. If it weren't for you—'

She put her hand to her mouth.

'You think it was me, don't you? My God, Jesus.'

'Think what was you?'

'That I called the cops. That I'd do such a thing.'

I felt my insides drain away, my bones become liquid. My mother's head was lowered. She was stroking her fingertips up and down her tea mug, worrying at her lower lip.

She was thirty-two and beautiful, but in that moment she looked like an old woman. The pink had gone from her cheeks, her shoulders were stooped. Her eyes pale and watery.

There's no use trying to hide it. I can always tell when you've been doing something you shouldn't, Nanna G used to warn me, stabbing at the air with her forefinger. *It shows in your face.*

I'd scan the mirror searching for the clues that had given me away, but although I could never find any, it was true, she could always tell.

I can read you, just like I can read your mother. The pair of you are books. Isn't that right, Amelia-Rose? Books . . .

I'd never had the knack, but now I read my mother, the emotion painted on her face. Pain. Fear.

Guilt.

'Did you?' I asked, voice trembling. 'Call the police?'

'How can you even ask that?' she replied, whip quick.

But she didn't say 'no'.

And I didn't answer her question.

FIFTY-TWO

I turned the light off, watched the car parked across the street. A dark blue saloon with a rusty fender. Two men inside, both watching our flat. Same way they had been for the last ten minutes.

'Trust your instincts,' Matty used to say. 'If you think something's wrong, it probably is. Don't wait till it's too late to do something about it.'

'Mum!' I called.

She'd gone to her room for 'a lie down'.

'Mum, come here. There are men watching the flat.'

Her door opened, she shuffled out wearing a pink robe and slippers. Her eyes were red from crying, her hair a tangled mess.

'What do you mean, watching the flat?'

I pointed.

'Over there.'

We watched as the men got out of the car and crossed the road. Thirty seconds later, our intercom buzzed.

She shot me a wide-eyed look.

'I'd better get dressed.'

It buzzed again. I picked up the entry phone.

'Hello?'

'Mrs Brennan?'

I didn't correct him.

'Who is this?'

'Detective Sergeants Duckworth and Jones from Scotland Yard. May we come in?'

Scotland Yard? My flesh tightened, the air solidifying in my lungs.

'Do you have ID?' I asked, Matty's training kicking in.

'Of course.'

I wanted to tell them to go away, so I could run and hide under my bed. For Matty to tell me this was just a bad dream, and that he'd stay with me till I fell back asleep.

Instead, I told them to come up, we were on the second floor.

When the doorbell rang, I looked through the spyhole, asked to see their badges. They held up their warrant cards. I thought of Matty putting ADT stickers up on our windows to trick the bad guys into thinking we had an alarm. Of him telling me real crooks don't have horns like Disney villains.

'How do I know those are genuine?' I asked.

The men didn't look like police officers. They looked like my maths teacher.

The taller of the two, Duckworth I later learned, suggested I phone Scotland Yard, give their names and shoulder numbers.

My mother emerged from the bedroom in jeans and a sweater that looked like they'd been pulled out of the laundry basket. Her feet were bare. Her sleeves too long. It made her seem vulnerable somehow, like a child. Same as the day we came to London.

'It's okay,' she told me. 'Let them in.'

Her voice said she'd been expecting them. It made me wonder what else she'd done, what else she was expecting.

'Are you Amelia Brennan?'

He glanced down at the paint chipping on her toenails.

My mother nodded.

'And this is your daughter?'

'Yes. Sophie.'

I heard her saliva crack, her tongue peeling away from the roof of her mouth. My mouth was dry too, my heart thudding like a tethered animal trying to break loose.

'What's this about?'

I folded my arms across my chest, planted my feet wide the way Matty had done with Des on Parliament Hill. Damned if I'd let them see I was afraid.

Jones answered, addressed my mother.

'We understand that Matty Melgren is your boyfriend. Is that correct?'

She shifted her weight onto the other leg, pulled at the sweater cuffs dripping over her wrists.

'Yes, that's right.'

'And how long have you been together?'

She hesitated.

'About six years.'

Duckworth had taken a notebook out of his jacket pocket. He made a note of her answer. It made me uneasy that everything we said was going on record.

'So, Mr Melgren is not your daughter's father?'

My mother blushed, fiddled with her hair. It was lank, needed a wash.

'I was married to someone else when I had Sophie.'

Jones smiled kindly, explained that they simply wanted to clarify the relationship between her and Matty.

'And are you aware that he was arrested this morning?'

'In connection with the North London murders,' Duckworth added, watching us closely.

The room spun. But I refused to give them a reaction. I bit the inside of my cheek, concentrated on a fixed point on the wall to keep my tears in check.

'Yes,' my mother was saying. 'I heard.'

The detectives nodded as if it had been some kind of test.

'May we sit down?' Jones asked. 'We'd like to ask you some questions if that's all right.'

'Of course.'

I sleepwalked behind them into the living room, conscious of the galloping beat of my heart.

'Should I call a lawyer?' my mother asked.

Again I wondered, what have you done?

Duckworth smiled, shook his head.

'We just want to check a few facts, that's all.'

'Okay.'

'Where did you and Mr Melgren meet?'

Another pause. My mother tilted her head, scratched the side of her neck.

'Back in Massachusetts. He was over in the States looking for work.'

This was news to me. I'd always assumed they met the night she and Linda went out to 'let their hair down' – not that my mother was in the habit of picking men up in bars. As far as I knew, Matty was the first boyfriend she'd had since my father.

'And you reconnected when . . .'

'He moved to London shortly after we arrived, got in touch.'

'Were you involved with him romantically in Massachusetts?'

'I was seeing someone else.'

It occurred to me that she hadn't quite answered the question, though it wasn't till a lot later that I put the rest together.

'And you told him you had a daughter when you met again in London? A lot of men would be put off by that.'

'Not Matty.'

It's true, I wanted to tell them. But the words stuck in my throat.

'Are you engaged to him?' Duckworth asked.

My mother flushed again.

'We're going to get married.'

'So, you'd set a date?'

'Well, I mean, we talked about it. But . . .'

Jones smiled. His eyes were kind.

'Some guys take a while to settle down.'

My mother nodded gratefully.

'Yes, exactly.'

'Did he live here?'

'He stayed over a lot, but he likes his independence, says it's good to have space.'

'So how exactly would you characterise your relationship?'

Duckworth asked. His tone wasn't as warm as Jones'. More businesslike. To the point.

'We spent a lot of time together. He was always wonderful with Sophie.'

I wanted to tell them exactly how wonderful, to put what I'd done right, but still I couldn't speak.

'So you spent evenings together?' Duckworth asked. 'Weekends?'

'Often, yes.'

'Often?'

'Matty's very involved in the crisis centre his office runs.'

The detectives exchanged a glance.

'There is no crisis centre, Mrs Brennan.'

My stomach dropped to my knees. In my ears a dull ringing.

'There must be some mistake,' my mother said, shaking her head. 'He said he was there only a few weeks ago.'

Jones leaned forward; fingers interlaced against his chest.

'When was this?'

'The day the sketch came out,' I said, finally locating my voice. 'The witness account.'

Duckworth made a note in his notebook.

'I wonder if we could run some dates by you, ma'am. See if Matty was with you on any of them.'

My mother said of course, went to fetch her old diaries. When she came back her hands were shaking. Mine were too. I sat on them so no one would see.

Jones reeled off a list of dates I recognised from my clippings. The days women had gone missing. Butchered. Murdered. Dumped like trash.

The room wheeled. There was no blood in my head. My lungs were empty.

'To be clear, Matty wasn't with you on any of these nights?'

'I don't think so,' my mother whispered.

Jones was about to say something else when she cut him off; voice suddenly animated, eyes alive. Her hands moving like windmills, rotating madly on their stems.

'Matty can't have done it,' she said, practically tripping over the words in her haste to get them out. 'He was staying with his parents in Ireland when that poor girl was killed. If he'd done what you say, he'd have had blood on his clothes, wouldn't he? His parents would have noticed. He wouldn't have been able to hide it from them. You must have the wrong person. Same as last time,' she added triumphantly. 'With that odd-jobs guy.'

Jones moistened his lips, took a breath.

'They wouldn't have noticed,' he said in a gentle voice.

'Of course, they would. They were staying together.'

'Matty's parents wouldn't have noticed anything because they're both dead, Mrs Brennan.'

My mother's eyebrows moved together. She shook her head, stuttered.

'What? No, that—'

'His father died in a hunting accident in the seventies. His mother was killed a few years ago in a robbery gone wrong. Her head was bashed in with a hatchet. The culprit was never found.'

'A hatchet?' I whispered.

He looked at me sharply.

'Yes. What about it?'

I just shook my head, mumbled, 'Nothing.'

Haven't you done enough? Nanna would have said.

'He likes his camo, doesn't he?' Duckworth asked. It sounded as if he was talking to himself. Musing.

'I'm sorry?' my mother said.

'Camouflage trousers.'

'Matty doesn't wear camo,' I told him.

'Maybe you just haven't seen it.'

'It's not exactly his style. He's more of a cashmere and Oxfords kind of guy.'

The other detective cut in. 'Mrs Brennan, I wonder if we could ask you a personal question.' He flicked his eyes in my direction. 'It might be best in private.'

My mother nodded again, motioned for me to go to my room. She'd been rendered practically speechless ever since the revelation about Matty's parents.

I wondered whether she'd had the same thought as me when they mentioned the hatchet. If her brain had gone straight to the one in Matty's sports bag.

I hesitated a moment, thinking maybe I could persuade her to let me stay, then figured I'd learn more by appearing to acquiesce. I could hear plenty with my bedroom door open.

Jones waited till I'd gone, then cleared his throat.

'Did Matty ever hurt you, Mrs Brennan? Abuse you physically or sexually?'

I heard the embarrassment in my mother's voice.

'No, of course not.'

'And in your, erm . . . personal relations, did he ever suggest bondage or any sort of rough activities?'

'No. God.'

'What about anal sex?' Duckworth asked. Unlike Jones, he didn't have the manners to sound uncomfortable.

'I'm a Christian, detective.'

'So that's a no?'

'Of course it's a no.'

'And he never hurt your daughter? Never touched her inappropriately?'

'No, he did not.'

A swell of acid rolled around my stomach, a sickly feeling in my throat. I'd never told her about the night Matty couldn't find a towel, still didn't know what it meant. Or if it counted as 'inappropriate'.

'Ever notice any mud on his camo trousers?' Duckworth asked.

'What?'

'Ever seen—'

'My daughter already told you. He doesn't wear camo.'

'What about his apartment? Ever notice anything there? Stains, a bad smell. Anything strange.'

'No,' my mother said, but she'd answered too quickly. I suspect we were both thinking about those blocked drains.

'What about his relationships with women?' Duckworth asked.

They were jumping from topic to topic. I wondered whether they were doing it on purpose. Trying to catch her off guard the way they did on *Perry Mason*.

'Misogyny?' Jones prompted. 'Trouble relating?'

My mother scoffed.

'Hardly. He's the most charming man I've ever met.'

'What about cruelty to animals?'

'Do you think I'd want anything to do with someone like that?'

'His camo trousers, are they brown or green?'

'Why do you keep asking me about camo trousers?'

We didn't know it then, but a swatch of camouflage material torn from a pair of trousers had been found in the mud near where Niamh Keenan's body was dumped that matched fibres discovered at Hampstead Road Lock.

The detectives answered my mother with a fresh question of their own. A deflection tactic, one I've employed plenty of times myself since.

'Did he ever store anything here?'

'No.'

'Ever asked you to lie for him?'

'No!'

'Okay. I wonder if we could show you some photos.'

'Photos? Of what?'

'Perhaps we could invite your daughter back in. We'd like her to see these too.'

I came out of my room before they had a chance to call me. Jones grinned knowingly.

'I've got a daughter about your age,' he said.

I refused to smile back, to form any sort of alliance with this man.

They showed us pictures of several victims. Sheryl North wearing a single earring, gold like the one my mother had found in Matty's flat, though it was too long ago for me to be sure it was the same. Farah Lawson, fingernails torn from where she'd tried to fight off her attacker. Gemma Nicholls, her arm cut with a hatchet. *Do you have any idea how hard it is to cut through bone?*

'I realise these are hard to look at,' Duckworth said. 'But if they prompt any memories . . .'

I told him they didn't before my mother could say anything. Plenty of people have hatchets. The earring could have belonged to anyone. So what, that I'd seen Matty with a scratch on his arm?

They left eventually, each pressing a card into my mother's hand.

'We suggest you don't talk to the media,' Jones said. 'They won't leave you alone otherwise.'

'Why would they want to talk to us?' I asked.

He didn't answer, just said goodnight and advised us to lock our door.

FIFTY-THREE

When I look back on the days that followed, I see them only as a tangled mess of distorted shapes. My memories, a kaleido-scope. No order or sense to them.

I remember the guilt though; the way it tore at me. I felt it physically the same way you'd feel a broken leg or stab wound. I was crippled by it; couldn't move, couldn't breathe.

I'd wake in the night gripped by fear; gasping for air, covered in sweat. I couldn't eat, couldn't sleep. All day my body shook.

I tried praying, but after, 'Dear Lord . . .' the words wouldn't come. Not because I didn't know what to say, but rather because I didn't feel I deserved to say it.

What if it had all been a hideous mistake?

I thought about the earring in Matty's apartment, the hatchet, of him lying about the crisis centre. Of all the times he'd said he was there when he wasn't. I thought of Niamh Keenan, her face so mutilated even her parents struggled to identify her. And of Gemma Nicholls discarded in the bushes just minutes from where we lived. Of how Matty seemed amused when he heard she'd been mistaken for a mannequin.

I thought about the dead parents he'd pretended were still alive, and that it was him who'd suggested I collect clippings of the murders.

But then I thought of what my mother had said about the police arresting the wrong guy once before. What if they had done the same thing again? What if the killer really was that odd-jobs man after all?

I thought how much I loved Matty and that surely I'd have been able to tell if he was a serial killer. I thought about his warm eyes, the way they'd crinkle when he smiled, the way he always stuck up for me. A murderer wouldn't behave like that. They wouldn't be able to.

And what about the police profile? Matty wasn't a loner or socially inadequate. Frankly that label fit my mother better than him.

Then just as I'd persuaded myself he wasn't guilty, another memory would explode in my head making me question myself all over again. The night of the pizza. That terrible drive.

Matty had a knack for making you think you were over-reacting, blowing his 'games' out of proportion.

Do you seriously think I meant to hit you in the face with that ball?

I didn't realise you couldn't breathe.

Lighten up, Soph. I was only mucking around.

But what if he wasn't mucking around? What if he had meant to hurt me? To scare the hell out of me?

I didn't know what to believe or even what I wanted to believe.

'I've got a tummy ache,' I told my mother. Resorting to old tricks. 'I think I'm getting sick.'

She was lying in bed, a good half hour after she should have been up. She didn't look as though she'd slept any better than I had.

'You're going to school,' she said, even though it was clear she had little intention of going to work.

I decided the truth might get better traction than a phantom illness.

'I can't go,' I told her. 'Please don't make me.'

She sighed deeply, patted the bed for me to sit down next to her. I perched on the edge, picked at my cuticles.

'I can't face it,' I said. 'Let me stay off, just today.'

She didn't answer straight away, which I took as encouraging. A rookie error, I should have known better.

'Hiding under your duvet isn't going to make any of this go away. I won't lie to you, going to school today is going to be hard, maybe the hardest thing you've ever done. Which is why you've got to do it.'

'That makes no sense.'

She placed a hand on my arm, a sure sign there was a lecture coming.

'Being brave isn't about going to war and acting the hero. It's about being scared to death of a thing but doing it anyway because you know it's right. I get that you're afraid to go in today. Your friends will talk, some might even blame you. It's going to be tough as hell. But get through this and you'll get through anything.'

I chewed the side of my tongue, picked at a loose stitch on her sheets. Sunshine streamed through the closed curtains. I could hear birdsong, people laughing on the street below. It all seemed so out of place, an impertinent intrusion.

'But—'

'You're going,' my mother said. 'And that's final.'

I wanted to tell her everything. *A problem halved is a problem shared. Talk to me Soph . . .*

I hadn't talked to her for years though. Matty was my confidant now, but I could hardly talk to him. I couldn't talk to anyone.

She gave my hand a squeeze, promised people wouldn't be as cruel as I thought.

What she didn't understand was that I was less scared of facing the judgement of others than of facing myself.

FIFTY-FOUR

Gossip is a sink hole. It pulls you under no matter how carefully you tread.

The police held a press conference exactly four hours after knocking on our door. Harry Connor sat up on his podium and announced to a roomful of reporters that they'd made an arrest in connection with the Shadow killings and had now charged a man.

'Following an anonymous call to the tip line, Mr Matty Melgren, a bereavement counsellor from Camden, was arrested for the murders of nine women in North London since 1981, as well as the murder of an eight-year-old girl in Brownstone, Ireland.'

There was no note of triumph in his voice, no sign of gloating. Only the droop of his shoulders hinted at what he felt. Recently, my shoulders had started to droop too. Metaphorical weight taking a physical toll.

'We can connect Melgren to at least eight of the North London murders, but we suspect he is responsible for dozens more,' Connor said, pausing to let the words sink in.

My mother pushed her chair back, poured herself a large glass of wine. No juice.

'Turn it off, Sophie,' she said. But I didn't.

It was like the time I'd watched *Friday the 13th* with Matty, against what my mother had called her 'better judgement'. I'd covered my eyes when the scary bits came on, but I couldn't help peeking through my fingers.

The day after his arrest, the whispers started. People I'd thought were my friends shunned me. When I entered a room it went silent. Walking down a corridor, I'd hear my name, but when I turned around, I couldn't tell who'd said it. It could have been anyone, they were all looking at me. Shifty-eyed glimpses. Hushed voices. Kids I was friends with. Kids I wasn't.

That's her.

I bet she knew.

How could she not have?

It was like being back in Miss Bacon's class. Sally Sniders and I were at the same high school, though up till now, we'd had little to do with each other. I figured she'd learned it wasn't worth getting on my bad side and secretly hoped she'd spread the word a bit.

'You got her to walk in your shoes. Good for you,' my mother said when I announced I'd sorted things out back in Miss Bacon's class.

'You mean, Sophie walked on hers,' Matty corrected. 'Your ma's right, pumpkin. Fair play to you.'

I liked his analysis of the situation better than my mother's, but whatever the cause, since the *Jackie*/sticker book truce, Sally and I had given each other a wide berth.

Now that berth was breached.

'You and your mother should be ashamed of yourselves,' she hissed as I lined up for lunch.

A porcupine rolled over my scalp.

'What?'

'All those women your father killed. Don't pretend you didn't know what he was doing.'

The porcupine gave way to a hot flush of anger. I shoved her hard against the wall, gripped her by the throat. The lunch hall went silent.

'Matty Melgren didn't kill anyone,' I roared, right up in her face. 'And he's not my father.'

Sally sneered.

'And yet here you are with your hands around my neck.'

I was marched to the headmaster's office, a grey-haired man with a philosophy doctorate from Magdalen College Oxford, rather confusingly pronounced, 'Maudlin'.

'You're a good student, Sophie,' Mr Osmond told me, after inviting me to please take a seat and making a show of capping his pen and interlacing his sausage fingers. 'We have high hopes for you. But if you're going to get on here, you need to learn to control your temper. I understand this is a difficult time, but you can't go around assaulting people just because they say something you don't like.'

'You don't understand . . .'

'There's nothing to understand, Miss Brennan. Your behaviour was undignified and unacceptable.'

'Aren't you even going to give me a chance to explain?'

The old man sighed, blew through his beard.

'Go on.'

'It's not fair. Matty hasn't even had a trial, but everyone's already decided he's guilty.'

I didn't add that they'd decided I was guilty by association. Or that I thought they might be right, albeit for different reasons.

He scratched his head, disappeared his lips. From his expression I thought he was about to lay into me again, but when he spoke, his voice was gentle.

'You're right. We can't know yet whether he's guilty or not.'

Which was precisely my problem. As long as that question went unanswered, my guilt would remain.

I was sent back to class with a warning rather than a detention. I should have been pleased, but I wasn't. A part of me wanted to be punished, to pay for what I'd done.

In Latin, I received another warning. A note from Sally Sniders, folded over three times and passed from desk to desk until it reached mine.

DON'T THINK IT'S OVER, she wrote.

I don't, I thought.

Twenty years later it still isn't.

FIFTY-FIVE

Unlike when he was in Ireland, Matty phoned constantly from prison. I'd come home after school to find my mother hunched up on the couch, the receiver lying in her lap like a dead puppy. More often than not, a wine glass in her hand, blistered pill packets strewn across the table.

I didn't put it together straight away. The phone, the pills. Her red-rimmed eyes.

I was more focused on why she was in the living room rather than at work. It had been years since she'd got home before me.

A latch-key kid, my grandmother called me.

'It's a bad idea, Amelia-Rose. She'll get up to no good if you're not around. It's a slippery slope. You remember what happened to . . .'

My mother was the one on the slippery slope, though Nanna G didn't know that. My mother hadn't told her anything of substance for years. I can't say I blamed her. If Nanna G was my mum, I wouldn't tell her anything either.

Tuesday afternoon was more of the same. I dumped my

school bag inside the door. She was in her usual spot on the sofa, staring into her wine glass.

'It's not a crystal ball, you know.'

I was in a scratchy mood. Mr Osmond had talked about the murders in assembly, made a big deal about 'innocent before proven guilty'. I recognised that he was trying to help, but also that it would only make things worse. For a man whose profession was all about managing kids, it seemed to me he might have understood them a little better.

'Run crying to Oz have you?' Sally jeered at breaktime.

'I don't know how you sleep at night,' someone else muttered.

'Do you ever think about the women he killed?'

'Or their families?'

I didn't have the energy to argue back, my hands hanging uselessly at my sides.

The end of school bell offered no relief. Going home was yet another gauntlet, one I had to negotiate alone since Bea no longer cared to walk with me. The media vans were double parked all the way along our street. The pavements swarming with journalists and looky-loos.

'We're on the front page,' my mother told me not long after the arrest.

'You mean Matty is?'

She shook her head, handed me the paper.

'No. Us.'

Somehow our names had been leaked, our address too. There was a photo of my mother and me coming out of our building. Above it the headline:

DID THEY KNOW?

'Guy from the papers said he'd give me a grand to dish the dirt on you,' Linda informed us.

'What did you say?' my mother asked.

'Go forth and multiply. Or words to that effect.'

That same evening there was a knock at our front door. A TV reporter had managed to get through the main door. My mother was sleeping. I looked through the peephole, saw a woman with an unflattering ginger perm and furry micro-phone standing poised next to a cameraman, his camcorder light already on.

The intercom buzzed constantly after that with other reporters trying to 'Give you a chance to tell your side of the story'. My mother took herself to bed with a sedative. I located a screwdriver and disconnected the entry phone.

Now I stood where it had been, giving my mother disap-proving looks.

'I just need a bit of time to myself, that's all,' she slurred, her 's's morphing into 'sh's.

I jush need a bit of time to myshelf . . .

Hard to believe this was the same woman who'd given that speech about courage.

Perhaps she read my mind.

'I'm trying,' she said. 'It's just so difficult with Matty calling all the time.'

I felt a crawl of adrenaline. My stomach tightened.

'You never said he was phoning. What's he say?'

She shrugged, spilled half her drink.

'That he's innocent. That they've got the wrong guy. That he loves me.'

I ground the carpet with my heel, tried to swallow down the lump growing in my throat.

'It makes it so hard,' she said. 'Every time he calls, I feel so guilty.'

'Guilty? Why?'

She swirled the dregs of her wine around in her glass. Stared at them as if she were reading tea leaves.

'Everything. Some days I'm just guilty to be alive.'

'Maybe you shouldn't take his calls.'

'It's not really as easy as that.' *Ash eashy . . .*

The bottles and pill packets continued to pile up. So too the reporters and catcalls.

That night I slipped into my mother's bed while she slept.

'I'm sorry,' I whispered.

But only the walls heard.

FIFTY-SIX

I wonder now how differently our lives might have panned out if we'd been at Matty's trial. If we'd been able to look into his eyes. If he'd seen us looking?

How much easier it may have been if his lawyers had prepared us for what to expect rather than leaving us to discover all the terrible facts of the crimes along with the rest of the watching world?

No day was the same. Sometimes I found I could hold it together, other times I felt like throwing up. Everything was a blur. Only my nightmares seemed real, so ghastly I was afraid to go to sleep.

I never wanted to go to court. I was too afraid of what I'd find out, too ashamed. If only I'd known sooner, if only I could have stopped him, I thought. And then always on the tail of that, what if they got the wrong guy? What if this was an awful mistake?

I drowned in 'what ifs'.

My mother was conflicted too, but unlike me, she had every intention of sitting in the gallery and supporting him. I remember her flicking through her wardrobe the day before the trial started, trying to find something suitable to wear. *An outfit that strikes the right note.*

'You're not serious?' Linda asked, horrified. 'You're not actually going to stand by that man after what he's done?'

'You don't know he's guilty.'

'I know he might be. Ten murders at least, one of them a child half Sophie's age.'

'Everyone's entitled to a defence.'

Linda's hand went to her mouth.

'Oh my God, Amelia. Tell me you're not . . .'

My mother shuffled her feet, looked at the floor.

'You are, aren't you? I don't believe it. Paying his lawyers! What are you thinking?'

'I'm just helping out a bit. Do you have any idea how much these things cost?'

Was that the real reason Matty kept calling my mother, to tap her for cash? And then following my outrage, a fresh wash of guilt. Always there, just beneath the surface.

'Jesus, Am. Standing by him is bad enough, but . . .' Linda grappled for the right word '. . . funding him? It's crazy.'

'I have to,' my mother said quietly, eyes trained on the floor. 'Don't you see? If there's even the slightest chance he's innocent . . .'

They went at it a while longer. Linda said she didn't know who my mother was any more. My mother said she was going to take a pill and go to bed. She'd started taking a lot of pills by then. *To help me sleep*, she said. But she didn't always take them at night. Nor did she always go in to work. *I might have to call in sick again . . .*

It was around this time she graduated to gin. *Wine just doesn't do it for me any more.* This from a woman who until only a few months ago hadn't been able to drink alcohol without sweetening it first.

'Still think she's the bravest person you've ever met?' I asked Linda.

'More than ever,' she said.

Linda must have got through to her eventually because although she continued to defend Matty to anyone who'd listen and send money to his legal team, she didn't end up going to court.

'He's upset,' she told me. 'He says it would show him in a good light if we were there.'

What about us? I thought. Would light would it show us in?

I was still persona non grata at school, although you'd never have guessed it from the crap the newspapers printed. They were forever quoting this or that 'unnamed source, a close friend of Melgren's daughter', who claimed to have the inside scoop on my life with a serial killer. Never mind that I had no friends now, that Matty wasn't my father. That a jury hadn't decided he really was a serial killer.

Although she didn't go to court, my mother kept the radio on all the time, even while she slept. She drank steadily, went to work sporadically. I took to making our supper in the evenings, cleaning up the flat when I got home from school. By morning, it was always a tip again.

I read the papers, watched the news, sobbed over the details. Pored over old photographs, trying to cling onto the man I was losing, to find in them the man I'd known. But the murders cast a veil over everything, so I no longer knew what was true and what was a lie. Even now, twenty years on, I still struggle to reconcile the memory of the man I'd loved with the picture the prosecution painted.

I couldn't bear that so many lives might have been destroyed by him. Didn't know how to deal with the shame. When Sally Sniders goaded me, I kicked back, but my heart wasn't in it and she could tell. It was like being back in Miss Bacon's class, only now I didn't give a hoot what people thought of me or whether my mother was married to Ronald McDonald.

A week into the trial, Grace Keenan, the sister of the eight-year-old Matty had supposedly killed in Brownstone, took the stand. Eyes lowered, she told the court how Matty had stopped her and her sister for directions, claiming to be looking for his lost beagle.

'He had a lead and a map, like. There was no reason to think he was lying.'

Niamh was apparently reluctant to help, anxious to get to their grandmother's birthday tea.

'Just think how terrified the wee dog must be all out there by hisself, I told her. And in the end she said, "Aye, okay then," and off we went. I—'

Grace broke off, lip quivering. The prosecutor said it was okay, just take your time.

'Niamh and the man were nattering away. I was a little ways ahead, calling after the dog. Niamh tripped, twisted her ankle. Made a holy show of herself, crying and screaming. "I can't move," she said. "I think it's broken." I didn't know how I was ever going to get her home.

'"You run on," the man said. "I'll carry her back. No point you both being late for your granny's party."'

'I thought he was being nice. I thought I was doing the right thing . . .'

The judge cleared his throat.

'I realise this is painful, young lady, but could you try and look up when answering questions?'

Grace went very pink.

'I find it difficult to look at people. I'm shy, like.'

And yet, when the prosecutor asked if the man was in the courtroom, she nodded and said in a loud, clear voice that yes, that was him in the dock. 'I'll never forget his face.'

That turned out not to be quite true.

Matty's barrister, Bob Hart, stood up, adjusted his robes.

'Let's talk about what you told the police, shall we?'

His cross examination resembled target practice, each question a bullseye by all accounts.

Despite what she'd told the prosecutor, Mr Hart forced Grace to admit she'd been a little hazy on the details.

He read out an extract from a transcript:

'He was wearing brown pants,' Grace told detectives interviewing her.

'Not camouflage?'

'Aye. That's right, camouflage.'

'Any facial hair?'

'Um, a moustache.'

'A moustache? Not just stubble?'

'I meant stubble. It made his upper lip area dark, like. That's what I meant to say.'

Years later, it came out in a magazine interview that it wasn't just the police she wanted to help. She felt so guilty, she said. If she hadn't left her sister, she might still be alive. *Identifying that man meant everything to our family. I felt very strongly that it was down to me to get Niamh justice.*

We weren't so different in that regard.

Matty phoned again that evening. I picked up the receiver and listened in.

'This was a good day for us, Ams. My barrister tore that girl to shreds. The police don't have a case. They've clearly been fabricating evidence right left and centre.'

All I heard was, *This was a good day for us*. I thought about all the evidence that had come up since the trial started: the crime scene photos, the footmarks that matched his feet, newsreel of the victims' families crying on the steps of the Old Bailey.

My hands wouldn't stop shaking. I had a permanent blockage in my throat. And yet here was Matty talking with the same cold detachment as if he were discussing the weather.

Ironically, to other people he didn't seem cold at all. Every day women lined up to get a seat in the gallery, star-struck by his charm and good looks. Many of them groupies who curled and dyed their hair in line with the Shadow's preference, turned on by his notoriety. A psychological condition known as hybristophilia apparently. Bonnie and Clyde Syndrome. It could have all the labels in the world, and it still wouldn't make any sense to me.

'He just doesn't seem the type to kill,' was said a lot. 'He's the sort of guy you'd be proud to introduce to your parents.'

It wasn't just women who were taken in by him though. The

longer the trial went on, the more people questioned whether he really was behind these crimes. The cross examination of Grace Keenan was only part of it. The prosecution case was largely circumstantial they said, a term I had to look up and yet still have explained to me.

Beyond reasonable doubt means you have to be completely sure a person is guilty, as one legal expert put it on *Radio London*.

'By the time the defence finished with her, even Grace Keenan couldn't say she was sure Melgren was her sister's attacker.'

My mother clung to the possibility of Matty's innocence. Hope, a bauble dangled in front of a baby ready to be snatched away as soon as she reaches for it.

'They've got to acquit,' she said. 'It's going to happen. I feel it in my bones.'

I didn't know what to feel. I longed as much for a guilty verdict as an exoneration. I'd been so sure of his involvement that day in the café, but now I wasn't sure of anything, which is what made it all so difficult. I craved certainty. A resolution in whatever form.

'How can you be so confident he's innocent?' I asked my mother.

'Because I love him,' she said, as if it was the most obvious thing in the world.

Extract from the Evidence Re-Visited Project

Between 1981 and 1983, a wave of signature killings spread through North London. Apart from an
eight-year-old girl, the victims were all similar in
appearance – slim, petite brunettes in their late teens
or early twenties with shoulder length curly hair.
Many were discovered dumped in garbage disposal
sites, undergrowth, ponds or canals. Although police
believe there are many others whose bodies have
never been found.

As horrifying as the crimes were, they have long
been overshadowed by the perpetrator, Matty Melgren's, charisma and good looks, along with his
refusal to admit his guilt and the controversial testimony that led to his conviction.

At the heart of the prosecution's case was footprint
evidence (the impressions on a surface made by unshod
feet rather than shoes). These prints can indicate certain skin features, particularly crease marks and ridge
detail as well as other characteristics such as gait.

However, whilst research in this field has suggested that the shape of a footprint is very individual (though not unique in the way of fingerprints or DNA*) the weight it should carry is still a matter for debate.

In fact, in 1999, a new study found that although footprint evidence is of value within crime scene investigations, it is not a hard and fast science, and examiners should approach it with caution.

* DNA was not a factor in Melgren's trial. It wasn't until 1986 that genetic fingerprinting would be used in a criminal investigation.

FIFTY-SEVEN

Matty's trial lasted two months. The jury deliberated for two weeks.

'It's a good sign,' he told my mother. 'Shows they're undecided.'

He still called most days.

'Speaking to him keeps me going,' she told me. 'But it undoes me too.'

Her hair was limp, her skin dull. Her big eyes raw and bloodshot.

'Keeps you going for what?' I asked, but she didn't answer.

I was getting ready for school when the phone rang. Early spring and freezing cold. The Ides of March, as our drama teacher had informed us the day before. We were studying *Julius Caesar* in class. I was reading the part of Brutus.

It was seven fifteen in the morning. My mother and I looked at each other. No one ever called at seven fifteen.

Her hand was shaking when she picked up, though I suspected only part of that was down to nerves. She was 'taking the edge off' all the time now. She didn't start before I'd left

294

for school, but I don't suppose she waited till long afterwards to pop the first pill.

She leaned against the wall, winding the telephone wire around her finger. I watched, every muscle primed. A pulse beating hard in my carotid.

'Today?' she said, voice barely a whisper. 'Are you sure?'

Her eyes flitted to the bottle of Gordon's on the side. The caller said something I couldn't hear.

'Right,' my mother answered. 'I see.' Then, 'I can't make her.'

'What?' I mouthed. I knew 'her' meant me.

She cupped the receiver.

'Mr Hart says they expect a verdict today. Matty really wants us there.' She paused. 'Both of us.'

'No,' I said, suddenly shaking all over, a body on the end of a rope. 'I can't.'

'It would mean a lot to him, darling.'

'No,' I repeated, more forcefully. Practically shouting.

I went in the end though. Penance, probably.

The air in the courtroom was dry as sand. It stuck in my throat so I couldn't breathe. A headache drilled through my left eye. My lumbar ached.

My mother and I were seated at the front of the balcony. I had the sense of being watched, thought I heard my name whispered. But even so, I felt invisible, like a ghost. Like I wasn't really there.

Matty was in the dock. He looked up at the gallery and winked. My mother sent him a reassuring smile back, though I'm not sure it was her he was winking at. The viewing area was packed, she and I were sitting pressed together so close I didn't know if it was her trembling or me.

'All rise.'

Judge Krause came in, an old man who looked as though his robes had outgrown him or else he'd shrunk inside them. He said a few words I didn't take in and then asked the foreman if the jury had reached a verdict.

An angular woman who reminded me a little of Miss Bacon stood up and said, yes they had. When the judge asked if it was unanimous, she told him it was.

I reached for my mother but her hands were clutched together and pressed to her lips. From the way she was staring fixedly ahead, I knew she was praying.

'How do you find the defendant?'

'Guilty,' the Miss Bacon lookalike pronounced.

My mother gasped as though winded. The murmurings in the gallery got so loud the judge had to call for order. I covered my mouth, thinking I might be sick, uttered a single word.

Matty glanced up again. This time he was looking directly at us.

His face had gone very white. His lips peeled open.

Caesar bleeding out.

Et tu, Brute?

FIFTY-EIGHT

Regardless of which way it went, I'd been sure the verdict would give me closure. So sure, so stupid.

My mother stuck a Post-it note up in the living room not long after we moved to London—

The biggest mistake a person can make is being afraid to make one.

'It's wrong,' I told her. 'I can think of plenty of things worse than that.'

'What it means is, you'll never realise your potential if you're scared of messing up.'

'Potential?'

'What you're capable of. Think of all the great scientific discoveries. Antibiotics, vaccinations—'

'Televisions . . .'

She laughed.

'Yes, even televisions. If people had been afraid to try something new, we wouldn't have any of them.'

'So, you're saying mistakes are good?'

This boded well.

'I'm saying you can't live life without making a few. Mistakes are okay so long as you learn from them. And as long as you make amends,' she added.

She was as keen on saying sorry as she was on teachable moments. Nanna G was the same. Back in Newton, she found something I should apologise for most days. *You have to mean it though, or it doesn't count.*

When the verdict was read out, 'sorry' was the word I whispered, though, as my grandmother was fond of remarking, *Saying sorry doesn't always make things right.*

But how could I make something right if I didn't know whether what I'd done was wrong? Had I screwed up? Or was my real mistake not acting sooner?

Matty's lawyer read out his statement to the press on the steps of the Old Bailey, reporters and camera crews jostling for position.

'A terrible miscarriage of justice has taken place here today,' he intoned in his deep courtroom voice, wispy hair fluttering in the wind. 'I am innocent of these murders which have rocked the world and caused women everywhere to fear going out alone.'

It brought to mind Judge Krause's pronouncement just before sentencing:

'The jury could have gone either way . . .'

It was almost as though he and Matty had conspired to raise questions over the verdict, questions that would continue to be asked for decades to come.

I looked around at the swarm of placards and protesters milling around the courthouse steps. Matty's supporters turned up every day. It didn't seem to matter to them whether or not they got a seat inside the chamber. They were able to make their presence felt just as well outdoors.

MATTY IS INNOCENT, their notices read.

POLICE STITCH-UP

TRIAL BY MEDIA

Then on the other side of the road, the two groups separated by uniformed police officers with truncheons at the ready, were all the folk who thought he'd got his just desserts. They carried placards too, and homemade banners painted on bed-sheets.

MONSTER, they said. And, STOP VIOLENCE AGAINST WOMEN.

'Come on,' my mother urged, pulling me by the sleeve – voice and hands quivering.

She'd been the first to doubt Matty, but now she believed a terrible injustice had occurred. As we staggered away from the Old Bailey in the same way we'd staggered out of our building on the night of the fire, we passed a knot of men who plainly hadn't been rooting for our guy.

'Murdering scum.'

Ptah. A slug of phlegm hit the pavement.

'I hope they castrate him.'

'Castration's too good for that maggot.'

My mother stopped dead, eyes glittering like she was going to deck the lot of them.

'Pathetic creatures. You don't deserve to even say his name.'

I stared at her in open-mouthed admiration, scampering after her as she marched off.

At home, she locked herself in her room with a bottle of gin. She didn't emerge for the next three days. When I knocked, she didn't answer. The sound of her crying the only way I knew she was still alive.

I wished I could I cry, but the tears wouldn't come. Instead, they built up inside me, a dam waiting to burst. A boulder on my back, rocks in my throat. And all the while, the same black thoughts circling in my head.

What if Matty wasn't the killer? What if the real culprit was still out there? What would that make me?

What if women were still in danger? What if more died because of what I'd done?

And if he *was* guilty? What did that make me then? If I'd been less of an ostrich, if I'd looked beyond what I wanted to see, how many women would still be alive? How many families still intact?

If he was innocent, I was guilty.

If he was guilty, I was too.

Matty may or may not have been a murderer, but whichever way I sliced it, there was blood on my hands.

Lives had ended because of me.

FIFTY-NINE

Des Banister's life ended at six-thirty in the evening, exactly three hours after Channel 1 interrupted *Yogi Bear* to announce that Matty had been found guilty of the Shadow murders. It would take us another twenty-four hours to discover our neighbour had shuffled off this mortal coil. We never found out why.

Shortly after Matty's arrest, he'd returned home from wherever he'd been holed-up. I came downstairs as he was unloading his van; black bin bags that gave off a yellow smell of cauliflower cheese. His clothes were filthy, his army boots and trousers caked in mud.

'Where have you been?' I asked.

I hadn't laid eyes on him since the 'fries in the puddle' incident.

He just mumbled, 'Away,' and kept on walking.

It was the last time I ever spoke to him. I'd hear him clunking about downstairs late at night and his godawful rock music drifting up through the floorboards. But I didn't hear his van pulling up in the early hours any more, or the pipes chugging as he drew a bath.

I got up one night, needing the toilet. As I sat there, a movement in the window caught my eye. A black shape shifting in the dark garden.

A burglar? Someone trying to break in?

My whole body tensed. I was both hot and cold at once. I wanted to call my mother, but I was turned to stone, couldn't speak.

The shape moved, a figure looking up. Before I could duck, I saw its face, Des Banister's white skin seeming to glow in the moonlight. He hadn't seen me though. The light was off, the slats were down.

He turned back to what he was doing; something with a shovel. Digging, patting the earth flat.

I watched him wipe his hands down the side of his trousers, pick up a can of beer from the ground and raise it to the sky as if he were toasting it. The following day, I went out there, curious as to what he'd been up to.

I figured he must have been burying something, but there was no sign of disturbed earth and I couldn't be sure where exactly I'd seen him. *Oh well* . . . I turned to go back inside.

As I reached the back door, I sensed him watching me. A face in the window that quickly disappeared. The next time I saw him, he was dead.

Bailey had been whimpering non-stop. Des' van was parked outside, but there were none of the usual noises to suggest he was home. Matty had just been found guilty, I had other things on my mind, but as the animal's whining got louder and more persistent, I started to worry. Not about Des, about his dog.

Reluctant to speak to him if I could avoid it, I lifted the letter-box flap and peered in rather than ringing the bell.

I'm not sure what I expected to see, only that what I saw wasn't what I was expecting.

'People see what they want to see, not what's really there,' Matty told me once. 'It's called Motivated Perception.' Something I expect he relied on a lot.

I don't know what motivated me that day, only that I saw Des' feet poking out from behind a wall, Bailey standing over him. And as my eyes adjusted to the light, blood on Des' white socks. A red rose blossoming in the snow.

I saw, but I didn't want to see. My brain refused to catch on.

'Des,' I called through the flap. 'It's Sophie.'

Bailey raised his head, and then lowered it again.

'Did you hurt yourself, Des? Des?'

My chest was tight, I couldn't take in enough air. The edges were closing in. I knew what had happened in the way a lion knows it's time to leave the pride, and yet I couldn't acknowledge it to myself. Wasn't ready to make it real.

'Let me in, Des. I know I was rude to you before. I didn't mean it.'

Des obviously felt remorseful about something too. When the ambulance men came, they found a note next to his body written in the same block capitals he'd used on the newspaper clipping. Two words: *I'M SORRY.*

To this day, I don't know why he took his life or what he was apologising for. He suffered from depression apparently, blamed himself for his mother's death and for a road accident involving a child when he was in his teens.

His cryptic note could have been about either of those things. Or it could have been about something else altogether. Framing Matty, as conspiracy theorists have suggested. The Shadow murders. Having urges he couldn't control.

We'll never know for sure, not least because he hadn't addressed the message to anyone.

That night, I finally cried. For myself, for Matty, and for all the sorrys I couldn't say.

SIXTY

Matty didn't phone the first few weeks he was in prison. It takes time to get put on the 'officially approved' contacts list, as I found out later. I also learned that prison staff would likely be listening in to his conversations and recording his calls. I recall he was rather outraged about that.

'I'm entitled to privacy,' he told my mother.

'Apparently not,' she replied.

She acted tough when she spoke to him, didn't want him to know she was falling apart.

'I can't bear for him to think less of me.'

'Isn't what you think of him more relevant?' I asked.

'When did you become so hard, Sophie?'

I considered suggesting that perhaps she should try being a bit harder too, but thought better of it. Linda had warned me she was fragile, that I needed to handle her carefully or she might break.

'Just be nice, Sophie. Cut her some slack.'

As if it was my fault she was crying all the time, that she could never seem to get stoned enough. That she tortured herself with a never-ending loop of questions: *Who do you think called the police? Do you reckon he thinks it was me? You don't believe that, do you?*

'It's the phone calls,' I said. 'They're killing her. She says he's going to die in there. That it's all because of her.'

'How's she figure that?'

I shrugged up to my ears.

'Hell, if I know.'

'It doesn't make any sense.'

I shook my head.

'Nope.'

I tried persuading her to take a break from speaking to Matty.

'You need to stop accepting his calls. Can't you see what they're doing to you?'

She'd just ended yet another conversation with him, Niagara Falls down her face.

'It's all I have left,' she said.

'All you have left of *him*, you mean?'

'What?'

'Because you know, I'm still here.'

'Yes, I know,' she said, but she clearly didn't.

She was so tightly blindfolded by grief, the rest of the world had ceased to exist. Me included. Some days she'd look at me as if surprised to see me sitting there. More than once she seemed to forget my name.

'You've got to put a stop to this, for both our sakes.'

She began to sob, shoulders shaking. I touched her and she flinched.

'I can't stop. I need him. He makes me feel so loved.'

'A love that's destroying you.'

'I know,' she repeated. And again I knew she didn't mean it.

He made reverse-charge calls two or three times a week. My mother always accepted them, but never the toll the calls were taking on her. She went in to work late, stopped eating, rowed with Linda. When our car was stolen, she couldn't even be bothered to report it to the police.

'You have no idea what it's like to hate yourself,' she told me.

I said yes, actually I did, but she didn't hear. She didn't hear much of what anyone said any more, anyone apart from Matty.

He phoned one night when she was 'having a lie down', code for drinking to blackout. I'd long given up trying to stop her, but maybe I could stop this.

A prisoner from HMP Huntersville is trying to make a reverse-charge call. Do you accept the charges?

I hesitated a moment, then said yes, I would.

'Well, hey there, pumpkin,' Matty said. 'What a nice surprise.'

His voice, his manner. He sounded just like he always had, as if the intervening months hadn't happened. I felt my insides melt. It was an effort to keep my resolve.

'Mum's packing,' I said. 'It's why she can't come to the phone.'

'Packing?' He sounded put out. 'You're going on holiday?'

'Didn't she tell you? We're moving. A fresh start. Tonight's our last night here.'

He gathered himself quickly. I suppose he'd had a lot of practice with that.

'Can you give me your new number? I'll need to get it approved with the screws, see? You wouldn't believe the bureaucracy in here.'

I glanced at my mother's closed bedroom door, heart strumming against my ribs.

'I don't think that's a good idea. She doesn't want you calling any more.' Then for good measure, 'If you must know, that's the real reason she didn't come to the phone now.'

The silence that followed went on so long I thought he must have gone. I was about to hang up – hands trembling, underarms pricking with sweat – when he spoke again.

'Is that why she didn't answer my letter?'

'I expect so,' I said, though I had no idea.

I didn't come across the letter until years later when I was sorting through my mother's things. A declaration of undying love that I'd have urged her to burn had I found out about it sooner:

Life has no meaning without you in it. My dreams are nothing if I can't share them with you. Believe in me, in what we had and what we will have again. I'm going to fight this verdict until it is overthrown – which it will be. Our journey together hasn't ended, my love. It's only just begun.

He was right about their journey just beginning, I thought when I read it. The moment he was convicted, my mother was on a one-way train to the grave.

Matty took a long, deep breath. I could picture perfectly the way he'd look as he did so. How he'd press his lips together, eyes cast down as though travelling deep inside himself. I knew him so well I could draw his face from memory, and yet in other ways I didn't know him at all.

'Does she think I'm guilty?' he said.

'Are you?' I asked.

Another pause, and then the line went dead.

SIXTY-ONE

The line is dead, though I'm not sure what I was expecting. I put it back in the holder, smooth down my hair for the umpteenth time. Rebuke myself for caring how I look for the umpteenth time too.

Matty still hasn't been brought in. I'm both pleased and disappointed. The sooner he's here, the sooner this will be over. And yet, I'd do anything to put the moment off.

It's as though I can feel the blood coursing through my veins, the charge of adrenaline. Every sinew is taut, every muscle flexed. I feel like I'm going to hurl.

In an hour this will all just be a memory, I tell myself. One of Janice's little tricks to get through things that make you anxious.

This isn't just anxiety though. It's pure, petrifying dread.

'Remember you're in control,' she coached me the other day. 'If it gets too much, you can walk away. You're not a little girl any more. He has no power over you.'

He does though. Twenty years after his conviction, and I still can't go past the running track. I'm still living in the same flat.

Still talking to my mother every day, the same circular conversation, the same recriminations and guilt.

I sit up a little straighter on the plastic chair. There's no lumbar support. My back aches. But I won't let him see I'm uncomfortable, that I'm scared. Damned if I'll give him the satisfaction.

My eyes go back to the phone on the wall. There's another one on the other side of the glass. I try to imagine him picking it up, what he'll say. I can't picture it though, which frightens me further. I have no idea what to expect.

In some ways, my whole life has been building to this moment. Or perhaps it would be more accurate to say, it's been frozen until this moment. Everything put on hold.

If we are our memories, what does that make me? A woman who doesn't know what was real and what was a lie, who doesn't know what or whom to believe. You can only move on from your mistakes if you know what those mistakes were. You can only grow if you have a place to grow from.

I'm a bicycle wheel stuck in the mud. Thirty-two years old and I'm still spinning in the dirt.

I said that to Janice once. She laughed, told me I might have come up with a more flattering metaphor. She writes self-help books, guides to managing trauma and the like. Language is important to her.

I pick at my nails, then sit on my hands so Matty won't see me fidgeting when he comes in. Straight away I'm chewing at my lip, shifting about in my seat. Trying to seem strong is a losing battle.

What's taking so long?

Just as I'm thinking about getting up and finding someone to ask, I hear the quick march of approaching footsteps. The sound echoes down the empty corridor, reverberates off the walls.

My heart is a battering ram. I feel it in my throat as my abdominals tighten. I'm absolutely sure now I'm going to puke.

Focus on your breathing, Janice would say, but I can't. I can't focus on anything apart from the drumbeat of those feet. A steel gate bangs shut, making me jump, the clanging resounding loudly in the hollow emptiness.

What am I doing here? What was I thinking?

You need closure, Janice told me, but I'm not going to get that here. Matty's hardly going to change his tune now. And if he really is innocent, how will I know?

Looking into his eyes? What a crock.

The footsteps slow and stop on the other side of the door. I taste pennies, the sharp tang of copper. It's a moment before I realise I've bitten my tongue, that it's leaking blood.

On the other side of the glass, a door opens. Two men walk in, one of them uniformed, one of them cuffed.

The cuffed man holds out his wrists for the bracelets to be removed. As he does, he looks at me and smiles. His blonde hair is greying. He's lost weight. There are lines on his face. But his smile is the same, his eyes too. The colour and shape a mirror image of mine.

He sits down without removing his gaze, raises the phone to his ear and gestures for me to do the same.

Hand shaking, I pick up the receiver.

'Hello, Sophie,' Matty says.

SIXTY-TWO

My mouth is so dry, it's a few seconds before I can speak.

'Matty,' I say.

No hello, just his name. As if I can't believe it's him, and in a way I can't.

The intervening years are a mist quickly clearing. He is just the same. Twenty years he's been locked away, but his eyes have the same sparkle, his voice the same baritone, the same Irish lilt. I lost my accent within a term of starting school. He has lost nothing of himself.

With that thought, I am a child again, the twelve-year-old girl who idolised him, loved him more than anyone else in the world. And again, I think there's been a terrible mistake, that I've made a terrible mistake.

We didn't visit him after he was sent to prison. My mother said she wasn't up to it and, having seen what the phone calls did to her, I didn't push. As I got older, I could have gone myself, Huntersville was only a few bus rides away after all. But I didn't. Like my mother, I couldn't face going, not least because that would have meant facing myself.

'You came,' Matty says, as if reading my thoughts.

I feel my cheeks redden.

'They said you're dying.'

My mother would have scolded me. *You can't just blurt things out.* She was always so careful with what she said, so precise. I often had the impression she tried out sentences in her head before saying them aloud. *The spoken word is a spent bullet, Sophie. You can't take it back.*

Again, Matty seems to read my mind.

He chuckles softly, tells me I always did say it as it was.

'So uncontrived. It's refreshing.'

I won't let him get the upper hand.

'You've got cancer?'

He nods, doesn't look particularly upset about it.

'I'm sorry,' I say, and I find it's true, I am, though I'm not sure why.

Time running out to put things right, maybe. Or basic programming. Only psychopaths take pleasure in other people's pain. They say Matty is a psychopath. Is that why he became a bereavement counsellor? I find myself wondering for the first time. Getting off on his patients' grief?

I make a point of looking at my watch.

'I don't have long.'

I want him to know I can leave whenever I want. That if he's got something to say, he'd better hurry up and say it.

He smiles that smile from twenty years ago.

'Me neither, so I'm told.'

And just like that, he's got the upper hand again.

'I was sad to hear about your mam.'

He holds my eyes with his to show he means it. I believe him.

I shrug, bite my lip to stop the tears coming. From him, the words cut the scars wide.

'You must have been what, seventeen?'

'Eighteen,' I correct him. Then, 'How did you know?'

'My lawyers can do some things right apparently. What happened?'

I consider not telling him. My mother's death is the last thing I want to discuss with Matty, given he set her on that road. But then I think there are things I want him to tell me, so maybe I have to give a bit too. Or at least, appear to.

'Her heart,' I lie.

He doesn't need to know everything. Some days even I doubt what I did, the line I crossed.

I don't tell him that I still talk to her every day, still hear her voice in my head. That I have conversations with her in death that I never got a chance to have with her in life. That I see her in my mind's eye, as a ghost. A phantom poring over photographs, drinking gin and popping pills. That I would do anything to have her back, to reclaim the woman I lost almost as soon as he came into our lives.

She changed when she met him. He lit her up in ways I never could, destroyed her in ways I never wanted to. I still needed her, but she didn't need me.

We're like Bonnie and Clyde, she used to say. It didn't escape me that Bonnie and Clyde were a pair not a trio.

'Her heart,' Matty repeats. 'Is that so?' And I realise he knows I'm lying.

I shuffle in my seat, swallow hard, but my throat is arid and the saliva catches, making me cough.

'Do you want a drink?' he asks, although there's no way he can get me one.

Just another game. So many games.

I'm about to remind him that I don't have long. Perhaps I'll invent a boyfriend I have to get home to. Or children. But Matty gets there first.

'I won't keep you. I'm sure you're very busy. I just figured it's time you knew. Before it's too late.'

A jolt of electricity passes through me. I place my free hand between my knees so he won't see it tremble.

'Time I knew what?'

He leans back, ankle resting on his left knee the way my grandfather used to sit.

'About the skeletons,' he replies, a smile cruising his lips.

SIXTY-THREE

Everything goes very still. I hear the static in the air, the breath moving in and out of my lungs. My heart. My pulse.

'You mean . . .'

'It's time you knew,' he repeats.

He's enjoying this, but all I can think is Matty Melgren has spent the last twenty years exactly where he deserves to be. That I've been torturing myself for nothing. That I did the right thing.

I need more though; why he did it, why he didn't hurt us too. Were we just a part of his scheme, a wall to hide behind? Or did he genuinely love my mother and me?

Was he off killing women all those times he cancelled on us? What was he doing the day of my Prize Giving? What was the champagne he brought around afterwards really to celebrate?

He was a father to me, but was I a daughter to him? Was I anything?

I need dates and details. I need to understand him.

I'm afraid to speak in case it breaks the spell and he clams up again, and yet there's something bothering me, niggling like a nugget of corn caught between two teeth.

'Why are you telling me this now?'

I don't buy his spiel about time running out. That implies a compassion I'm pretty sure he's incapable of.

'I've been talking with a priest,' he says.

I cock a brow. Yeah right, I think, but I don't challenge him.

'You must have suspected . . .'

I shake my head.

'Not till—'

He scoffs, shakes his head, eyes half shut.

'I still can't believe it. I mean, after everything . . .'

My chest tightens as it slowly dawns on me. He's known all along. Is that why he's brought me here? To confront me, to pay me back?

'It took a long time to truly believe it,' he says. 'And even then I had my doubts, but of course it was the only thing that made sense. That dark streak. Self-preservation too, I suppose.'

My cheeks burn, my mind going back to the past we shared. I think about how much I secretly enjoyed crushing Sally Sniders, a truth I'd shared only with him. The snarky comments I made about Des, how cruel I was about him. And then of course the thing with my mother that he can't know but may very well have guessed at.

I did it for her, I tell myself.

You still did it, the other voice inside me whispers.

He's talking, I force myself to focus. This is the last time we'll speak. I can't afford to miss a word.

'. . . hated me deep down. Resented me for having all the fun.'

'Fun?'

I'm nauseated, a pulse throbbing dully in my carotid.

'I fought it for a long time, tried so hard to suppress the urges. It took such effort just trying to appear normal. All the while this force was building inside me, a pressure like I was going to explode.'

He pauses, looks at his lap, and for the first time his bravado fades. He almost looks ashamed.

'And then,' he says, looking up again but not quite meeting my eyes this time, 'then I met your mother. It was as if an angel had answered my prayers.'

'She made you seem normal,' I say, my theories confirmed. 'That's why you wanted to be with us. A ready-made family was the perfect disguise.'

He gives a one-shouldered shrug.

'I suppose it was an advantage.'

'An advantage?' I sound like a parrot. 'You're sick, you know that?'

He grins, clucks his tongue.

'Aye, it's what they tell me. But she was sick too. Every bit as much as me.'

She?

'What are you talking about?'

His face changes again. The expression that looked like shame has disappeared, in its place eye-twinkling amusement.

'The police think the murders started in '81, but they're years off.'

I wonder if the cancer is affecting his brain. He's all over the place. I try to keep up with him, I came here for answers after all. And if there's a chance I can get him to identify more victims . . .

'So, when did you start killing?'

'1977. The Charles. Pretty brunette with a charming little gap between her front teeth. You'd have been very young at the time. Just a wean. Your mother and I had reconnected. We'd tried to stay apart after she got pregnant, but this thing we had was intoxicating, electric. More powerful than both of us.'

He watches me for a reaction but I'm slow to catch on.

'I don't understand. You said she was the answer to your prayers. That she helped you suppress your . . . urges.'

The word sickens me, sticks in my gullet.

Matty's smirk broadens, a flash of white enamel appearing between his lips.

'What I said was, I was struggling to fight my urges and then I met your mother . . .'

The tone of his voice, the tilt of his chin. The drawn-out pause.

My stomach clenches, a wave of acid rides up my oesophagus.

'I don't understand,' I say, but I think I do.

'I was convinced there was something wrong with me, that I was an alien, a species apart. And then I met Amelia-Rose. I thought I was dark, but my God, I was nothing compared to her. That ruthlessness, her contempt for everything that breathed.'

I slam my fist down on the ledge, hard enough to make the pane rattle.

'Don't you dare. Don't you dare try to pretend—'

319

I'm shouting but he's as calm as a summer's day.

'I'm not pretending anything, Sophie. Don't tell me you fell for that holier than thou act of hers. You mustn't judge anyone till you've walked in their shoes,' he says, mimicking my mother. 'That old chestnut was straight out of *To Kill A Mockingbird*. You studied it at school. Surely you recognised the line?'

My shoulders relax, my breath comes more easily.

'So, she wasn't particularly original. It's hardly the crime of the century.'

'No, but it speaks to character. Only those without morals have to hide behind the morality of others.' He chuckles. 'Your poor dad.' He makes air quotes. "Dad", and straight away my shoulders are back around my ears.

'What's that supposed to mean?'

He actually looks surprised.

'You never suspected?'

I don't answer, just narrow my eyes at him. He's holding all the cards though.

'Poor sop was only too happy to put a ring on her finger when she told him her expanding waistline was down to him. That was the one thing I could never give her, and the one thing she could never understand about me. To your mother, marriage meant freedom. To me it was a deathtrap.'

I push my chair back, start to stand.

'I've listened to enough of this crap.'

Matty cricks his neck, pushes his sleeves up.

'Didn't you ever wonder why Jamey boy left you, Sophie? It was a pretty big deal in those days, a nice Christian boy walking out on his wife and kid.'

I lower myself back down, tell him my parents weren't suited. Can't help adding, 'And clearly he was a chump.'

'A chump who was terrified by the woman he married. She burned the notebooks after he'd left, but not before he'd read them. Your grandmother did too, I'm told. God, how they freaked her out. I mean it wasn't the first time she'd had reason to question the purity of her daughter's soul.'

I snort derisively.

'You're many things, but I never pegged you for quite such a storyteller, Matty.'

He brushes a bit of lint off his sweater, flicks his nails.

'Why do you think she had the pair of you living under your granny's roof?'

I haven't thought about my grandparents for years. They passed away shortly after Matty's sentencing, dying within a few months of each other. *A sign they were soulmates*, my mother said, which made little sense to me. *I expect it wouldn't*, she replied when I told her as much.

'Bills,' I say now. 'Saving on rent. A kid to bring up on her own . . .'

He shakes his head. *Uh-uh.*

'She was keeping an eye on Amelia, making sure she stayed in line. Of course, when the rumours started, she had enough. Told your mother to pack her bags.' He tuts. 'It's a sorry state of affairs when a person's reputation is more important to them than their granddaughter's well-being, don't you think?'

I'm not interested in his take on Nanna G or his societal judgements.

'What notebooks?' I ask.

321

It's as though the words are coming out of someone else's mouth. Certainly, they haven't filtered through my brain first.

He smiles, pleased I'm paying attention, and immediately I hate myself for posing the question.

'Fantasy fiction mostly. Shades of *Frankenstein*, the Marquis de Sade. There were sketches too, pretty graphic from what she said to me. And stuck in at the back, a photo of Cindy Bowman cut out of a newspaper, along with a bloodstained swatch from her dress.'

My veins chill.

Cindy Bowman was a three-year-old girl whose body had been discovered by Crystal Lake in Newton when my mother was a child. The medical examiner ruled the death as accidental. Cindy had been playing by the rocks, he explained. She'd slipped and cracked her skull.

It was in the local papers of course, but the story wasn't of sufficient interest to make the news overseas. The only way Matty would have heard about it was if my mother had told him.

I try to look unimpressed, ask him what he's getting at.

'Your mother had urges too. The difference is, unlike me, she didn't have the guts to go through with them.'

My blood settles, I gave him a look of contempt.

'You've just contradicted yourself. First you imply she was involved in Cindy Bowman's death. Now you're saying she didn't have the guts to follow through on her fantasies. You can't have it both ways, Matty.'

'I never said she killed the kid.'

I push the hair off my face, exhale deeply.

'Well, then.'

Matty's eyes are hawkish.

'She didn't kill her, but she did watch her die. That's what gave her the taste. She showed up on Cindy's parents' doorstep the day of her funeral.

'"Can I see her?" she said.

'The girl's father explained gently that Cindy was dead, in heaven now with the angels.

'"I know she's dead," your mother answered, as if the guy was a potato short of a pie. "I want to see what she looks like in her coffin."'

'I don't have to listen to this,' I say, but something keeps me in my chair.

'Amelia was the one with the big dreams. I was the one who carried them out. Life's a game, the only limit our imagination, she said. The victims too, of course. We had to limit ourselves there, that was her rule.

'They couldn't have any personal connection to us. Pickups in bars or clubs were off the table given the obvious risk of witnesses. And they had to come from all walks of life and not just one particular area.

'Harder for the cops that way, she said. They'll never know where you're going to strike next.

'I had to stick to North London though. She figured it might raise suspicions if my car was pulled over south of the river.' He smiles to himself. 'I wouldn't have thought of that, but she was smart your mam, and with twenty boroughs to choose from, there were plenty of rich pickings.'

I'm rendered mute, and then I spot the hole.

'All those times you were off killing, she had no idea where you were. If what you say is true—'

'Ah, that's what made it fun. She never knew when it was coming. The murders were rituals, marriage ceremonies binding us together. Proof of my devotion, that we were meant to be together. It's why I selected victims that looked like her. They were an homage, you see? Gifts I tied with a bow.'

I remember how she'd laid into Matty when he'd found it funny that Gemma Nicholls' body had been mistaken for a mannequin. The disgust on her face.

I say this to him, dare him to respond. He does so without missing a beat.

'She was always careful in front of you. Kids repeat things, she used to say. Just look at Nazi Germany, all those brats dobbing their parents in to the Gestapo. You never know who they're going to talk to. What they might say.'

I shake my head.

'You've got an answer for everything, haven't you?'

'That's because I'm telling the truth.'

'You wouldn't know the truth if it kneed you in the balls.'

I say it so forcefully a speck of saliva hits the glass.

He smirks.

'That violent streak, you really are a chip off the old block.' Then before I can respond, 'Go on, ask me anything you like. I've nothing left to hide.'

I should ask about the other victims, of course. The ones who have never been found. Later I'll kick myself for not doing that. But right now, all I can think of is my mother, what he's accusing her of.

'I'll never forget how upset she was after the Brownstone murder. She could hardly talk to you that day in the café, was convinced you were involved. You have no idea how it tore her up. Hardly fits with everything you've said, does it?'

Matty chuckles softly.

'You're right. She was torn up about Brownstone. But it wasn't because she was upset I was a part of it, it was because she was furious about what I'd done. I slipped up, telling that geebag in Kilburn I was a bereavement counsellor. Cocky, your mother warned me. Pride comes before a fall.

'My addiction was getting out of control. I realised I needed to get away, let the dust settle a bit. I thought Brownstone would be a sleepy enough place I could dial things back, but that force just kept building inside me.

'I couldn't contain it, and in the end it got the better of me. Your mother was mad. She felt there was nothing sacrificial about that murder. The girl didn't even have curly hair, she said.

'She liked me stopping that woman about the cardigan though, figured it was a great joke how someone so strongly matching my victim type was thanking me for helping them out. Things were a little better between us after that. It still worried her though, all the details coming to light. The fact I'd gone rogue, as she put it.'

I massage the base of my throat, trying to ease the building sickness.

'Bullshit,' I tell him.

He's not listening though, on a roll.

'Brownstone is why she shopped me. She thought I was out

of control. Or perhaps she just decided it was her turn to end a life. Better to live a moment as a lion than a lifetime as a lamb, she used to say. It's why I insisted she pay for my defence. Amelia owed me, and she knew it.'

I shake my head, I won't listen to any more of his lies.

'She kept looking for connections between you and the killer, agonising about them. Discussing them with Linda, my grandparents. Why would she have done that if what you're saying is true? Why would she have drawn attention to you like that?'

Again he responds without hesitation.

'To test what other people thought, I expect. To work out how badly I'd tripped up, if I'd implicated her somehow. Which is another reason she went to the police, I imagine. She was saving her own neck. Your mother was nothing if not a survivor. And of course, she always did have a jealous edge. I'd say ask Jame Brennan, but I guess you can't really do that now, can you?'

I look at this man I once loved and now hate. He wants to stick the knife in one more time before he dies. But I won't let him stick it in me.

I meet his eyes, angle the phone away from my mouth so he can read my lips.

'My mother didn't go to the police,' I tell him. 'I did.'

I take in the pall that passes across his face, the surprise slackening his features. And then I buzz for the guard.

'We're finished here,' I say.

SIXTY-FOUR

It was after that afternoon at Ferko when Matty noticed the woman's cardigan and made the slip about what the Shadow did to the victims' toes.

I waited till my mother was in the bath, 'Hey Jude' pumping through the door. Her favourite Beatles song, the one she and Matty used to dance to back in the days they danced.

I wasn't sure I was going to do it. Even as I dialled the tip line number, I didn't believe I'd actually go through with it. That I'd be able to.

The detective manning the phone sounded tired. A bored voice roughened with a smoker's rasp. Every so often he'd take a drag, blow it out.

'North London Murders tip line . . .'

The police never used the Shadow nickname, the hyperbolic moniker likely beneath them.

I glanced over my shoulder, worried that my mother would come out of the bathroom and catch me.

'I, er . . .'

I'd planned what to say but now it was time to say it, the words wouldn't come.

'Do you have information?'

'I think so,' I whispered.

'Well?'

He was irritable, no idea what was at stake – for either of us. The murders had been going on for over two years, the investigation team privately wondering if the perpetrator would ever be caught, as I know now from all the documentaries I've watched.

'I think I know the killer,' I said, barely audible.

The detective must have thought it was a hoax, or maybe he'd just heard the line a few too many times before. Both Matty and Bea had spoken about a bottomless barrel of cranks each after their five minutes of fame.

'Name?' the detective asked.

I didn't realise he meant mine.

'Matty Melgren,' I said. 'He's my mother's boyfriend.'

He didn't correct me.

'Address?'

I gave it to him, mentioned the proximity to Hampstead Road Lock. That got his attention. So did my reference to the fact Matty had been in Brownstone at the time of the murder there. And that he'd joined the search to find Niamh's body.

'What's your name?' he asked more gently, the kid gloves going on.

I hesitated a moment, then hung up. Giving Matty's name was bad enough.

The phone rang again seconds later. Some animal instinct told me not to answer.

When my mother came out of the bathroom, she found me

sitting by the receiver, hugging my knees to my chest, rocking backwards and forwards.

'You're white as a corpse,' she said. 'What's wrong?'

Quickly I changed the subject.

'Have you ever seen a corpse?'

'What a funny question . . . Now how about fish sticks for supper?'

Ever since I'd made that fateful phone call, I've agonised over what I set in motion. Matty was convicted on evidence that was largely circumstantial, the key piece of which was footprint evidence that recent studies have since called into question.

If it weren't for me, he'd still be a free man. If I'd got it wrong, I was as guilty as he was supposed to be.

Now at last I have the answer I've longed a lifetime to hear. But rather than giving me closure, it's raised yet more questions, even more terrible than the first.

SIXTY-FIVE

'Bastard,' I say, turning out of the prison a little too sharply. 'Bloody, shitting bastard.'

A pair of teens in hoodie tops and low-slung jeans amble past. One leans in to the other, whispers something, and they both laugh. They're not laughing at me, but I can't help feeling that they might be.

'Bastard.'

I say it louder this time, smack the side of the steering wheel. My nose starts to fizz. The pressure builds behind my eyes, a lone tear slinking down my face.

In the rear-view mirror the prison buildings start to shrink and fade.

It's over, I tell myself. You did it.

I should be jubilant. Finally, I have the answer I've waited a lifetime to hear. Matty was responsible for the Shadow murders. I was right to go to the police. He'll die behind bars, just as he deserves.

And of course, there is a relief knowing that, but it's not the relief I was looking for.

'There's no happy ending,' Janice told me once. 'Even if you ever find out for sure whether he's guilty or innocent, it'll come at a cost.'

It didn't stop me hoping though, searching for the truth. But turns out she was right. I know the truth, and yet my chest is still filled with rocks.

'He's a liar,' I say to my mother. 'How could he say those things about you?'

I didn't start talking to her straight away, too much resentment had built up over the years for that. I found it hard to forgive her drinking and pill popping, the way she'd retreated into herself after Matty's conviction. That what mattered to her was who she'd lost not who she still had.

But after she died and with each year that passed, I started to forgive her more. For what she'd done, for what she had me do. Time, rubbing the rough edges smooth. There was so much I'd never asked her, so much left to say. As many unanswered questions as beta blockers mixed with her dinner, I thought, tidying up that day.

It was Janice who suggested I write her a letter.

'It can be very therapeutic,' she said. 'You could try writing yourself one too. All the things you'd like to tell your past self. Child you.'

I said I would, but I never did. Instead, I began to speak to my mother without really meaning to. I found myself whispering her name into my pillow, or when I went out for a walk. Then gradually, I started asking her things, reminiscing.

Do you remember such and such . . . Or, why do you think

he did this, that and the other? Before I knew it, I was holding whole conversations with her ghost.

I'm not a nutcase, I wasn't hearing voices. It was more that I was able to imagine how she'd respond, or perhaps I just let fantasy fill in the blanks.

Janice was right, talking to her was therapeutic. I began to do it more and more so that now rarely a day goes by without us speaking. It's almost like having her back again.

Although I always picture her with a glass of gin, or looking at old photographs, the woman I talk to isn't the woman I knew in those later years. Rather, she's my mother from when we first moved to London. When she and I were all each other had. The version of her that I loved best and miss the most.

That's why I'm so mad at Matty. He killed those women and, although I'm not kidding myself about my role, he killed my mother too. She never recovered from what he did. It was because of him she knocked back pills and drank to blackout every day, because of him she longed to die.

And now he's trying to kill the only thing I have left of her, the memory of the woman who brought me to London in search of a better life. Who made us bed picnics and organised scavenger hunts on Parliament Hill. Who taught me the meaning of pathetic fallacy and the importance of putting yourself in another person's shoes.

'Bloody, shitting bastard.'

'Language, Sophie.'

I don't hear voices, but I can hear her saying it.

'Did he really think I'd believe those lies?'

'Who knows? He's told so many.'

I press down harder on the accelerator. My eyes burn. I swipe at them to clear my blurred vision. I won't cry, not over him. Not any more.

'To make out you were the reason he killed all those women. That the two of you were playing some twisted game, that you were more ruthless than he was. Jesus.'

I shake my head, but as I say it, a dark memory pokes up, baring its teeth.

A photo frame. A wooden case.

Amelia's Treasure Box – Hands Off

SIXTY-SIX

I don't believe Matty, of course I don't.

The man is a consummate liar. When I think how he protested his innocence all these years, how he suckered so many people in. How well he kept up his 'normal person' act with us.

No, I can't believe a word he said, never mind that this is my own mother he's talking about. As Parliament Hill comes into view, my mind goes back to the day she helped Lucy Allen find her dog. The way she refused to give up even when my friend was flagging.

A person with dark urges wouldn't act like that. Psychopaths can't empathise with other people, let alone animals.

Same as that business with Sally Sniders. Matty was all for teaching her a lesson. Frankly, so was I. It was my mother who encouraged me to have compassion for a bully, to try to understand why the cow behaved the way she did.

Hardly the hallmarks of an evil mind.

Even so, Matty's words have left a mark. I find myself going over what he told me, finding new ways to refute him even though I know I shouldn't be giving him head space. He's taken up enough space in there to last a lifetime.

And yet . . .

When I think about it, she did look angry rather than upset that day in the café.

There was a private look that passed between them when she told Matty I thought the victims resembled her.

And she did glance at me as if to gauge my reaction while telling Matty off for being amused that Gemma Nicholls had been mistaken for a mannequin.

I push the thoughts away, curse him for being so manipulative. Curse myself for letting him play me.

He played you your whole childhood, I rebuke myself. You going to let him play you now too?

And yet, and yet . . .

I remember Mrs Coates teaching us the best way to get a person to think about something, is by telling them not to.

Human beings are designed to look behind the curtain, she said.

Is that what Matty's done? Made me peek?

A drop of rain trickles down the windscreen. The sky is crying too.

'Tell me it's a lie,' I say to my mother's ghost.

Straight away I'm angry with myself. Of course the bastard's lying.

Buster greets me at the door, his wet nose pressing against my leg, letting me know he wants his ears rubbed. I drop to my knees and bury my face in his fur. He nuzzles against me, understands my mood in the way only an animal who spends all day watching you can.

Matty watched us too, I think. He learned our ways, knew exactly how to push his agenda. How to get inside our skulls. Twenty years have passed and he's still doing it.

And yet . . .

I get to my feet, pat my flank for Buster to follow. I mean to go to the kitchen to get him a Bonio, but I must be on some kind of autopilot because I'm walking to the bedroom that used to be my mother's.

I open the door, go inside. I haven't kept it as a shrine, but I haven't cleared it out either. Laziness more than anything else, same reason I bought the flat after my inheritance came through from Grandad and Nanna G. Buying the place seemed easier than looking for somewhere new. Change too daunting.

The carpet in here needs vacuuming. There's a thick layer of dust on the shelves. But it's more or less how she left it; minus the empty pill bottle I chucked before calling the ambulance. *Give it five minutes after I'm gone, Sophie. Just to be sure.*

I move as if in a trance; my body and brain not communicating. I approach the dresser against the far wall, pull open the top drawer. It sticks a little then gives. Buster is watching me from the door, his ears flat against his head.

The photograph of my father is long gone, but the other one is still there. The image of a little girl cut out of a newspaper and stuck in a frame. Hair worn in pigtails. Snub nose. Freckles. Three years old at a guess.

I hear Matty again—

She didn't kill her, but she did watch her die. That's what gave her the taste.

He's a liar, a manipulator. A slayer of ten. More probably.

And yet . . .

I don't articulate the thought to myself, just reach into my pocket and pull out my iPhone. I Google 'Cindy Bowman', hit the image tab.

Ten, fifteen, twenty pictures pop up. All of them just like the girl in my mother's photo frame.

A pulse throbs in my neck, the breath sticks in my lungs. I hear the crack of saliva as I swallow, the beat of my blood.

I turn the frame over; unclip the fastenings, remove the back.

From my mouth, a howl. Low. Wolfish. Wild.

I vomit, double over. The frame drops to the floor. With it the flutter of cloth, white polka dots on blue.

Stained with what I know is Cindy Bowman's blood.

SIXTY-SEVEN

The liar told the truth.

DNA analysis, unheard of back when Cindy Bowman died, confirmed that the blood on the polka-dot fabric was hers. While trace fibres and adhesive residue showed it had indeed been stuck into a notebook; a notebook which I now have every reason to believe once contained the perverted fantasies of a disturbed mind.

After my visit with Matty, I struggled to reconcile the woman I thought I knew with the woman I now know she was. My ability to hold it together came in fits and starts. I tried not to drink, tried to pray. Failed on both counts.

To begin with I felt myself falling back into the abyss, but it was a different sort of darkness to the chasm I inhabited after Matty's arrest. Back then, I had to accept my hero might be a killer, along with the fact I'd betrayed him. It was my fault he was locked up and I had no way of knowing whether I'd acted justly or not.

The uncertainty was a poison that slowly killed me.

The netball team, friends, grades – none of it mattered any more. From the moment he was escorted into custody, I didn't so much live as move through life. A robot going through the motions. A person without purpose. Soul-sick. Lost.

I needed to know for sure whether he was innocent or guilty. I needed to admit to him what I'd done. And I needed to know I'd made the right decision rather than being a hothead who had destroyed everything good.

The day I visited Matty, I finally got the closure I'd waited twenty years to achieve. I knew what he was. He knew he was in jail because of me. And I knew he belonged there.

I'd found out the truth about my mother too. And now I'm clawing my way out of the depths as more and more memories start to click into place. A picture slowly taking shape like the jigsaw puzzles Nanna G used to send on my birthday.

How my mother reacted when I told her Matty took me on that terrible drive, for instance. She didn't try to persuade me I was overreacting. Instead, she took me at my word, believed me instantly.

Only one explanation fits. She knew what he was capable of because she was capable of it too. And because she knew all about his deadly urges, because they were in it together.

There's also the way she kept saying it was her fault he was in jail. How she pooh-poohed my pleas for her to take a safer route home and change her hairstyle. How closely she fitted the police profile; a loner, socially awkward – even a history of cruelty to animals if that little box of bones in her nightstand is anything to go by.

I've been thinking a lot about her little sayings too. Put yourself in someone's shoes. Don't let anyone else define you. It's what's in a person's heart that counts.

I hate to admit it, but Matty has a point. The lessons she

taught me were largely off the back of a Post-it note. He said, only those with no morals have to borrow the morality of others. A mask of decency. He should know.

As hard as it all is to accept, being in no doubt about who she was makes this journey easier than the pot-holed path I stumbled along after Matty's arrest. The truth will set you free is a cliché, the sort of gem I might have found stuck up around the flat. But the truth *has* set me free. I no longer blame myself for the past. Now I'm just trying to come to terms with it.

I recently learned the truth about Des too. Hannah, the woman who lives in the apartment downstairs, was doing some gardening the other day. She wanted to plant an olive tree, had to dig deep.

'You'll never guess what I found,' she said, brandishing an urn, *Mum* painted in faded letters on the side.

She showed me where she'd unearthed it and, as she did, I saw Des in the dark holding a shovel, patting the soil down. He hadn't been burying bodies that night, he'd been burying his mother's ashes. He must have already been planning his own departure and wanted to lay her to rest first.

The old me would have gone straight to my room, masked my emotional hurt with physical pain. Not any more. I've been in recovery for over a month. I've joined a fellowship, say the Serenity Prayer. The blade still calls to me; particularly at night when the ghosts start crowding in. But in a strange way, I've found it's easier to deal with my grief when I'm not trying to block it out with a knife.

'It's a process,' Janice says. 'A tunnel. You have to go through it to get to the light on the other side.'

My sponsor tells me cutting doesn't help, that it only gives you more things to be remorseful about.

Both of them are right. I have my bad days when I struggle to get out of bed, when I have to remind myself to breathe. But I'm moving in the right direction. Owning my past. Recognising that whilst I may be a victim, I'm a survivor too.

Today, I'm taking Janice's advice and writing a letter to my childhood self. For so long, I've yearned to go back in time and warn girl Sophie what was coming. I want to tell the child I was that fear is the brain's early warning system. That my mother lied, I *should* have been afraid.

I sit at the kitchen table, sucking the end of my pen while my coffee goes cold. Buster is curled up in his bed, snout resting on his front paws.

'I don't know where to start,' I say.

He raises his big head, points his nose at the window. With Buster, the answer to every question is, 'Walkies'. Why be indoors when you could be outside?

Outside . . .

I take the pen out of my mouth and write.

Sophie—
There's so much to tell you, I don't know where to start. The kite, maybe. It's not the beginning exactly, but it's as good a place as any . . .

Something shifts inside me as I reach the end. My breathing is easier, the cement on my chest breaks up.

This isn't the end though, I think. It's the beginning.

And as the thought forms, I'm filled with a surge of energy

341

that literally blasts me off my feet. I get up, pace around the kitchen talking to myself like a mad thing, the idea I have growing along with my resolve.

'This isn't his story,' Janice said one time. 'It's yours. You get to write your own ending, not him.'

All these years, I've resisted telling my version, felt I didn't deserve to have a voice. But it's not about what I do or don't deserve. It's about what I need to do.

Matty wanted to hurt me. That's why he summoned me to Battlemouth, a final act of domination. Telling me about my mother was his last hurrah, one last way to wound.

But, in revealing her secret, he had to reveal his own – that he was guilty despite all his protestations of innocence. And that his murder spree began in 1977, four years earlier than anyone thought.

Now I know the truth, the rest of the world must know it too. If I'd gone to the police sooner, fewer lives may have been lost, but at least now I can finally bring some closure to the victims' families and shine a torch on disappearances that have never been attributed to Matty. Or my mother.

A part of me is frightened how people will react. They'll likely hate me, blame me for not coming forward sooner, just as I've blamed myself. I have to do it though, to make amends, to face what I've been running from. To move on.

And so, I sit back down in a sudden shaft of spring sunshine and begin to write the tale I've waited so long to tell—

You think you know this story. I think I do. But how much do any of us really know?

ACKNOWLEDGEMENTS

There are some stories you think might be fun to write. And others you burn to tell. From the first line, *Truly, Darkly, Deeply* had me in flames. Without these people that fire would have flared unseen:

My agent, the tour de force that is David Headley. There is no cheerleader finer, no champion I would rather have in my corner.

The Quercus Team: My brilliant and eagle-eyed editor, Stefanie Bierwerth who has always had such an innate understanding of what I wanted to achieve with this novel and whose passion, enthusiasm and insight I appreciate so much. Andrew Smith who designed the breathtaking cover which perfectly captures the book's essence. Kirsty Howarth and Charlotte Webb. Kat Burdon, Jon Butler, Hannah Robinson, Hannah Winter, Bethan Ferguson, David Murphy and everyone in the sales and marketing department.

Helen Edwards at DHH Literary Agency who has taken this book into so many international territories and Emily Glenister for being a rock star.

To the people who keep me smiling: Harriet Tyce and Dominic Nolan for encouragement in the early days that this was the novel I needed to write. James Delargy for answering my very many questions about Irish slang with such patience and grace. And Alison Barr for Scottishisms and a therapist's view on Sophie's mindset. Niki Mackay, Elle Croft, Adam Southward, Simon Masters, Polly Philips and everyone in the 'Criminal Minds' gang for virtual water cooler chat and making this thing we do less solitary. And my non-writer friends who put up with me talking endlessly about my books and still go out to buy them.

My sons, Max and Joey whom I love to Heaven and back and who know there's no point lying to me because I'll profile them and be able to tell. See boys, it's in print so it must be true . . .

Charlie whose cold, wet nose is a constant joy and whose early morning demands for breakfast are not. And Maggie whom I miss every day.

My parents, Carolyn and Martin, and my siblings, David and Henrietta, for being such great supporters, always.

My husband Tim who believes in me even when I doubt myself. Who makes me laugh when I feel like crying. The wind in my sail.

And finally YOU, my readers, for picking this up and letting me tell you a story. Do let me know if you enjoyed it, I'd love to hear from you!

Contact:

Drop me a line on Twitter @VictoriaSelman or sign up to my newsletter at VictoriaSelmanAuthor.com.

To be the first to hear about my next book:

Visit my website for all the latest news by scanning the QR code below.

I hope to share another journey with you soon!